ONE HU
ONE HUN

CW00503107

Also by Christopher Bigsby

Hester: A Romance
Pearl
Still Lives
Beautiful Dreamer

ONE HUNDRED DAYS: ONE HUNDRED NIGHTS

CHRISTOPHER BIGSBY

Methuen

First published in Great Brtain by Methuen 2008

1 3 5 7 9 10 8 6 4 2

Methuen & Co. Ltd
8 Artillery Row
London SW1P 1RZ

www.methuen.co.uk

Methuen & Co. Ltd Reg. No. 5278590

A CIP catalogue for this title
is available from the British Library.

ISBN: 978-0-413-77656-3

Typeset by SX Composing DTP, Rayleigh, Essex
Printed and bound in Great Britain

For Bella and Frank

ONE HUNDRED DAYS:
ONE HUNDRED NIGHTS

A Note On Translation

Translation, always difficult, is especially so in a country in which everything is possible, providing it is not. How to convey the aptness of puns, the ambiguity of words which mean one thing in Sagrado Dios and quite another elsewhere? To be honest, language slides around a little in Sagrado Dios itself, while one part of the country does not always understand another. Hence, some approximations are required. For purists, this text doubtless falls short. Sometimes one English word is preferred when another might be thought more accurate. Sometimes the spirit of an exchange is preferred to a literal transcription. How else are we to understand one another, however, except through seeking to transpose into our own experience that of another? I quote, of course, from the late Archbishop Juan Carlos who died so recently in the convent of the Sisters of Small Mercies.

Sail down through the southern ocean, towards the blue-green ice of Antarctica, and to the west, where the sky and the sea meet as one, is the green mystery of a land whose history enfolds myths and whose myths contain history. To the south, ice a mile thick; to the north, heat that can bend the air. And in between a thousand stories never before told.

But for the earthquake of 1912, which took the lives of a Papal Legate (temporarily and secretly cohabiting with the opera singer Dolores Del Largo) and three thousand men and women of no particular significance, except to themselves and Almighty God, it is possible that the name of Sagrado Dios would have remained as obscure as it had for centuries. But sudden death, provided it is on a significant scale, has a way of forcing itself on our attention. So Sagrado Dios featured, for a day or two, in newspaper headlines and on the Marconi radio. But 1912 is a time ago and while the *Titanic*, which in that same year took it into its mind to sail vertically rather than horizontally, has never left our consciousness, who now recalls Sagrado Dios and its Disaster?

Fondly regarded by philatelists (its one peso stamp of 1897 having removed a President's nose, an error punished in kind when the printer found his own similarly removed), it features

1

on few people's travel plans, at least not on those of people easily deterred by poisonous animals and virulent diseases. Only Mormons are regular visitors, seeking retrospective salvation for their dead of whom there are rather more after their visit. It is a country, however, that bears more than passing attention.

When Pedro Romerez went to the moving picture show, in the chapel of the undertaker Hernando Juarez, he never minded whether the film had already started or not. He watched it through to the end, saw the second feature, and then watched the beginning of the first film until it reached the point where he had come in. Then he put his hat on his head and walked out into the night where the moon shone silver and the darkness pulsed with life. He understood that you can enter a story at any point, that it will wait for you and then carry you forward as a boat is by the sea.

So let us enter this story of Sagrado Dios in 1944, and not in its capital city of San Marco (capital cities having attention enough) but where simple people lived a simple life until one day a miracle occurred and a ship rose from the depths of the sea.

Over the ocean a war was being waged. It meant nothing to the people of Anzuelo until a U-boat surfaced one day in the dazzle of the bay and the Captain was rowed ashore, sitting upright in the bow as though he were made of wood. He was watched from the hillside as he stared ahead, his eyeglasses glinting in the sun. It was that sudden flash, indeed, that was his undoing for, to more than one of the watchers, rays seemed to stream out of him. Montezuma may have assumed such strangeness to be a mark of the gods. Here it was recognised for what it was: the mark of the devil.

He was greeted by the Mayor and Father John, who flicked nervously at black robes filmed with dust. The Mayor saluted and the Captain shot his hand up towards the sky as though he were reaching for the golden disc of the sun. That, too, stirred anxieties in those who watched this encounter at the water's edge.

He had come, he explained through his first officer, who spoke a halting Spanish that seemed to owe more to Cervantes than Berlitz, to seek assistance with the repair of a small component of the boat's engine, imagining that all towns, no matter how small or remote, must have someone who is a master of machines. His own engineer, he added, had been lost overboard and his assistant had damaged his hands. The Mayor shrugged in sympathy. Father John brushed his soutane once again. Nor was the Captain wrong, though there were, in truth, only two vehicles in Anzuelo. One was a truck whose rusted body had been slowly replaced by pieces of wood on which grew soft moss, green and yellow with a tinge of black. The other was a Citroën, left by a French mining engineer who had found no mines but had succumbed to the sins of the flesh and then to the consequences of such, being taken by mule first to the hospital in San Marco and then across the ocean to die within an hour of being off-loaded from a steamer at the port of Toulouse.

That these two machines continued to function was a testament to faith rather than engineering skill, of which, to be honest, there was none within a hundred miles of Anzuelo. They were blessed each year by Father John, who was rewarded with a little spirit distilled from the root of a local plant which the Spanish had discarded as a weed, and inspected by a sewing-machine salesman who had never sold a sewing-machine, though he fell in love with a woman with thighs of steel and breasts of pigeon down. To those in a small town by the sea, whose principal transport was either a boat or a mule, a salesman smacks of oil and mechanics so his blessing was regarded as no less significant than that of the priest, but to a U-boat commander it is doubtful whether a similar conviction would have obtained. As it happens all this was beside the point, for there was no way that anyone would assist him in his dilemma.

Why should this be? One might as well ask why Señora Rico rose each day at five and wrote a passionate letter of love to the Mayor, only to destroy it at eight as she walked towards his imposing home, freshly painted each spring, meaning to slide it under the door and enter his heart as she was afraid to enter his house. One might as well ask why sinners confessed to their sins in the knowledge that confession would be followed by sin. Some things are possible, others are not; some things are necessary, others are only desired. Some things may happen with time and good weather and an absence of calamities; others will never happen even if the Pope and all the angels in heaven decree it. In particular, this captain would never secure a repair to the broken part which he placed on the ground in the heat of the noon sun.

A U-boat is a kind of miracle belched up from the depths only to lie like a dead seal in the oily water. It is also a disturbance in the cosmos, a mistake, an abberation, an abomination. The people of Anzuelo were not so ignorant as never to have heard of U-boats. Newspapers arrived, if not regularly, then at least with some frequency. So late were they in arriving, however, that news was never news and hence there was a lack of urgency. Indeed there was a kind of miracle which accompanied their arrival: for if the headline announced that a crisis was feared, the likelihood was that the crisis would have been resolved long before the citizens of Anzuelo read of it. Lost children were found, injured people recovered. News was a branch of history, like the light which floated down from the stars and which was silver white because it was time's bones bleaching in the night sky. So, U-boats were no mystery. They existed to kill unseen, like the jungle fever that occasionally swept down from the fetid forests of the north. Now one was here, a stick thrown onto the sea. And a man had come asking them to join themselves to his undersea voyage, to contaminate them with the death he carried in his eyes.

They knew about appeasing gods. It was in their blood. Others with fire in their eyes had rowed towards the coast and history had reversed itself. Such events must never be repeated. A spell had no power until it was pronounced three times, but even the second set the world vibrating like the air at noon over the metal sheets of the boathouses. They knew that this god must be received and entertained, that all courtesy must be extended. But they knew, too, that he must never be allowed to return to his vessel, for if he did the beast would reanimate and devour everyone. They had seen the rays stream from his eyes.

So, he was seated at the head of a table, with the Mayor and the priest looking into his dead eyes, knowing what must be done. They fed him with the best food they had to hand, which was a long way short of what he must have had on board his miraculous ship, but he received it with courtesy. They offered him the flat red wine of the region, which is deceptive in its strength. It deceived him. He began to speak in his own language, oblivious to his hosts. He threw his hand up towards the ceiling several times and saluted. They passed him another flagon of wine. He hardly seemed to see them. At last he had to be supported when he left the table. The two officers who had accompanied him stood awkwardly on either side, themselves none too secure on their feet. The enlisted men who had rowed him ashore and stood guard outside while their superiors caroused, sprang to attention as he passed and then relaxed a little as they realised that he could hardly register their presence, let alone their military correctness. He waved a hand vaguely in their direction, leaving them to their fate as they left him to his.

5

He never felt the knife that passed gently from ear to ear under his chin and smiled even as a red mouth opened where no mouth had been. His men, too, met their deaths with a certain ease and grace, irrigating the dry earth with their blood, the drops beading with dust until they resembled so many pellets of dung, such as a beetle might roll along the ground for no better reason than that necessity compels. The work done, the bodies were eased into the ground and wooden crosses banged – clang, clang – with the flat of a spade.

A sudden light swept and swelled across the water from the distant boat, low in the dark water, as though to mark the passing of the men. Then it was gone, like God's grace withdrawn in the face of human depravity. The Germans were looking for their captain. Fascist light was penetrating the darkness, caressing the waves, sliding lubriciously over the land. But nothing was revealed beyond the pure white circle of light, a silver pool like a wayward moon looking for a home.

In truth the town was empty. The citizens of Anzuelo had gathered up food in bright shawls and coloured handkerchiefs, picked up jugs reassuringly heavy with wine, and removed themselves into the cool of the jungle. All that remained was a three-legged dog and a blind cat which had formed a confederacy not easily threatened by the presence, or otherwise, of undersea Nazis now trying life underground for an eternity or two.

At dawn three inflatable boats set off from the slug-like submarine. Each was rowed with startling precision by sailors dressed in the neatest of uniforms, as if their clothes alone would command respect and obedience. From a distance the three looked like black beetles dragging themselves over winter ice. The menace lay all in the movement, oddly symmetrical, strangely metronomic. The sea was a deep blue-black ink. The sun had only just begun to flood the sky with a sudden flush of crimson.

At last they neared the harbour, where the hulk of a freighter lay on her side, sparkling with rust and neatly blocking access to anything but the smallest craft. Her plated sides were so thin that in certain lights it seemed possible to see through them, as a hand held up to the sun will appear to glow transparently. She had sunk from sheer exhaustion, her owners happy to secure the insurance and disinclined to remove the obstruction. No scrap company regarded it worthwhile to salvage her and so she stayed where she had sunk. It was no inconvenience to the fishermen who, after a time, had grown used to her. Indeed a species of small fish, green and scarlet, had colonised the wreck. To the approaching sailors, however, she must have seemed ominous, for though her name had long since been eaten away by wind and tide her port of registration remained clear: Hamburg. The sailors pulled on their oars and finally raised them vertically as they approached the harbour's edge. The raised oars resembled nothing so much as the banners of a defeated army, with the colours torn from the masts.

They were ashore before the sun had climbed halfway up the church tower, before light had flooded any city street except that which fronted the harbour itself. They swung round the town to the landward side and ran along the streets, their shadows cast behind them as though they were themselves pursued rather than the other way about. They stopped for a moment in the city square where the fountain, which had long since dried up, its pipework corroded by salt, rose up, half angel, half devil, like us all. It was to have been the figure of Anzuelo himself, a saint who had been devoured by wolves which had pursued a young man and his bride. His life had been sacrificed for others. The sculptor, however, was an atheist, one of the town's few

7

Marxists, who saw the story quite differently. To him the saint was a credulous fool destroyed by the wolf of capitalism, a victim of the bourgeois institution that is marriage. He sought, therefore, to build his implied criticism into the statue. The result was a somewhat deformed figure who seemed to wish beyond anything to return into the rock from which he had been prematurely hewn. The figure, further deformed by the deep shadows that still enshrouded the town, brought the sailors to a halt. But discipline soon exerted its pull. They broke into small groups and disappeared into the labyrinth of sidestreets.

At first they ran, kicking open doors and nervously searching rooms left neat and clean by those who now lay asleep in the nearby forest. As time passed they slowed, confident now that they would not be shot in the street or ambushed in an abandoned kitchen, but certain, too, that they would not find what they sought. These men, used to the confines of a metal tube, to breathing air laced with diesel oil and sweat, felt exposed, like so many turtles flipped on their backs and unable to recover their feet. But they also breathed fresh air, air perfumed with the scent of flowers. For all the urgency and indeed danger of their position they were relieved to feel the land beneath their feet and the warmth of the sun on their faces. They searched, it is true, but by degrees they did so with ever less attention, the silk of the breeze gentling their fear and softening their trepidation. For no sooner should they find their missing officers than they would return to sea and face the daily possibility of death beneath the waves, where neither sun nor breeze could penetrate and where their fate would be known to none who cared for them.

They sat, that first night, in a defensive circle, their cigarettes glowing in the blackness like May bugs floating in the still air. They awaited an attack which never came. At dawn half of them returned to the ship. The others watched the sun climb over the

8

white houses, flooding their souls with a hope that had no foundation. Yet each day that passed must bring them closer to the end of a war they had begun to understand they could not win. Each day that passed without the regular thud and churn of a destroyer's propellers meant that they might survive to see that war's end.

And so, one day, they laid their weapons in the town square in a circle, ammunition clips at the centre, the whole design like a dark sun with black rays extending outwards through the dust. Within an hour the villagers began to return, walking past the men as though they were invisible. Father John, however, crossed the shadow of the church and stood for a moment looking at the new flower that had bloomed black in the white square. He stared up at the church tower, where the bell vibrated silently in the heat, and nodded before indicating to two villagers that they should pick the dark petals one by one, carrying the rifles into the church. She loves me, she loves me not. Eventually only the heart of the flower remained, until even this blank hole in the earth had disappeared.

Later that day two houses on the edge of the village, abandoned and empty, were opened and cleaned. Fruit was placed on the table and a goat was tethered to a post at the rear. It was two days before the former mariners realised that these houses were for them, and then only when a young girl took one of them by the hand and led him, and them – for where one went the others followed, for fear – to their new lives. From that moment they were treated as though they had no existence. No one greeted or abused them. Once a week fruit would appear and once a month a goat would be tethered; but no one so much as glanced in their direction. They had survived and, little by little, abandoned their uniforms and relaxed until anyone entering the village would not at first have noticed them, except that when they walked they did so with a brittle precision which betrayed them. They retained, in other words, a little of the arrogance that had led their captain to his death.

They never looked for their captain's grave, but there were days when they would gather at the water's edge and look out at the sea where their fellow officers and men had rowed out in the dazzle of day and opened the seacocks of an undersea boat which obliged by slowly sliding under the sea, leaving only a series of vortices, swirling whirlpools of iridescence. Their voyage had found its destination in the cool waters of the South Atlantic, where the current gathers up the detritus of a continent and hurries it south towards a purifying ice.

When the war ended all but one of them left, walking out of the village the day after news of the surrender arrived. The news itself was already three weeks old when it reached Anzuelo. It meant nothing to the villagers, whose only contact with it had been a low black boat that appeared one day on the still waters of the bay and a smaller boat which glided across the sparkling sea full of sailors, exploring a continent, voyagers preparing to greet the natives of an alien world.

The man who stayed lived alone in one of the two houses set aside for the sailors. Still the fruit appeared, but the goat did not. Instead a spade and a hoe and a sack of seed were left beside his door and one day, as he passed through the square, a young girl dipped a metal cup in a bucket of water raised from the well and offered it to him.

He took the hint and in the small section of land behind the house, a section marked out by broken tiles laid in the red-brown dirt, he planted seed which, thanks to the winter rain which for once did not fail, grew into corn and peppers and gourds of different colours. When the harvest was gathered in he took a selection of all his crop and carried it in a sack into the middle of the village and laid it outside the church door. The next day a bottle of sharp-smelling alcohol was placed outside his house. That night his voice echoed in the cool air, a voice singing sad songs in a language which none who heard it understood.

Meanwhile, in the pleasantly cool study of a small house off the main square of San Marco, Professor Mario de Cervantes was writing the history of the novel in his country. This was a more demanding and fanciful project than it might have been in some other place, on some other continent, for the fact is that the novel had been banned for three hundred years as seditious and anti-Catholic. However Professor Cervantes, a small man with a large ambition, had a theory about that, which meant that his history, on which he had already been working assiduously for some twenty years, would be some time more in the making.

His theory was that since the impulse of the fiction-maker could not be so easily suppressed, it had simply transferred itself into all other aspects of life in a country which so hungered and thirsted for stories that mere prohibition could serve no purpose. So, the myth-making powers of the novelist bled into the rituals of the church, which were elaborated, which developed sub-plots, spawned characters and uttered dialogue not to be found in any of the conventional documents of the faith. The one true church fragmented into dozens of sects, each one of which developed its own theory of creation, its version of the fall, its commandments, its litany. The priests, in turn, became shamans, tellers of tales in much demand both for the familiarity of the stories they told and for the subtle variations they spun. And what was true of religion was true also of politics. Though the government party remained monologic, reciting from a single text which had to do with country, duty, sacrifice, development

11

and all the familiar clutter of language recycled by each new dictatorship, literally scores of other parties came into being, each one of them illegal and therefore the more powerful since they constituted mysteries, had their own narratives, imagery, heroes and styles.

Business, likewise, suddenly developed guilds, societies, associations in which staid citizens dressed up in strange costumes relating to the supposed origins of their crafts and professions. Those joining were required to recite from memory the stories that passed as history, to tell of Carlos the Silversmith who had encountered a giant one day on his way from the village where he was born, a giant who had demanded that, at penalty of losing his head, he should ask the one unanswerable question in the universe, a question to which the silversmith replied by asking, 'What is the one unanswerable question in the universe?', a piece of logic which led the giant to cut off his head, thus proving the unreliability of strangers, the disadvantage of being on the short side, and the lack of justice this side of the grave. Then there was Pepe the Great, the magical baker who had first discovered the properties of yeast and used it to entertain the court ladies by getting them to roll imitation phalluses and then watch them rise, an experience which readied them for his own tumescence, which is why bakers' hats are the shape they are and why women always feel a shiver of guilt when they plunge a cake into their willing mouths.

For Professor Cervantes the whole world was one interlocking complex of stories. Indeed the novel itself seemed ever less significant to him. The air was alive with plots which made the efforts of writers, once they were released from three centuries of silence, seem poor indeed. Nor was he unaware that his own history had something of the shape and interest of a story. There were evenings when he amused himself by reading aloud from the manuscript pages, noting, as he did so, subtle foreshadowings, powerful symbolism, enduring themes.

He suspected that there might, beneath all the diversity of the materials that he presented, be some underlying tale, a master story of which all others were but offspring, a story as dense with meaning as the universe itself, which, it was rumoured, had once been a single atom into which all of existence had been compacted. Such a story had exploded, sending fragments in all directions, with every particle containing a trace of that original. And since we must be formed of material that had once been squeezed into that singular atom then we, too, are made of story. And who can doubt that, he asked himself many a time, when we survey our lives and recognise their shape, so like that of a book, their progress so like that of a narrative wending its way towards an inevitable end.

Of course the Professor was mad. It was, indeed, twenty years since he had been required to leave the university, an unprecedented move in an institution where insanity was always thought to carry a certain charm and even to be a sign of a profound intellect. However, his habit of summoning the fire brigade to change broken light-bulbs in his office should the university caretaker prove too tardy was thought to go beyond the usual bounds of abnormality. He retained his title, the words 'professor' and 'mad' seeming natural bed-mates, though now he was Professor Emeritus, a curious distinction which seemed to imply that his previous title had come about through nothing more than inadvertence. A nurse came once a day to administer medication, which he took without demur. He felt no different than he had those years before, and since his behaviour appeared no stranger than that of many of his colleagues who had not been required to retire or to take medication he was treated with respect by all he encountered. Besides, it is not only primitives who suspect that the insane may be blessed in a world in which mass slaughter, torture and the regular ingestion of alcohol, not to mention breakfast cereal, are evidently regarded as perfectly normal modes of behaviour.

He went each day to the local baker to buy his madeleine, occasionally stopping to tell the proprietor the story which lay behind the small cake which, he assured him, owed its name to a young woman of Paris who had once intervened to save the life of a man threatened with the guillotine. The proprietor had long since learned to close his ears and offer a smile. The world, he knew, was full of stranger men than this and there was no more regular customer than the Professor. Sometimes, indeed, those who had never heard the story before would enter the shop to listen, buying half a dozen madeleines themselves on their departure, no doubt intending to tell the story to their wives or husbands that very evening. From there he would go to the butcher, but why tell what he said there? Sufficient to say that he was a man who so absorbed himself in his work that he carried it with him wherever he went, that he, in a sense, became the thing he studied as some people are said to resemble the dogs who trot beside them in the street.

But the point of this story is not the Professor, nor his vast and ever-expanding project which, like the PhDs he had once supervised, threatened eventually to incorporate all the known universe, but the fact that this man, this strange and yet affecting man, had a daughter. This daughter was conceived late in life, and evidently in a way which quite baffled her father. One day he had discovered a maid, an attractive young woman, her skin coffee-coloured, her hair blond, naked on his bed seemingly singing to herself in a strange voice. She had immediately grasped him to her with such passion that he was greatly tempted to summon the fire brigade or anyone else who might relieve him

14

of the embarrassment he suddenly felt as, for a second, he so forgot himself as to recall, if only momentarily, his biological function. The maid left nine months later, having presented him with a baby daughter who was raised until her sixteenth birthday by a distant relative summoned to his house. Thereafter she looked after herself.

None knew of the child's true origin, assuming her either to be an orphan or the offspring of the relative, banished from her own community and sent to suffer for her sins in the house of a madman. But her origin mattered less than her appearance, for she was of such unsurpassed beauty that there were those who would submit to several hours with her father in order to gain even the slightest glimpse of her. That, perhaps, is the master story which he sought but was too blind to see: that the universe continues because we believe that beauty will whisper the truth in our ears and breathe life into the driest heart. And are we so very wrong?

The Professor, who thereafter, and unaccountably, kept a photograph of the vanished maid, projecting onto her the romantic feelings he could never acknowledge he felt, had an assistant, Manuel, whose job it was to visit the National Library there to find the earliest examples of narrative art. His interest, however, lay not in the books, fading, with the must of mould and the mottle of age on their pages, but in the Professor's daughter, Justina. At night he lay in bed and burned with love. He pictured her blond hair, yes blond like that of her mother, her pale face, yes pale and not olive or tawny like that of most citizens in a country where the sun bathed all in its promiscuous light, her soft body. . . . Her eyes were blue, another miracle as it seemed to him, blue as the ocean, as the sky, as . . . his vocabulary failed him, though not his imagination, which pictured her walking towards him, loose-limbed, smiling, unbuttoning . . .

but, no, some privacy, some respect, were we not all once young and foolish and wish that we might be again?

Manuel had studied at the university. He came from a poor family but the university charged no fees to those whose fathers and grandfathers had served the state – there being no state, as such, before the time of Seamus O'Grady, the Irish soldier of fortune (and still greater misfortune) who had founded it and done his best to populate it through epic fornications which left a trail of red-haired, quick-tempered children, raised to venerate the Pope and despise all atheists. His father had been a clerk in a regional office of what became the ruling party when it seized power to rescue the country from the radicals who had, by some misfortune, so misled the electorate that they were elected by a landslide vote. Such loyalty was rewarded.

Manuel had no politics, beyond gratitude for the change of fortunes that must surely come with a degree from the country's only university. Accordingly, he played no role in the various factions rife on the campus. He hardly saw the posters calling for reform or revolution and was scarcely aware of the soldiers who, from time to time, drove their half-tracks along the dust-lined campus roads and plucked half a dozen students from their rooms as if gathering ripe plums. The vehicles were called half-tracks because, it was said, of their propensity to shed one of their tracks, subsequently turning in disconsolate circles like some ballerina doomed to pirouette for ever for some obscure offence against Terpsichore, Muse of dance, provided that there might be ballerinas given to belching out smoke from recycled cooking oil.

He did have arguments with his fellow students when they insisted that the function of literature was to transform society. 'Art is a weapon,' they cried, 'a weapon with which to smash the state.' 'No,' he cried, 'it is beauty and truth.' 'And why are beauty and truth in a prison cell? What are beauty and truth to

16

the peasants who labour all day under the hot sun to keep the rich rich and themselves poor?' 'I was poor,' he replied, who was, in truth, still poor, but anticipated being otherwise. Then he regretted saying such for they replied, as he had known they would, 'Those are not poor who have dictators on their side.' He said nothing more and avoided such arguments thereafter, returning to his books.

When he graduated he had no job to go to. Unemployment, declared by the ruling party to be non-existent and falling, was high and rising and his father's contribution to the state had, in truth, been small, too small to guarantee preferment for his son. But, as luck would have it, and luck, in this country, at this time, was a substitute for almost everything, from ambition and hope to logic and faith, he encountered the Professor one day. The Professor had dropped his papers, which flew into the air like so many doves released at the dictator's regular and compulsory rallies in favour of the peace which would come once radicalism had been stamped from the face of the earth. Manuel ran back and forth snatching at these flying words, picking paragraphs from the branches of stunted trees, recovering sentences from the gutter where cigarette ends and food wrappers were tumbled by the wind. Seeing that the Professor could hardly hold the pages once they were no longer contained by the scarlet ribbon that had been wrapped around them, he accompanied him home.

The housekeeper brought him a glass of lemonade, beaded with a fine mist and containing pieces of ice which tinkled reassuringly in the dark quiet of the Professor's study. How he came to be offered the job of researcher he was no longer sure; but after a time it was simply assumed that he would come each day to receive his assignment before going to the library, where he would work until the sun no longer shone through the circular window in the roof.

He had been working for a month before he first saw Justina. He had completed his report of a book he had found, a book by an unknown author written at the turn of the century, and was placing it on the heavy mahogany table at the centre of the Professor's study when she opened the door. It was as if the sun had suddenly shone fully in his eyes. And, indeed, the sun did shine through a window in the hall so that her blond hair was lit from behind. An angel might have wandered onto this earth and sought him out. She stood for a second but before his eyes could accustom themselves to the sudden light, turned on her heel, muttered something that expressed irritation, and closed the door behind her. He stood a full minute, as if doubting what he had seen, as should he who had visited this house many times and never suspected the jewel that lay concealed within. Her voice still sounded in his mind like music and the perfection of her form left him shaking.

At which point we leave him, though only for a while. The fact is that there are so many stories and each one connects to another. How may we understand one story if we do not explain how it relates to others? Connection, connection is all. It is what drives us. Even in our dreams, when we step into those stories as heroes or heroines, in fables seemingly unrelated to our lives, there is a needle which stitches the bright fragments together as a shaken kaleidoscope displays a pattern seemingly immanent in no more than shards of coloured glass.

Federico Martinez was born in Anzuelo in the same year that the U-boat had broken the skin of the sea. He was the son of a fisherman, but in his blood swam not fish but ambition; and ambition and Anzuelo could only with difficulty be contained in the same sentence. At the age of eight he walked the three hundred kilometres to the capital, with nothing but a loaf of bread and a bottle of papaya juice to keep him company. His mother, who had eleven other children to care for, let him go with regret, for she loved him no less than those others and, if truth were told, a little more, but she saw in him a strength and resilience, even at so young an age, that she felt would suit him better for the world than any of his brothers and sisters. Besides, this was a country in which everyone was a relative to everyone else and hence there were cousins and uncles and aunts aplenty, both in San Marco and even in the villages along the way.

Federico lived in his imagination. His lies were ten times more vital and inventive than those of his siblings or of his schoolmates. If he was late for what passed as a school in Anzuelo it was because he had been challenged by a dragon and lifted up into the air until he was giddy, before being set back on the earth at the forest's edge. That he felt a deal more giddy as a result of a clip on the ear did little to blunt his talent or enthusiasm for invention. To him, Anzuelo was peopled by marvels, and if Anzuelo then how much more so San Marco, remote and hence more mysterious by definition.

Even when he arrived in the capital, tired and feeling more alone than ever before, he was not disillusioned by the banality of the streets, for what is banality to one is wonder to another. And miracles are always at hand for those who look for them. The first door he knocked on, to seek directions to his aunt's, or was it his cousin's (he had so many relatives he was often confused as to which might be which), was opened by a man who seemed to expect him.

'Late,' was all he said, as Federico began his well-rehearsed question. 'Inside.' Knowing it impolite to refuse the instructions of an adult he stepped over the threshold, so named for the distant days when it restrained the wild wheat ready for the threshing, and walked forward over the angled flagstones, grey and cool.

19

'Are you hungry?' asked the man, who bent down and stared into his face as though eager to penetrate a conundrum.

Federico nodded. The word 'hunger' hardly encompassed his feelings, for he had been walking a day and a half with nothing to satisfy him but a pebble which he rolled around his mouth to keep the saliva flowing.

He was seated at a wooden bench in the kitchen, a bench long enough to seat a dozen such as he, and a woman of more than generous proportions placed a bowl in front of him and filled it with cold soup that tasted of potatoes and onion and fennel. Then, squeezing his cheek painfully between thumb and forefinger, she retreated before returning a moment later with a wedge of coarse brown bread. He picked up a spoon and, pausing only to look about him with wonder, began to eat as though the meal might be his last, as he did not doubt it would be in this house. In the distance he heard the ring of the front doorbell, the very bell he had sounded only a few minutes earlier. It was a bell which rang with an unusual clarity and seemed to touch something deep within him. Nonetheless, hunger is hunger and he continued with his meal.

A few minutes later the man returned. He was short and thin, with a small grey moustache and a flurry of hair which stuck out at all angles and seemed a little singed at the ends. You might have taken him for a shoemaker, if your image of a shoemaker were of one such as he. He shook his head in some perplexity and addressed the woman who had returned to remove the soup bowl.

'It was another boy. He had come for the job.' He shook his head again. 'I sent him on his way, though there was something about him that I seem to remember.' This was clearly offered as a statement, but it had the sound of a question and was surely received as such by the woman who nodded in response.

'It hardly matters which one does the job.'

Again she nodded her head and picked up the bowl, only to replace it with a plate on which was a slice of pie.

So it was that Federico became apprenticed to the country's leading bell maker, indeed the country's only bell maker. And for the next ten years and more he worked with wood and metal, developing muscles and a sense for sound and its relationship to size and shape and thickness and the presence of impurities. His head rang with carillons, echoed with peals, reverberated with a music lost within the single stroke of metal on metal. All sound, he grew to know, was imperfect. Indeed it was the nature of the imperfections that was the source of its true beauty. If only he had learned the lesson that what is true of bells is true, too, of people he would, perhaps, have suffered less disappointment in life, though disappointment, on the whole, was not to be his lot.

He also learned patience, for the art of the bell maker is not one congenial to those who love rush and haste. Even the smallest error will affect the sound; and if there were few with ears subtle enough to detect such yet there were those who did, and were the bells not made to speak to God more than to men and could such a conversation be conducted in any but the purest tones? So, as he listened to the city's many bells he fancied he could detect which ones had been flawed by a failure of concentration, a lack of craft or even by a necessary laying aside of the business of making while a mother or wife came to the moment of her death, for who, he asked himself, can be allowed to make that journey on their own? Nevertheless, a day or two spent at the bedside and not the forge had allowed the temperature to vary by a crucial degree so that now, and for as long as the bell summoned the faithful to worship or struck the hour, the fact of that death, and the crucial desertion it had

21

imposed, was contained within the sound, as a bubble will be trapped within a crystal glass.

A bell that has been cast must be left to cool over many weeks and months. When the bell is as large as that which boomed each day from the top of the cathedral, whose walls were white but whose many pinnacles were the colour of clay, it must be left for several years. The metal must set, he learned, consolidate its strength, purify itself, though never entirely, settle into its final shape before emerging from the sand. So it is with people, he might have thought, were he prone to philosophy, which he was not, being a young man, now, of some seventeen years.

'It is amazing,' said his employer one day, as the metal flowed into a mould, sending a cascade of sparks around their feet as though they walked on a lake of fire stirred up by the wind, 'that broken bells can be more famous than those that are whole. In Moscow there is one that cooled for three years and yet even so a piece fell out of it like a slice of cake in a café. Now it is one of the wonders of that city. In Philadelphia, in the United States of America, the Bell of Liberty is cracked.' He nodded to himself, seeing, perhaps, the irony of a freedom bell that could never ring. 'But those are failures. They are a warning and not such as should be celebrated.'

His young pupil, who knew nothing of Moscow or Philadelphia, nodded his agreement and they continued to pour until the last glowing drop fell, like a shooting star across the night sky.

As was inevitable in a city which, though the capital, was still little more than a village that has outgrown its shoes, one day, as he crossed the central square where pigeons and people gathered, men sold trinkets and women their souls, Federico saw Justina. The world has a limited supply of seventeen-year-olds and San

Marco, despite its citizens' enthusiasm for lying together in the cool of dark bedrooms lit by bright slices of afternoon sun cut by wooden shutters and laid across white coverlets and golden bodies, had as limited a supply as the world at large. It followed that those who did exist would seek one another out. And so it was this July afternoon.

Justina was returning from the cathedral where she had lit a candle for her mother and, it has to be said, for the cascade of pearls she had seen in the window of a jeweller's shop and which she was anxious to see cascade around her own neck and nestle on the swelling slope of her breasts. Her mother's prayers, added to her own entreaties, might, she calculated, perform what must surely be a minor miracle in the pantheon of miracles. As she left the church the old men and women who camped out in its entrance, and who made visits there so uncomfortable, lifted their hands and raised their sad eyes to the young girl in white. Normally she would have walked past them, for which seventeen-year-old, as we surely know, can see his or her own future in the poverty and antiquity of others and which seventeen-year-old can swim against the current of self-regard which flows so strongly, if not silently, in the pulsing blood of youth? But on this occasion she opened her purse and took a few coins out, coins of little value, to be sure, but enough, put together with others, to buy the thinnest of candles in the sacred darkness of the cathedral beyond. She placed one in the hands of a man who looked up at her as the faithful look up at the sad smile of the Virgin Mary. She did so perhaps to add a little magic to the prayers she had just offered to possess the cold beauty of the pearls, but such an act of charity made her step into the light and stride across the square with a spring to her walk which caught the eye of a bellmaker's apprentice who stood waiting for the noon bell to toll.

So caught up was she in the thoughts of candle, prayer, charity and pearls, that Justina walked directly into the young man who had been staring steadfastly up at the mud-coloured pinnacle waiting for a silver sound.

'Oh,' she shouted petulantly, glancing down at her shoes to see that they had not become scuffed.

'Oh,' he echoed, recovering from the soft encounter with her young breasts.

They stood for a moment and looked at one another; and in that moment her dreams of a young lawyer, who might shower her with presents and comforts and babies, slipped away like a lover at dawn, the lover of whom she also dreamed, who was not a lawyer but had the hard, muscled body of a peasant. Who can explain such a moment when we first discover what we never knew we sought and discover that of which we never knew we were ignorant? They stared, oblivious to those who moved past and around them. He opened his mouth but said nothing. Instead the great bell of the cathedral sounded and its many hidden harmonies slid effortlessly into his heart, so that ever after he would associate her beauty with that other beauty that had transformed his life. The sound floated on the wind. But here was its embodiment in flesh and blood, except that he doubted that such beauty could indeed be human.

Then the moment passed. She dropped him a curtsey – though why she could not have said – and began to walk away, who would have stayed but was captured by the sheer logic of motion. He remained fixed in his place, the great bell reverberating in his head and his heart swelling with joy at the beauty that had appeared before him and which was the sweeter for being so swiftly withdrawn. The hands on the Town Hall clock behind him continued to move on, though perhaps they trembled for a moment or two. It had no bell, however, and hence no interest to a young man who listened for harmony in the universe but who had never thought to find it in the form of a young girl though, now he came to think of it, there was a similarity in the shape of both and had her voice not sounded out with that same silver beauty he detected in the finest of the city's bells?

It was an encounter that seemed to pass unnoticed by anyone in the square, with a single exception. For crossing on the way back from the library where he had been digging for a vein of fiction in the dull soil of histories, philosophies and theology was Manuel, the pupil of the Professor whose theories were outlined, free of charge, to the city's bakers and butchers. He had seen the young woman emerge from the cathedral, a white angel dispensing charity to those in need. He had noted the spring in her step as she moved across the square like a dancer, speaking with her body, spelling out her needs and desires with nothing more than pure movement. He had seen, too, the moment of collision when unadorned beauty had encountered brute fact, for how was he to know that the young man had beauty ringing in his ears as well? The moment came, the moment went, but it left a stain on his soul.

A cloud of pigeons rose into the air with a sound like the pages of a book being ruffled by a student aghast at how much remains to be read. They hung for a second as though they might be about to arrange themselves into a message to the world, and then settled back, forming a pattern determined solely by the handful of seed thrown by a visitor to this capital of a republic seldom visited by strangers, seldom acknowledged by the itineraries of tourists seeking in movement what they should have sought in stillness.

And was there truly only one other who noticed Justina's meeting with destiny? This is plainly not so: for who would not

25

notice a young woman of beauty, dressed all in white, on a summer's day? There can have been few indeed who did not see and, having seen, few who did not store the memory of that moment, one more image, detached, perhaps, from context, to be filed away for no other reason than that it might spring unbidden into their minds and cause a momentary smile to lighten their lives at a dark time of day.

One such was Hernan Cordoba, who stood on a small box and spoke of justice and equality and the toiling masses. He noticed because he was watching with care for the arrival of the military or police. So just was his society that anyone who questioned his freedom to speak was liable to find himself swiftly deprived of it. He, too, was a student, or had been until he was dismissed from the university for disrupting the serenity of study with public meetings and demonstrations. He had also, it must be said, failed his examinations but, as he had asked his fellow students who scanned a list pinned on the library door to discover their results, what are examinations but the concrete evidence of authoritarianism, requiring, above all, the recitation of information and views approved by those sanctioned as teachers precisely because they were believers in authority?

Since then, he had gathered a small group around him. It was smaller than that which he commanded before he had been dismissed, for then he was briefly popular with fellow students who cared nothing for his politics but themselves had no great liking for examinations or, indeed, the state which determined the syllabi which were the primary source of their anxieties and the cause of their labour. Once banned from university property, however, he quickly lost his influence and now faced the difficult task of speaking to the enlightened working class in a country in which the working class refused to identify themselves as such and in which enlightenment did not seem to be their principal characteristic. Ironically, however, there was no one quite as convinced of the importance of education as he who had previously denounced it, or of the need to inculcate facts and history as he who had seen such as merely agents of power and authority. The difference was that now he was the teacher and what he taught, by definition, the truth.

Nor was he wrong about authority and the lack of freedom and justice. Should he ever begin to doubt the truth of what he preached from the steps of public buildings, in bars, or in the jolting aisles of those few buses travelling somewhat sporadically and with frequent breakdowns through the countryside, then he was constantly reassured as to the accuracy of his analysis. Those who protected the buildings would move him on or simply punch him in the face; owners of bars would take him by the ear and throw him in the street for ruining their trade. Bus drivers would stop their buses (those which had not already stopped of their own accord) and force him off miles from anywhere, so that he had to beg lifts from truck drivers who alone seemed happy to listen to him if only because he kept them awake, he and the regular explosions caused by inferior fuel and still more inferior servicing. He had even been arrested by the police and knocked around a little and once was taken to prison by the military, who did nothing to him but stood him in the central courtyard so that he could hear the screams which cut through the air like whips.

Today, as Justina dispensed charity and walked so vibrantly across the square, he had been talking about the forthcoming election whose sole candidate was the President. No one listened, or at least no one gathered around his box as he gesticulated, his shadow a black pool around his feet as the noon sun beat down. He did not even have the satisfaction of provoking the police into justifying his comments about their behaviour. So, as Justina left the square and Federico stood trying

27

to distinguish between his rapture at the bell and his new and undefined feelings for the girl who had just literally walked into his life, Hernan stopped speaking and climbed down from his box. A man nearby applauded him and Hernan turned gratefully towards him, only to recognise one who for many years had conducted the traffic, wearing a pair of orange gloves, and who would engage anyone who would listen in conversation about the connection between red meat and lust.

In Hernan's old college briefcase, presented to him by his rich uncle when he was accepted at the university, an uncle to whom, naturally, he no longer spoke, were a dozen posters and a small pot of glue. The posters were hand-drawn, except for the small imprint of a hammer and sickle he had stamped on them with the help of a piece of old linoleum cut with a chisel, a skill he acquired at school. The posters called for a boycott of the elections and he meant to stick them up a little later in the day when people had withdrawn to their houses for a siesta, the police included. Now, however, he had to go to a bar and wash dishes and glasses for two hours, for he had no money to sustain himself. The bar was a hangout for writers and artists and as a result he did not feel compromised, as he might have done had he been washing the dishes of the bourgeoisie, a class which he found doubly infuriating because they failed to acknowledge that description of themselves and because he had to admit that he was himself, by birth and upbringing, a member of it.

It was not the lunch-hour. In San Marco and throughout the country lunch was taken in late afternoon and lasted much more than an hour. It was not so much a meal as a way of life, a way of being. It started at around three or four and could occupy the truly diligent until six or seven. Food was simple but plentiful, provided one had a liking for fish, which came in every shape and colour and size. They were grilled, baked, poached. They came with or without heads, swimming in a piquant tomato sauce or crusted in pepper. Some came from the shallows, where they had skimmed and skittered, leaping into the limpid air, silver flashes against a blue-white sky. Others had been pulled from the frosted green depths, frill-finned, eyes bulging, jagged barbs lifting them into an air they could not breathe. There were blue shrimps raised in bulging nets, water cascading down, a spill of diamonds; crabs and lobsters were snared, transported from cold to boiling water to satisfy those who, as the afternoon drew on, drank glass after glass of wine and talked of nothing they would remember, with those who kept their privacies concealed by a spill of words or congealed in their clotted hearts. Time was thus suspended for a simple meal, anxieties laid aside, truths conveniently brushed away.

Then would come the paseo as half the city took to the streets, especially to the Boulevard O'Grady, ablaze with lights and as clean as the President's whore who was herself washed three times each day and drenched in perfumes and oils, though she still smelled of the fish which her father's family caught in the distant village of Anzuelo and sent each day to grace the table of the President.

O'Grady, of course, was Seamus, the County Cork philanderer who had arrived on the eve of the Revolution in 1848, *the* revolution according to the O'Gradyistas, who celebrated his birthday by painting the fire hydrants green (which caused little danger since it was many years since any of them had functioned) and wearing sprigs of lettuce, shamrocks proving impossible to come by and equally impossible to cultivate.

Others preferred to celebrate 1872 or 1881; still others showed a preference for 1902 or 1913 or even 1929 when Guiseppe Florida, son of an itinerant opera singer (and is there

29

any other kind?) and the former Miss San Marco of 1909, led his peasants over the mountains and down into the city shouting their slogan – 'Chickens Know Best' (a reference to rustic wisdom) – and waving green ribbons signifying spring wheat (thereby, it was said by some, endeavouring to associate themselves with O'Grady and thus win doubters to their cause). Admittedly they had been cut to pieces by the ancient Gatling guns that were still the mainstay of the army under President Juarez, and had been since a division of the Confederate Army had retreated to Sagrado Dios in the War Between the States, taking rather too literally their commander's advice to 'get as far south as you can and get there as fast as possible.' But such was the sympathy of all for his simplicity that after he had been executed in the main square the soldiers took up his body and paraded it to the cemetery where heroes of all previous revolutions had been laid to rest, along with archbishops, presidents and leaders of the city's Guild of Grocers, this being the most powerful of the city's guilds.

The principal boulevard was called O'Grady because, fresh from a boat he had signed onto in a state of some intoxication, and still somewhat unsure which country this might be, having only recently exhausted his not inconsiderable supply of illicit liquor – brewed in the woods of County Cork and said to have driven many a man to madness and matrimony – he had found himself at the front of a charging mob and, though fighting to release himself from their grasp, was thus the first through the presidential gates. When the defenders threw down their weapons, it seemed to him that he was being called upon to make some remarks, though quite why, at this distance from those events, it is hard to say. Thus he made an impromptu speech from the top of the palace steps. He spoke in a strange language – stranger still to those who might be presumed to speak it but who in truth recognised little that he said beyond repeated references to 'Mary O'Rourke' and a certain 'Big Bill Cahill' – but the very strangeness was no doubt what impressed. He was cheered up the remainder of the steps and cheered again as he fell unconscious, with a beatific smile, before the portraits of the eighty-four previous presidents.

It was widely assumed that he had been wounded and the next morning prayers were said for his recovery at six, seven, eight and nine o'clock mass. And recover he did, with the help of a small glass or two of cordial. He made a second speech, no more coherent, perhaps, than the first but just as stirring to those who listened to the unfamiliar but affecting rhythms of his Irish voice. He stood on the palace balcony and looked out over the people gathered in the square though, lacking his spectacles, crushed when he had collapsed, saw nothing but a moving pattern of colour that made him feel a little sick. The following day he was elected President, a triumph of which he was unaware having discovered the pleasure to be found in the cordial he had been offered to cure his hangover of the day before.

His period of office was characterised by a sudden profusion of public holidays declared on days that had no special signifi-cance on this continent but a good deal, it was assumed by all, in the history of his native Ireland, which history was now overlaid, as it were, on that of the country in which he so unexpectedly found himself. He introduced a game that involved a ball, large sticks, and the kind of violence until then rarely seen outside the context of genocidal wars. He had a succession of 'wives' or 'companions' (problems of translation preventing a more precise designation) of stunning beauty who lit up the lives of all in the capital until the Catholic bishop instigated 'the revolt of the duennas' which instituted a brief and regrettable period of almost puritanical zeal which banished women from the palace and liquor from all festivities. The latter was swiftly seen as a mistake even by the Catholic hierarchy and rescinded, but the other injunction remained in force until Seamus O'Grady did what he had never believed he would do. He married. His bride, as it happened, was from Anzuelo, which was why this otherwise disregarded fishing village ever thereafter had a place in the heart of all the country's citizens which it would otherwise not have occupied, its reputation for squid not exactly qualifying it for such affection, though later the country's most famous poet would choose this as a place to die or, strictly speaking, have it chosen for him by an assassin.

Esmeralda was hardly beautiful, though in a poor light she could be said to have a certain charm. It was presumed, indeed, that O'Grady had wooed and won her in just such a light, for his favourite places of assignation were the capital's bars. That aside, the rise of a fish gutter to the President's palace was seen as a gesture of some political shrewdness and was certainly applauded by those who wished to see the country's many divisions healed. The marriage took place in the cathedral. The fish gutters of Anzuelo formed a triumphal arch with their gutting knives while bride and groom alike wore sprigs of lettuce at their breasts, as did all those who gathered at tables in the square to celebrate the occasion.

Seamus O'Grady was the only president to die in office, which was why his name was revered, or if not quite revered at least not effaced from history by those who followed. He never learned the country's language but continued to give speeches on public occasions in a language in which all statements had the sound of a question and nothing but proper names were easily distinguishable, and then only with a certain guesswork on the part of listeners. In the few years he was in power, however, the citizenry became used to Mary O'Rourke and Big Bill Cahill,

32

almost as if they were new saints to be added to the calendar, and who is to say they should not have been, given how strange some of those already included are admitted to be? They grew used also to a villain called Cromwell, who they could tell by the tone of O'Grady's voice, as from the huge fist he shook in the air, was a kind of Antichrist.

Seamus died, finally, one Sunday morning following a celebration which involved his engaging in a drinking bout with ambassadors from Finland and Russia. This was stiffer competition than he had met with in many a year and it was thought that it, combined with his over-enthusiastic attempt immediately thereafter to breed either a second-generation president or fifth-generation fish gutter, had finally strained his heart. Whatever the truth, he died in the ample arms of his wife. He was buried next day and, it is said, the people cried for a week, frowned for a month and lamented for a year, at which time they renamed the main boulevard, until then called the Avenue of the Americas (one of many doomed attempts to use the same name in many a country on that continent), Boulevard O'Grady. It was here that the paseo took place and whenever a particularly beautiful girl walked past, swishing her hips from side to side like a thoroughbred horse, she was known as a Mary O'Rourke, and whenever a young man, of haughty looks and with a glint to his eye, paused for a second to watch the passing women as if he were selecting the ripest peach from a basket of fruit, he was known as a Big Bill Cahill. And somehow it was assumed that they would come together, the perfect couple, a product of nature, of myth and of the vivid imagination of one of the country's most famous citizens.

As month gave way to month and then year to year, there was a special blend of pleasure and pain for Manuel, who came each day to the house of the girl he loved, even if she looked on him with contempt or, perhaps, even worse, simple disregard. He was, to be sure, a scholar who breathed more easily in the must and dust of a library and kept his life, like his work, in the strictest of order. But it would be a mistake to believe that a young man who reduced his knowledge to index cards and annotated even his shopping list must be immune to the tender feelings which afflict all others. He kept a diary in which he recorded the details of his day, the money spent on paper-clips and pens, coffee and bus fares, the hours at which he must attend the Professor, his dentist, his lectures. There came a day when he began to record other things. He created a kind of Thesaurus for her hair: silky, soft, flowing, bright, shining. Her eyes were almond, bright, shining (his vocabulary was not particularly wide or inventive). Her teeth were, well, bright, shining. To be honest he inhabited a world that was largely inanimate. What was he to make of a girl who swept through the house and whose laughter echoed everywhere? Beside the piles of books, like the solid bars of a cell, she was quicksilver. She had but to look in his direction for him to feel the ground move beneath what he had come to believe were his somewhat ample feet. What was he to do, one might ask, when nothing had prepared him for anything but taxonomy? For there were times when it appeared that he believed the whole world created so that he might assign its different parts to discrete categories. His was a world whose coherence was assured while mystery only existed to be resolved: now here was one who transcended all boundaries and was herself a mystery not to be explained away. She was a fact, right enough, undeniable and implacable, but beyond that she was a shifting code, a cipher to which he lacked the key. He watched her as she moved about the house, uncertain what she might mean to one whose life was defined by study, library and a solitary room.

34

He loved her. He had read that word in books but now learned that there is a gulf between a mere word and the thing it signifies. For what he felt was beyond the power of words to define or explain and he had never believed that such could be true, for he had previously thought that words were what held the world in place. Now there was a gap and with what could he fill it except bewilderment, a despair deeper than he could imagine or an exultance that had no definition?

She gave him no echo, no hint or suggestion that she was even aware of his existence, no matter his passion, no matter how he felt it must shine in the night. Her eyes would pass over him as her feet moved over the cool stones of the floor. Yet there was a pleasure even in that and there were times he envied the floor.

The Professor saw even less, for his eyes were focused on his books as his mind was fixed on the shifting patterns he sought or projected. He would have missed her had she not been there, but missing and loving are not the same. She was a presence in his life and his life was different because of her presence. So far he loved her. It was something more than familiarity but something less than life's passion. That he reserved for the past where there was one he saw through his memory's eye. His one-time maid had been reinvented as the very image of a lost possibility he could never define, a lost love which in truth he had never found.

Thus Justina lived with two men, one who loved her but lacked the words to express that love, the other who existed in the warmth of her glow much as he felt the sun on his back as he walked in the morning to buy his madeleines without questioning the source of that warmth. The one burned with a flame invisible to the girl whose life he would illuminate. The other lived in the light of a life that had been his inadvertent

35

gift. How much wasted energy is radiated by those who burn alone.

So this young man did what others have done who find themselves in the same situation. He drowned himself in work. He stayed long hours in the National Library where more than one revolutionary had written his testament and drafted his manifesto. Here, Jacomo Toledo had written of the need for cobblers to acknowledge their solidarity and protect themselves from the imports that were destroying their jobs. 'NO SHOES RATHER THAN FOREIGN SHOES' was his slogan. He and his followers went barefoot and the peasants were so confused by this symbol that they thought his interests were theirs. In the revolution which followed he thus had their support until the import taxes he imposed raised prices and left the poor poorer than they had ever been.

Manuel Pinero likewise, many years since, had sat on the leather chairs of the library and developed his Theory of Eternal Recurrence which saw history as the turning of a great wheel whereby those who at one moment were at the apex were next at the other extreme. The rich must inevitably plunge to poverty and the poor rise to plenty. His party, too, had a slogan: 'TURN THE WHEEL,' they would chant at their rallies. It is never wise, however, to announce the inevitable decline of those in power and he was thus tied to a literal wheel one day and sent spinning down the Boulevard O'Grady and into the city's principal canal where, unfortunately, the wheel landed wrong side up and he drowned. His supporters on the bank chanted 'TURN THE WHEEL', but those who had perpetrated the deed plainly had no intention of doing so.

Our student sat now in this same circular library, where all the country's knowledge was brought together in a single place. Here, too, were secrets: for if only a few were given access to this echoing hall, where even a whisper would chase itself around the walls and the sound of a leather book being set on a leather table top could sound like a muffled gunshot, still fewer were allowed to progress through a narrow corridor to the room beyond where books were kept which could only be consulted by those judged worthy and discreet enough to suffer the potential corruption implicit in the subversive and the erotic. Since it was assumed, no matter the evidence to the contrary, that the rich and the intellectuals were incorruptible, along with policemen, judges, masons, doctors and dentists, these were occasionally to be found researching the tomes known only by their reputation to the populace at large.

Manuel was not there, however, to read *The Sexual Adventures of Donna Maria* or *The Diary of the Woman of San Isidro*. He was concerned to search out novels published when no novels were allowed, for it seemed to him, if not the Professor, that to ban an object is not to eradicate it but only to grant it scarcity value. To be sure, most of the volumes to be found behind the wire mesh of the Protected Shelves had been imported illegally or poorly translated from some foreign tongue. But there were a few, crudely printed, which had been written in the years when the Church believed that fiction was sanctioned lying, lubricious in content and deceptive in intent. A few of the authors had been executed for their pains by those who found the very concept of fiction hard to grasp. If a character expressed a belief was that not necessarily the view of the writer and when that same writer, carried before the court, suggested it was otherwise, such a defence was, of course, exposed as the merest casuistry.

'Where did these figures come from who disport and blaspheme in your account? Are these their true names and where are they to be found?'

37

'The book is a novel, sirs. The characters are conjured from the air.'

'Conjured, do you say? So there is witchcraft here?'

'No, sirs, I mean no more than that they are an invention, a creation.'

'God alone is the creator. Who or what else may be the source of invention?'

'Why, my mind.'

'So these people never existed in the world. They are phantoms of your mind. And you say they are not your responsibility? Whose responsibility, pray, might they be but his who commits them and their blasphemy to the page? What experiences do you have to guide you but your own?'

'All writers draw in some degree upon their own experience, transformed, of course, by art.'

'Quite so, and thus the blasphemies and naughtiness contained herein can be none other than your own.'

'They are imagined.'

'By you.'

'By me. But . . .'

'Do you accuse any other of writing what is to be found on these pages?'

'A writer, when he writes, is not himself.'

'Not himself?'

'He is capable of writing things he would never say and showing things he would never do because his characters are of a mind that they should do so.'

'And do these "characters" of which you speak invent themselves?'

'In a sense. At times.'

'Who invented man?'

'God.'

'Yet this is a function you are content to put on yourself or ascribe to the creatures you conjure into being. Can you not see that you are challenging God himself?'

'But who gave me my talents but God himself?'

'That you should use such talents, if talents they be, to produce something of worth, as a carpenter builds a house.'

'As I build a book.'

'There is only one book with the authority to tell us stories and those stories have the force of truth.'

'There are stories everywhere. Whoever keeps a diary is a storyteller. Whoever renders an account is a storyteller. Stories are in the air.'

'But these are facts.'

'There are no facts but those we choose to recognise as such. We select and already, thus, are creating stories to be believed or no.'

'It is a fact that you stand before us. It is a fact that you are plainly guilty of the offences with which you are charged and it is a fact that you will now be taken to the gallows and hanged by the neck. How say you to that?'

'How say I? I say that you might as well try to stop the waves as arrest the creation of stories. Show me the mother who does not tell such to her children.'

'Their names. Give me their names.'

But, receiving none, the inquisitor waved his hand saying, 'This is one storyteller who shall speak no more.'

He was wrong, of course, because the books survived as the cleric who judged the author so severely did not. It was these books, indeed, that Manuel held in his hand because he could not hold the woman he loved who cared nothing for such as he.

The story he read – entitled 'Innocence and Virtue Redefined' – blended magic with the real until each seemed a part of the other. Indeed all divisions seemed to dissolve as a man, half Indian and half something from another world, crossed a country described in loving detail, so that the reader would feel that he could find his way there with nothing more than this text to guide him. This man, if that is what he was, had the power to transform himself into other shapes, becoming at one moment a washerwoman and the next a goat on a high crag. There were those who travelled with him as companions on the boats which journeyed up and down the River Panes without ever suspecting what he might be. He did evil to no man but could masquerade and to be truthful had an eye on a woman, and since he could change himself into a bar of soap or a soft towel he could caress her naked as she went about her toilet.

This was not a book for a young man to read who already burned with desire. He looked around embarrassed lest anyone should see him reading it, but he was alone; for reading attracted few in a country which preferred its stories straight from the tongue.

The hero came to consciousness beside a lake where the water mirrored the sky so that it was difficult to tell the one from the other. He had a memory of another place, but that swiftly faded as the smell of papaya and mango pulled him down into this life. He came on a mission. He sought a pure woman, a woman unstained by sin and uncontaminated by sensual thoughts, for he had surfeited on the sin which his talents opened to him. And how else to test such a woman than by insinuating himself into her presence and seeing how she might react to his whispering voice and searching hands?

He soon discovered that most were coarse by his demanding standards. They stretched in the sun, proud of their bodies, and blushed at the gaze of those who caught their eye. Even the nuns, who he had been told would end his search, described the sins they would abjure with such obvious relish that he could sense they were drawn to the very darkness they denounced. They were, he discovered, no less women for the fact that they were cloistered in their cells. Indeed in one scandalous chapter of the book the author described the passion they felt for one another, the passion with which they embraced and . . .

Manuel looked around once more and was observed by a shrewish woman whose eye he hesitated to meet. He felt perspiration bead his forehead, even in the cool of this dimly lit room, and understood a little why the Church had chosen to proscribe the wild imaginings of one who could describe the subtle patina of a woman's skin and the damp treasures they stored for those who should seek them out.

There was a note at the beginning which assured the reader that what he or she was about to read was no fiction. The title page itself referred to a 'True Story' while an epigraph indicated that the book was written with moral intent, for, as a brief note observed, unless we look upon vice, how may we recognise the face of the Devil? Yet to such a scholar as Manuel it carried the mark of fiction, while its account of gratified lust was presented in such profusion, detail and variety as to make it plain that its author had little interest in narrative or character but only in the coarser arts. And yet what are all narratives, he might have asked himself had he been French, but seductions? The reader was surely no more than the object of the writer's passions, to be stirred, engaged, provoked or satisfied. There was an act of surrender involved, a mutual contract in which to become complicit.

Did he think of Justina as he read about rosy thighs and shuddering sighs? Not at all. She was not as these women. She was an idea and an ideal. For all her attractions, indeed, she was barely corporeal, though he had watched her as she walked past

41

him in the house or strolled in the shadow of the courtyard. He read, he told himself, out of duty and, indeed, wrote careful notes on a number of cards he had brought along for the purpose, yet the urgencies which drew him on from paragraph to paragraph and page to page had nothing to do with his feelings for the girl whose very existence was to him a kind of miracle.

The protagonist of the book now transformed himself into a wisp of smoke and in this form drifted through the keyhole of a huge oak door which enclosed that part of the city given over solely to women. Here the Sultan's wives and concubines lived out their lives in luxury, bathing in ass's milk, and learning the arts of love. But since there were so many of them and so few nights in the year, each was visited seldom by the man their charms had once captivated. Where, then, should their affections turn but to each other? They must take what pleasures they might in the cool alcoves and the baths fed by warm springs, unaware that the steam which misted their bodies had now intermingled with the smoke which but a moment before had been flesh and blood. When they felt a soft caress pass down their bodies, therefore, what should they think but that a thin film of water flowed gently over and under and into them as the air itself enfolds and envelops?

There was a sharp intake of breath behind him and a bony hand descended on his shoulder.

'Such filth,' said the librarian, seeking at the same time, as it seemed, to reach round him and remove the book.

He blushed and looked up at her guiltily, although aware that he did no more than the Professor had urged him to do. He indicated his index cards, only to note that written boldly on them were such words as 'Thighs', 'Breasts', and 'Coition' (he was not a student of classical languages for nothing).

'It is my work.'

'Indeed,' she said. She took off her glasses, removed a pin from her hair and shook it free so that it caught the dull shine from the windows high above. 'It is my work, too.'

'You have read it?' asked the student, aghast.

Her severe face softened as she smiled, her teeth as white as the snow on the San Mateus mountains. 'I am a librarian,' she said in a low voice.

'I work for a professor,' he said, unsure as to why this seemed relevant.

She eased the button at the top of her blouse and then ran her hand downwards over its white lace front. 'A professor,' she echoed.

'Yes,' he replied, looking around the empty room.

She followed his gaze. 'Monday,' she said.

'Monday?' He looked at her blankly, as though the word might be a code and he the one who must decipher it.

'Yes,' she said, taking a step towards him. He smelt, as he had not before, the delicate perfume of her body. 'The library closes at three on Mondays.'

They both turned towards the clock which looked down from above the balcony. It was a clock that had been salvaged when a privateer wrecked off the coast, a privateer whose captain was an horologist as well, it so happened, as the worst of navigators. Its mechanism moved a moon round in a circle so that at one moment it was a crescent and the next full, pregnant with significance. The clock indicated that it was two minutes to the hour.

'Closed,' she whispered, putting her hand on the book which he had indeed closed the moment she had surprised him in his research.

'I must go,' he said, half raising his hand to point at the clock.

'Oh, no,' she replied, 'the hours of the Reading Room can be extended in special circumstances. Do you want an extension?'

He looked at her as she slowly undid a second pearl button which slid so easily through the embroidered hole.

'Indeed there are no particular restrictions on the Restricted Reading Room beyond the restrictions on who is permitted to enter here. I have seen your application,' she said, passing a pink tongue over wet lips.

'The professor signed it,' he replied, anxious to return the conversation more unequivocally to the details of bureaucracy while watching, nonetheless, as a third pearl button was unfastened.

'I know,' she said, 'I am intimate with your details.'

Suddenly it struck him that she seemed to have walked straight out of the text he had been studying. There she stood, compliant, provocative, demanding.

'Could I order another book?' he asked.

'Perhaps you would like me to recommend one.' She paused. 'Now that I am familiar with your tastes, and I am familiar, am I not?'

There were only two more buttons to go and already the curve of her breasts was open to his view. He could bear it no longer. Nor did he have to, for the privateer's clock began to strike and as it did so he opened his eyes and found in front of him not a tale of lust, with naked women, but a history of the corsetry trade in the 19th century, and by his side not a supple temptress, slowly disrobing, but a woman with a broom, asking him tetchily if he would lift his feet so that she could sweep under the desk. But it was the same woman and he saw that her blouse was indeed held closed by a row of pearl buttons, one of which slipped through its restraining buttonhole as she bent forward beside him.

He ran back to the Professor's house as if his true vocation were to be an athlete rather than a scholar. He ran through the empty streets, for all others had retired for their afternoon sleep. He ran in the sunlight and in the shadow but he blushed as much whether the sun shone or not. And when at last he reached the house he slammed the door behind him forgetful that there might be those who still sought to sleep. He leaned back on the door, panting, and was still there a moment later when Justina passed, her naked feet making faint sucking noises as she walked across the cool stone floor.

'Oh, it's you, she said. 'I suppose you've been in the library. Reading, reading, reading. You know, sometimes you should drop everything and try to live a little.'

What could he do but nod as she walked away from him, each foot in turn unkissing from the marble only to kiss again with each step she took?

When Hernan arrived at the café there were no more than half a dozen people present, though there seemed tobacco smoke enough for twenty, this being a country where smoking was a vocation, a religion into which all were inducted at the age of twelve. It was a habit presumed to safeguard against mosquitoes, dysentery and those diseases acquired in cheap hotels, in alleys and the back seats of taxis (of which, in truth, they were only two, though not at any one time). It followed that women did not smoke and, interestingly, seemed untroubled by mosquitoes or dysentery, but who can tell since none were likely to keep others informed of such, particularly in the case of the last named. The Green Parrot – so called because all parrots in the country were a vivid red (irony often constituting a large proportion of the Gross National Product of countries which are aware of their true insignificance) – was small and undistinguished, but its walls were covered by paintings whose colours were only muted by decades of cigarette and cigar smoke. These paintings had been offered in lieu of money by artists temporarily or permanently destitute and willing to trade the products of their talent for a glass of inferior wine.

But one painter was different. Pedro Almevar was a genius, a surrealist before surrealism, a vorticist before vorticism, a dadaist before Tzara. He was a modernist, an imagist, a futurist; he was all things in one and there were those who spent their time in the Green Parrot for no other reason than to see the products of his genius. And if they were lucky they would see the man himself, though it was many years since he had offered a painting for a bottle of whisky or even for Francesca who, in truth, could be had for a good deal less than that. He drank free, as why should he not who attracted those who paid not only for their own drink but also for the drinks of others, and had difficulty in telling how many zeroes should appear on a banknote in the smoke and gloom of a room where some sat and wrote their novels or poems and others gently strummed guitars or cleaned their teeth with spent matches.

Pedro Almevar, of indeterminate age, was there when Hernan arrived. He looked up. There was a flicker of recognition in eyes that were not so much blue as turquoise and not so much turquoise as red. As befitted a surrealist/dadaist/vorticist, he had a reputation as a radical and Hernan found a certain inspiration in paintings whose images seemed to betoken the violence of the state and the dreams of an aspiring class, though he had never heard the artist express his radical convictions except through the medium of his art. The oddity was that those who sought out that art were anything but radical, and there were times when Hernan could not but smile at the thought of so many rich people's homes and national museums permitting such corrosive images to work on their sensibilities.

It was not entirely clear, however, that Pedro Almevar was overly concerned with such ironies. His mind seemed focused on something closer to hand, though focused is perhaps not quite the word. He gripped a bottle of local *eau de vie*, and not the most expensive, either. That very same spirit had been used to power modified taxis when a strike of dock workers had prevented the importation of gasoline. The experiment had not proved entirely successful as a result of impurities, however, so that the taxis (more usually, taxi) so powered had the disturbing habit of making farting noises or sometimes rumbling belches, and this can do little for one's tourist trade, even if such a trade is as yet barely getting under way, hotels breeding rats, cockroaches and diseases in equal proportions.

Such impurities, however, did not inhibit Pedro Alvemar, though, interestingly, they had much the same effect on the human digestive system as had been so quickly exhibited with the internal combustion engine, both sharing the same physical properties and objectives. He had, after all, been powered by essentially the same fuel since the death of his wife in an accident nearly twenty years before. She had been pregnant with her tenth child and decided that she could not bear to bring another baby into a marriage in which the smell of oil paint mixed with that of alcohol and in which her artist husband, renowned for his abstract art, nonetheless insisted on retiring to his studio with a bottle and an artist's model each afternoon, emerging a little flushed some time later and with nothing more than a jagged line or splash of yellow added to the canvas when she crept in to see what he might have accomplished. Accordingly she had visited an elderly woman who lived in the Old Town and who had a certain reputation when it came to moderating the population, and submitted first to the herbs and then the instruments with which she sought to remedy her situation. The one had no effect, the other an effect so profound as to carry this mother of nine and soon to be mother of ten to her grave, so that mother and child together were interred in San Isidro's cemetery, along with the hopes and dreams of her children, four boys and five girls who held hands around the grave and watched as their father slipped and fell into the orange-brown soil, never losing his grasp on the bottle which he held tight to his chest like a secret he would share with no one.

The following day he gathered his children about him, as a hen does her chicks, and with tears in his eyes told them that they were his life. And so they were. He could not release his grasp on the bottle, clutching it, indeed, even more tightly than he had before, but he could forsake his sessions in the studio with a woman who posed for his jagged lines and vital colours. Each day when they returned from school, thereafter, he was waiting for them, even if the rest of his time was spent at the Green Parrot drinking away his memories beneath the pictures he had painted in the time of his youth.

Towards the front of the room, where the air was a touch less impregnated with contemplated despair, sat a gatherer of Indian myths whose book, *Los Indios*, sold steadily year by year to those who preferred their Indians safely contained between the covers of a book. It had, to be sure, little to do with the genuine stories of those who were to be seen, occasionally, in the fretted shadows of the forest or drunk on the streets of the villages which fringed it, but the blend of peasant wisdom and romantic strangeness had earned him a reputation with those who yearned for the supposed simplicity of primitive life without the inconvenience of actually experiencing it. Happily the Indians themselves, who would have rebelled against the very title of the book, which took as one what in truth were many, could neither read nor write and hence took no offence, being more concerned with those who chose to burn them out and slash their trees to open clearings where they could sow a handful of seeds and a deal of trouble.

He sat with a friend, a poet of some little reputation, at least among the followers of a poetry whose regular metre and rhyme made it sound like the simple songs sung by children in the street as they skipped with ropes or jumped on numbered squares which they had chalked on the heavy flagstones laid by the Spaniards, like tombstones over the civilisation they had destroyed. The two men were lovers, even if their love lacked constancy, each retreating, with regularity, to dark assignations on the still darker streets once the children had withdrawn for the day and other, older, children come out to play.

They met in what had once been the Jewish quarter before the Jews were driven out several centuries before for supplying the money demanded of them and hence incurring a sense of obligation which could only be discharged by repayment or deportation. But there was a certain constancy even in their inconstancy and the two men sat opposite one another for many hours a day, entertaining themselves with brittle observations about their contemporaries. The lover, however, resented the success, no matter how limited, of his companion; for though he was, to his own mind at least, the more brilliant of the two he had not had the good fortune to secure publication of his poetry, deeply experimental, indeed admirably opaque though it was. A year later he would batter his friend to death, using an onyx paperweight shaped into the form of two young boys embracing one another on a rock, before slashing his own wrists, feeling, suddenly, an irremediable sense of abandonment.

Hernan stood for a while and breathed in the stale air of what, lacking comparison, he believed to be the purest radicalism. Then he lifted a section of the bar, smooth and silky to the touch, walked through and clicked it satisfyingly back into place. The morning's dishes were piled high in the sink beyond. It was not a job he liked but he consoled himself by recalling the dignity of labour as he slipped a pink pinafore, with a green parrot rampant, over his head before rearranging the dishes, emptying the sink and turning the tap on the boiler quite as though he were a general disposing of his troops or a politician reorganising society.

On leaving the Green Parrot later that night, he walked down the rua Martinez past the convent/hospital of the Sisters of Small Mercies. The order owed its name to the experience of Sister Maria, eighteen of whose family had been wiped out in the earthquake of 1912, along with many of their friends, their property and animals. However, as Sister Maria declared at the time, and frequently thereafter, her crucifix had survived and hence one must be grateful for small mercies.

Their hospital dated from the influenza epidemic which struck just six years later. So overwhelming was this that the Sisters decided to do what little they could to address the national calamity. As a result, for a year they tended to the sick and dying, rather more of the latter, it was noted, than the former, their skills having more to do with embroidery than medicine. When at last the scourge had passed they decided to maintain their hospital, for were there not always the sick needing assistance and consolation? Some, it has to be admitted, were reluctant to place themselves in the Sisters' care but the pious submitted to their ministrations believing that it might bring them closer to God, which indeed it did, though rather faster than many might have wished.

The Sisters relied heavily on herbs and plants which they found growing wild, believing that their very wildness was a sign of their utility. They had, of course, been placed there by God; and why else but for the good of mankind? They were thus experimenters pushing back the bounds of human knowledge. 'Take a little of this,' they would say to a patient, believing that it must restore him to health. And if it did not, well, that is the nature of science. After a time, their distinctive approach meant that word began to spread and those who retained the use of their legs would often walk, or hobble, to the civic hospital, for all its acknowledged deficiencies. But reputations, for good or ill, are not always justly earned and perhaps so many who entered the convent hospital failed to leave again because they wished to spend their final hours with nuns who dispensed their multi-coloured medicines with such radiant smiles, saying, 'Try a little of this,' with every assurance that God decides the fate of all, even if He might require a little assistance from those whose faith, rather than skills, constituted their chief claim.

The Mayor had come to his exalted position much as had all his predecessors. He was wealthy. It was a wealth derived from copper, or at least from those who laboured deep beneath the surface to extract it so that he might perform the alchemy of transforming it into cash. He inherited the mine from his father who in turn had inherited it from his who had acquired it by shooting the man who rightfully owned it. Such, a certain young man in the backroom of the Green Parrot might have reflected, is the way with capitalism and perhaps with human nature.

The Mayor was elected by those with the power to do so, namely those whose stature in the community had been acquired by much the same process. He was not evil, or at least not beyond the evil which comes from being blind to the pain we

51

cause others when we fail to enquire what their lives might be. He was proud of his position, and he was generous, when it paid to be. He was proud, too, of his wife, without wishing to be with her more than was necessary for strictly civic reasons. Coming, as she did, from the slums of the capital, she had a natural relationship with the people when she appeared on the balcony of the City Hall. She had raised herself from her humble origins by working as a dancer and then an actress, at which time she met a young man, heir to a copper fortune. It was a familiar route out of despair. Its sheer familiarity was what drew the people to her, for they admired anyone who escaped what they feared would be their own imprisonment.

Meanwhile, he had a friend of his own, for his marriage had sprung from an affair that had burned in the spring of their lives but which by the summer had cooled and by the autumn was cold. The friend had the power to blow on the ashes of his passion until they burst into flame. She was the wife of an ambassador and understood that her function might be to do rather more than assist him to lie for his country. She might have to lie, too, though as a matter of fact he did not mind where or with whom she chose to lie because his interest lay in another direction entirely, she being no more than a function of his office, like the plumed hat he wore when presenting his credentials.

The Mayor's wife was a woman of poise and accomplishment, at least in her own mind. Why, then, stay with a man who owed everything to a stain in the earth and who lived in a country that most of the world found difficulty locating on a map? For the same reason, perhaps, as anyone else who should forge a relationship they cannot later understand. Because she felt an absence in her life which she endeavoured to fill in any way she might. Because she wished to punish herself and perhaps another for a greater betrayal. Because she looked to find something in such a violation of her nature that she could find in no other way. Because we do things for which we would never find an explanation if we should live a dozen lives, which, incidentally, she believed herself to have done, having dreams of herself as Cleopatra from time to time.

Whatever the reason, and however strange the relationship might seem, the Mayor and his wife, for a while, discovered in each other whatever it was that they sought. She had her consolations, of course, for this sophisticated woman, sophisticated, at least, in her own eyes, could become quite other when placed in close proximity to certain men who drifted on the tide through her life. These relationships were kept from the eyes of the masses, as were his with a number of passing women who occasionally ceased to pass quite quickly enough for her taste, but she would not compromise her husband's position and he was aware of the love and even adulation with which the people regarded his wife. There had even been talk of the presidency, though that was an office few would wish to claim, for, with the exception of Seamus O'Grady, none had died in their beds, unless you count Don Phillipe who was shot as he lay with a woman's stocking on one leg, a rubber mask over his face, and an orange in his hand. His wardrobe had revealed a full array of women's clothes, including a little black number which the coroner removed for his wife. But human nature being what it is, the lure of fame and power has blinded many to the risks which accompany such ambition. For the moment, though, the Mayor was content with his position, content, too, with both his wife in her public function, and his mistress in her private one.

Nor was he without his sympathy for the poor. His wife, indeed, had the instincts if not of a socialist then of a populist who understood that the promise of good deeds may serve when the practice is beyond immediate realisation. Tears would come to her eyes as she described the privations of the city slums or spoke in public, as she did on the day of the great parade. Before the parade began the President, the Mayor and, latterly, now that she had, as she fancied, a certain leverage, the Mayor's wife, addressed those who gathered for the festivities. The President spoke on this occasion, as on all others, of the need for national unity in the face of subversion, of the country's greatness, its function as an international symbol of freedom to a world whose eyes were fixed on its destiny. He spoke, as he always did, of its generosity in opening its arms to the poor and needy while assuring his audience of the stringency of immigration policies that would exclude all but those genuinely in need, a group which, as it happened, had amounted to no more than fifteen in the previous year, each one being of sufficient wealth to contribute to the national economy. He raised his hand in acknowledgement of a silence broken only by the sound of an old man being sick in the square below, who was immediately arrested for offering an affront to the office of the presidency.

The Mayor cleared his throat, gestured to the policeman who was removing the old man with some care so as not to spoil his uniform since he had risen early to iron it, and then spoke into a microphone which sent his voice echoing back from the brightly coloured buildings on the far side of the square so that the crowd heard his voice twice, as though he sought to underline each point. He spoke of his civic pride in an occasion which celebrated their common heritage. Being no clearer than anyone else as to what the occasion was celebrating he kept his remarks general except when he drew attention to the new benches that had appeared next to the fountain, benches which he himself had donated to relieve the exhaustion of the faithful as they approached the cathedral. He knew better than to extend his remarks since those he addressed (and, indeed, he himself) were anxious for the parade to start and for the jolting of the vehicles to displace the skimpy costumes of those who brought up the rear in several respects. He stepped back from the microphone to the cheers of six men who had been paid sufficient to enable them to purchase a bottle each of the cheapest sugar cane alcohol.

He was replaced by his wife. A ragged cheer went up and a cry of 'Esmeralda'. She smiled and waved, lifting her breasts in pride and hoping that the sun would shine on her teeth which, after all, had cost her husband more than the annual income of an entire peasant family, indeed several peasant families, in truth a whole village full of peasant families. She spoke with the accent of the slums, exaggerated tones which in other circumstances she strained to modulate.

'Juanistas,' she cried, invoking the name of a leader of the slum dwellers, now dead a hundred years and hence charged with sentimental rather than political force. 'This is your day.' There were cheers from below. She flashed her teeth which felt, suddenly, a little loose as the new dental fixative proved not as effective as it was claimed to be. 'The great O'Grady dedicated this day to you.' This being as plausible as any other explanation, she was greeted with a cheer which urged her on to ever greater heights of rhetoric. 'This city,' she exclaimed (though her loosening teeth made this sound suspiciously like 'this shitty') 'is yours.' Her husband looked a little uneasily in her direction, while the President nudged an aide who looked distraught but did nothing since there was plainly nothing to be done.

'You built this shitty. This shitty is a monument to you.'

There was a certain shifting of the feet amongst those who heard this not once but twice as it rebounded back to them from the walls of the shitty for which, they were being told, they were responsible.

'I am one of you. I was born in this shitty.' She clamped her teeth together in an attempt to force the adhesive to do its work. The sound, amplified by the microphone, was like a rifle shot and must have inspired her next remark.

'We all remember Juan who led his people in revolt against injustice. It is to his memory that my husband has dedicated the new benches so that those who are weary may shit on them.'

Her husband kicked her ankle, but she was entranced by her reception: for the crowd had suddenly grown animated, cheering each statement, then falling silent in eager anticipation of the next. She clamped her teeth together once again. The crowd cheered even this.

'Shittizens,' she cried, tears forming in her eyes. 'This is my shitty too.'

The President leaned towards the Mayor and hissed into his ear. The sound engineer, however, having entered the general spirit of the occasion, had turned up the volume so that even though the two men stood several paces away the words 'crazy', 'dumb', 'fat', and 'bitch' could be clearly heard. Immediately boos, hisses and whistles sounded out. The acoustics were such, however, that while the crowd heard every syllable, the Mayor's wife did not and hence could not understand the sudden change in their mood. Accordingly, she redoubled her efforts to ingratiate herself.

'I was born and bred in the backstreets of this shitty. I shat by the river as a girl. Today I shit in the Shitty Hall.'

By now those on the balcony who were not tugging at her sleeve or gesturing at the Mayor had tears on their cheeks. The Mayor elect and his wife, who were no friends to the incumbent, clung together as though their legs might give way. In the square below even the pickpockets had ceased their trade and stood looking up at the balcony as if a new star had suddenly entered the firmament. A chant began in the far corner of the square and spread rapidly across it until all that could be heard was 'Esmeralda! Esmeralda!'

She beamed and turned to her husband, forgetting, for the moment, that she held him in some contempt. He gestured to her, pulling his hand sharply across his throat, a signal universally understood to be an invitation to silence or sudden death. She saw it as a gracious invitation to continue and turned back towards the people, opening her arms. There was a cheer which echoed around the square.

'My husband,' she cried, in a kind of ecstasy, 'is nearly at the end of his period of office. It has been four years we shall not forget.'

The crowd waited, its appetite only whetted by delay.

'We hope that we have done something to help you in that time.'

Still they waited.

'You know that in my heart I am one of you.'

The silence was palpable.

'And now it is time for the festivities to begin.'

They leaned forward in anticipation. She saw that they wanted something more from her. She obliged. 'But in years to come,' she cried, her voice developing a vibrato, 'I hope you will remember my husband and I whenever you shit in this square and that you will say that we did the best we could for the shitty we love. This is our shitty. This is your shitty. And now please shit so that the priest may bless you.'

At which the crowd roared, while her upper dentures finally detached themselves from her palette as her husband jerked her away from the microphone with such force that her teeth flew out of her mouth, for the briefest of seconds flashing a perfect smile to the assembled mass before, Cheshire cat-like, disappearing from view.

The following day the benches were removed since overnight so many people had carved their names on them, together with the simple message: 'Carlos . . . Maria . . . Otavia . . . shat here.'

That day was a public holiday. Special stalls had been selling lettuce for nearly a week and a green line had been painted down the Boulevard O'Grady, a line that marked the pathway down which a succession of floats and decorated trucks would pass. None knew and none asked what occasion it was they celebrated, it being the nature of celebrations that they soon detach themselves from their first cause and thereafter justify themselves through nothing more elaborate than habit. Each craft guild was expected to take part in the parade, no matter how perfunctory their display, while a certain licence was granted to those who wished, on this occasion if no other, to display such parts of their body as modesty more normally requires should be kept undisclosed.

This last was itself sufficient to guarantee a ready audience and, indeed, all looked forward to the day including those who, from time to time, felt obliged to denounce it from church pulpit or public stage, while smiling from day break to sundown when it came around. Besides, sin remains a disturbingly abstract affair unless it can be openly displayed and hence precisely designated from time to time. How much more moral, after all, to identify the very weaknesses against which it is so necessary to guard oneself. Perhaps that is why, it was rumoured, the Vatican maintained a library where suspect texts were kept and where cardinals could browse at their leisure when they were not, as was equally rumoured, conducting their passionate affairs with members of closed orders who offered the additional advantages of being sworn to silence. But such calumnies, of course, attach themselves to the virtuous in all ages.

It was anyway supposed that there were limits to the trans-gressions permitted on the day of festival. No breast was to be on display, no smooth and rounded bottoms to mock the city's modesty. But costumes often being but imperfect fits and the sudden movement of distempered trucks proving constant and unavoidable pitfalls even for the most virtuous, sending those on board staggering and reaching for support, breasts and bottoms would, from time to time, and with no calculation or intent, slip momentarily into view. And what if the applause at such occurrences should so distract those otherwise anxious to restore their modesty as to delay such immediate repairs? Was that, perhaps, not an essential part of the message that in their hearts many believed to be the secret significance of the gnomic speeches Seamus O'Grady had made in a language they did not understand? 'Mary O'Rourke' would call the crowd, shifting like some corporate animal to get a better view.

Such casual morality, or momentary failure of costume, was invariably, however, associated with those from the poorest part of town who by some miracle, having no money and frequently no work with which to earn it, nonetheless contrived to con-struct the most beautiful floats and to wear the most inventive, if minimal and unreliable, of outfits. They brought up the rear of the procession and were the more appreciated because by then the crowd had had to tolerate the staid and uninspiring offerings of the Banco St Marco, the Association of Lawyers and the Professional Union of School Teachers. That same crowd had otherwise sought to alleviate the heat of the day with regular and plentiful supplies of sugar cane alcohol, sold by street vendors whose cry of 'Sugar Heaven!' echoed from the shimmer-ing white buildings and colonial colonnades of the Boulevard. And if regularly there were those who woke up the following day stone blind from the wood alcohol employed by the less scrupulous of vendors, why that merely added a certain spice to the day.

At the front of the parade was the greatest decorum. The crafts displayed their wares. Here was a giant shoe and a shoemaker at his last. There was a wheelwright spinning a wheel as though it were the globe or the wheel of fortune which must point each to his fate as the spokes flickered by in the sun. Indeed there were numbers painted around the rim and each time the wheel came to rest the number was called out, for there were those who would use such numbers on their lottery cards, cards bought mostly by the poor. On one occasion the numbers shouted out by the wheelwright had indeed won the principal prize; but there were so many claimants that none had enough money to do more than buy a few drinks in the cantina.

The lawyers' float this year featured a woman, rather gone in years, dressed up as Justice with scales in her hand and a blindfold over her eyes, though the failing engine of the camión on which she struggled to maintain her balance ensured that the scales regularly oscillated up and down in a manner which would have alarmed any accused had this been a real court. Justice had also discovered the necessity to lift the blindfold of one eye a little in order to see where she was going and where the support might be, without which she must be constantly falling to her knees. It was, it seems, a parade of metaphors for those with eyes to see, though many were blindfolded by drink, prejudice or simply an unwillingness to recognise metaphors when presented to them in the guise of a somewhat ageing woman staggering around an ill-serviced vehicle.

At the head of the whole procession rode the Queen of the Carnival, the 'Mary O'Rourke', dressed all in white with young courtiers in pastel blues and greens and pinks. It was considered an honour in San Marco to be asked to perform this function which could only be undertaken by one of flawless beauty, presumed virginity, and good connections, though two out of three was regarded as a reasonable score in these days in which good connections were not hard to come by but other virtues were rather harder to find or, if found, to verify.

This year the choice had fallen on Justina, and since her father had no connections at all, not even with reality, it was clearly her natural loveliness that had earned her the right not only to lead the parade but to ride on the only truck which seemed to have survived the city's mechanics, whose familiarity with machines was no closer than the current Mayor's with his wife, which is to say slight indeed.

There is something about a young woman in the flush of her youth that commands both respect and attention, even from those whose motives for gathering in the heat of the sun are more base. Beauty has its own authority and it was generally agreed that she was the most attractive young woman to have graced the procession since Seamus O'Grady had inadvertently initiated the tradition. And, as luck would have it, the guild that won the ballot for second place was that of the bell makers and bell-ringers, which thus placed a certain young man in close proximity to the girl whom, he, and virtually every other young man she had encountered, had convinced himself he loved.

The bell-ringers' float made up in enthusiasm what it lacked in originality, what it lacked, it has to be said, in virtually every other respect. A large, and not altogether convincing, cardboard bell rocked back and forth from a wooden pole which ran the length of the truck, parallel to its floor. This was painted silver. Meanwhile, six young men, five of whom were bell-ringers, held a silver bell in each hand and at a given signal would play the first twenty bars of the far from memorable national anthem. Indeed, so unmemorable was it that after twenty minutes, during which they did not once succeed in getting any further than halfway through it, by agreement they began to play a folk song whose alternative, and altogether unauthorised, lyrics were known by everyone and acknowledged by none identifying, as they did, parts of the male and female body and how they might, with sufficient invention and a deal of dexterity, be brought into physical conjunction with one another.

Our apprentice bell maker had the ill fortune, however, to find himself at a distant remove from the young woman in white. But where love rules there may be no barrier, so that he changed places with the young man who stood immediately beside him. The effect, however, was unfortunate for there was another young man who stood in front of the great bell and conducted. And though he had handled the change from national anthem to ribald folk song with some aplomb, since they had often amused themselves in private and enlivened their rehearsals by playing it, his method of conducting depended on the ringers maintaining their accustomed places so that he could point to them in turn and they could respond with a silver note. This had the added advantage that it was therefore unnecessary for any of them to learn his part, with the exception of the national anthem in which they had proved so inadequate. Each had merely to wait until the conductor's baton was waved in his direction and then give a sharp shake to his bell. Indeed they continued to do so, except that their changed places created a new, improvised, music which had something of the rhythm of the original and a family resemblance but which could not be said to be wholly recognisable to any but those who had already taken sufficient sugar cane alcohol to hear harmony in everything.

Matters deteriorated still further when, clearly oblivious to the changing music and the increasing desperation of the conductor, and with his eyes fixed on the back of his new love as she waved to an enthusiastic crowd, Federico jostled his way past the final bell-ringer who stood in his way and was at last in the front of the truck. Still he played, directing an occasional glance at the despairing conductor who had now decided to try to restore the lost harmony by recalling who should be ringing his bell no matter where he should be standing. And he might have succeeded – though I fancy not – were it not for the fact that the other players in his orchestra had also taken it into their heads to solve this musical crisis by exchanging places in an attempt to restore the original order. As a result the music changed constantly, creating a series of discordant notes which an avant-garde composer in the crowd later took as inspiration for a new composition. When the work was first performed, it caused a riot and part of the town's small concert hall was burned down as competing cliques of music lovers contended over the virtues of so radical a departure from the country's musical traditions.

Our hero, however, would not be displaced from his honoured position in the vanguard of their company and accordingly rebuffed the others when they sought to re-establish their line. Yet for all this they continued to ring their bells whenever the conductor pointed his baton in their direction so that the resulting noise was quite unlike that which anyone had previously heard from a guild apparently dedicated to the production of perfect sounds.

At last, even Justina realised that something must be wrong for people ceased to point at her and pointed instead somewhere behind. Had she perhaps failed to close her dress? Were they laughing at her, for laughing they certainly were? She felt tears begin to prick at her eyes and might well have jumped from the peerless truck and run to her home were it not for the fact that she heard a stifled scream from the rear. She turned around, holding her white dress away from her as a swan will fan out its feathers, and was just in time to see a young bell maker, with a bell in each hand, tumble from the truck behind, followed a moment later, by a large silver bell which contrived to fall on top of him. The other boys, meanwhile, quickly regrouped in the proper order and began to play what she, even with a few notes transposed and a rhythm somewhat affected by a sudden braking of the vehicle, recognised as an obscene song which she had heard from time to time sung by gutter children as they played in the dust with marbles the colour of the rainbow.

The truck stopped so precipitately that the line of young men, only just reassembled, lurched into one another like a line of dominoes, very much so, indeed, since they had opted to wear black and white costumes. To save themselves they let go of the bells and reached instead for the pole from which the great bell had been suspended before it had upended itself on top of their friend. Nonetheless they fell one on another so that, in their black and white costumes, they seemed like a descending arpeggio. The bells hit the cobbled street one after the other, creating a dull music instantly stilled.

The leading float, meanwhile, with its figure in white, face now masked with tears as her moment of fame was thus snatched away from her, drew ever further away as the boys were helped to their feet and restored to the truck, all except one. He ran after his vision in white, but must have thought he ran in vain; for if he had ever lit a fire in the heart of the one he loved he had just succeeded in extinguishing it, for would she ever think of him without hearing the fractured notes of an obscene song, without recalling the humiliation which had attended her reign as Queen?

The atmosphere in the Green Parrot that night befitted the general air of benign fulfilment appropriate to O'Grady Day. Reality was what it ever was; but for a few hours, at least, it lost its edge. And besides, who can say what the real may be when no two people can agree as to its shape and content, and no one individual recall it with accuracy a brief while later. For those who saw the world as an eternal struggle between exploiters and exploited, however, there was no real surcease from toil and no remission of the real. So it was that while in the front room poets raised their glasses and their spirits and searched for metaphors by bringing together what nature had chosen to keep apart, in the back room, darker, as befitted their intentions, and with rather less in the way of spiritual or spirituous relief, there gathered together a group of men who spoke of revolution and retribution, who read from books whose language eschewed the warmth and simplicity of those whose simplicity they believed themselves to celebrate.

At the centre of this group was a professor, officially sane where another professor, who was developing a theory of fiction which made human life itself a story subject to analysis, was not. But who is to say who is sane when those who make the judgement are themselves at a particular point of the compass which they alone insist is due north? This professor was a professor of philosophy and as such might be thought to care more for the realm of abstract thought than concrete action, but there is a yearning of the soul, felt by all, for that which seems to be denied them. There had come a time accordingly when Professor Sanchez had begun to feel a deepening sense of guilt for what seemed to him to be his withdrawal from the world, trapped in language and increasingly bewildered by an avocation in which every proposition is countered by its opposite, each acuity further refined or refuted by those for whom such refinement and refutation is the essence of their trade.

Beyond that, he was fifty years old. Need more be said? Despite his title and his two books of moral philosophy, required reading in the university, he felt an overwhelming sense of futility. He had reached that age at which all stare into a darkening future and admit to ourselves what we have always known but never allowed to enter into our souls – that we will die. As the future shortens, indeed rushes towards us at unseemly speed, we become aware of how little we have done, how little time remains in which we may transform and hence redeem ourselves.

Professor Sanchez had experienced such a moment as he had come to the end of a lecture on Hegel and noticed that of the fifty students present for his reading of the register only fifteen now remained, none of whom was looking in his direction. Indeed one appeared to be reading a newspaper while two others were playing a game of chess. He stopped and stared at the yellowing pages in front of him, pages he had prepared some twenty years before. His life, he realised, had amounted to nothing. Nobody cared about so abstract a subject, including, he realised with a sudden shock, himself.

And what was he to those he had noticed on his travels to the interior, where he maintained a small cabin to which he retreated each vacation and where he could fish in the cool rivers that tumbled down from the high mountains? The peasants who tilled the irregular fields, who struggled to lift rocks from those fields and shape them into the low walls which marked the boundaries of their master's property, had been no more than a kind of background noise, but as a dripping tap will slowly stain a sink so what he had not even known he had seen began to work on his mind until one day he put down the book he had been reading and stared ahead blankly.

When he came to himself, he and the world had changed. He saw what it was he must do. He must start his life again; and what else should his society do but the same? It must begin anew and to do that all institutions must be torn down. And to do so was to require that all those who sustained them should themselves be set aside. Things should be returned to the state in which they had once been before greed and possessions corrupted man. And in his mind he saw clearly what his organisation should be called, the organisation which was as yet as abstract as the subject he had long professed. It was to be called the Thousand Points of Light. He knew, of course, that such a name had associations with another society, one which he must see as the enemy, but that was the essence of his method: to reclaim language as he wished to repossess the nation's soul. He was an intelligent man. How else could he have been a professor of philosophy? But he revealed what we often learn at great cost. Intelligence and common sense may be strangers while the mind and the heart are separated one from the other only at the greatest price.

And yet the Thousand Points of Light was little more than an idea, albeit one that attracted a number of the Professor's former students, they and a young man who earned money washing dishes but who spent his days, and sometimes his nights, sticking posters wherever he could and seeking to persuade whomever he might of the wisdom he had so recently acquired from a man whose eyes were bright with certainty and who spoke so casually of a necessary cruelty.

So it was that on O'Grady Day, as the writers in the front room piled glass upon glass and saucer upon saucer and began to sing tunelessly, romantic songs of love denied and sentimental ballads from the nation's past, in the back room others punched the air with their fists and sang the Internationale. This had been unknown until now and but recently translated by a man seduced by his own rhetoric and transformed by the fact that others were singing what he wrote and that for once there were

67

those who listened to what he said and might soon do what he required that they should do.

It was the writers, though, who sang the louder, their voices amplified by strong drink and strong emotions, while on the streets all were one. Peasant or politician, teacher or cleaner, all walked the streets and took a drink or two. Bars spilled their yellow light out into the darkness like pollen on the velvet petals of San Marco's emblem – a black narcissus. Tomorrow would see the return of toil and pain, but tonight was for celebration; and celebration is a natural instinct to those who understand that life is short and must be lived to the full whether their purse be full or empty.

Sagrado Dios was discovered, as was the case with so many other countries in the hemisphere, by accident. A Russian who had fled to Spain and made a living by lending money at high interest to those who believe that tomorrow never comes, financed an expedition to discover a chain of islands of fabulous wealth. These had been described to him by a sea captain who claimed to have been driven thence by a great storm and who was a more adept confidence trickster than Abramov was a banker. The Captain had meant to abscond with the money, but when the King of Spain declared the expedition to have papal warrant became obliged to give his fantasies some shape and form. He assembled a fleet of three vessels, salted away what money he could by sending his son, with six mules and some gold, across the Pyrenees, and set sail from Cadiz one March day feeling that he travelled towards his doom.

Abramov had chosen the ships with care and provisioned them well. Whatever his religious faith, and it paid to be somewhat vague in that regard, he was a great believer in gold and understood the need to invest in that future in which others chose not to believe.

The journey was much as others of its kind. It began with some optimism, degenerated into doubt, privation and near mutiny, and then, with the help of two storms of unusual ferocity, ended with the sighting of the coast of what was about to become Sagrado Dios, having as yet no name that a civilised man could recognise. The sea was a pale blue and the land lay like a welcoming arm. The Captain, El Cordobes as he preferred to be called, though his sailors had other names more apt, as it seemed to them, including Tonto, ordered two longboats to be lowered and an imperial army, consisting of fifteen sailors, El Cordobes himself with a tame vulture on his shoulder, and a priest who had been seasick for three months and was sick again now, approached the gentle coast of Sagrado Dios.

The boats sighed onto the pure white beach, where the subtle shells of sea creatures had been pounded into fragments. A small group of sailors was ordered to disembark and form a protective circle, pikes pointing, like some spiked animal, towards the forest which fringed the beach. They waited as the waves gently turned the boats so that they were parallel to the shore. At last, when nothing stirred, the Captain, the priest and some half-dozen sailors stepped into the cool water and waded ashore. Abramov remained on board. Capitalists usually provide capital and not themselves but he saw such a close affinity between the two that he was unwilling to separate one from the other. El Cordobes carried the Spanish flag, a little stained from where a cask of brandy had been breached by the second of the great storms. A ceremony was required. He advanced a few paces, careful to keep within the protective ring of his troops, and then thrust the flag into the sand. The pole struck a rock and snapped in two, sending a shock through his hands so that he dropped it and uttered a blasphemy which thus became the name of his new country. The priest crossed himself and, with a great deal more

69

care than his companion, pushed a cross into the ground. Church and state thus satisfied, they looked around for the gold that must be to hand, half expecting to find it scattered amidst the sparkling sand, for even El Cordobes had convinced himself of what he had convinced Abramov and which he had struggled so hard to convince others.

That first night they rowed back to the ship through water that had turned from pale turquoise to black as the stars began to appear like a promise of the wealth they sought, so many diamonds scattered by the hand of God. They returned to the ship for fear of what might await them once they should enter the forest to gather provisions for their journey. They were unclear what they would find. Would it be cities of gold, guarded by those who knew its value and were prepared to defend it against the world, or would it be no more than a handful of natives easily dazzled by glass beads and unaware of the significance of the metal which stained their rocks and glinted in their rivers?

They landed at dawn and gathered once more on the shore before venturing further. They had no animals to bear their burdens. The two horses they had brought on board at Cadiz had both broken their legs in the storms and proved a satisfying diet. Each man, therefore, loaded himself with packs which made him bow down under the weight. They carried food and goods and clothing and ammunition. Each man had a musket and a pistol, besides a sword and a dagger. They were thus ready to greet new friends as Europeans had always greeted those they sought to embrace for the good of their souls.

El Cordobes placed himself in the middle of the winding line of men who moved slowly forward, those at the front hacking at the tangled branches with swords which swiftly blunted. Later celebrated as the Great March, this was in fact a dispiriting and enervating advance over a bare fifteen leagues or so. As they splashed through the sullen rivers which cut across their advance they collected the glistening black scars of leeches along their legs, while small flies circled their heads, darting in to taste the blood of these white strangers.

When they were discovered by young men from a village which clung to the edge of a cliff, a village approached only along a perilous path cut into the sandstone, they were all but delirious with pain and despair. At first those who discovered them looked at them with wonder. Their skins were pale as though they might be spirits from another world, and several of them had blue eyes so it seemed that they might have fallen from the skies, for how else could they have come here to such a place? El Cordobes, by now delirious and uncertain where he might be, drew his sword and endeavoured to strike out against the bright light which almost blinded him. Those who watched stood in amazement, for one of the creatures was crying out in a strange tongue and in his hand was a piece of the sun which flashed in their eyes.

For some time these natives did no more than stand and stare. Then, one of their number gave a command and branches were cut from the trees and rough stretchers devised, with a lattice of vines, on which the strange intruders were placed. Some sought to resist, but were held respectfully but firmly in place until they could no more move than a caterpillar inside a chrysalis. Thus they were dragged and carried along the forest track, up the stone steps and along paths cut into the rock that were no more than a few paces wide, while beneath them was a sheer drop to the rocks below.

El Cordobes and his men were treated with respect and what might seem almost a superstitious awe; but if one of them moved towards the pathway leading down to the forest floor several of

71

the natives would drift, as though by some chance movement, to bar their way. And so it might have continued had not El Cordobes, inspired by a mixture of terror and frustration, risen to his feet and uttered a curse which echoed around the cave, raising the middle finger of his right hand in a derisive and obscene gesture. Immediately a sense of shock seemed to run through their captors, who stood immobile for a second before falling to their knees.

El Cordobes, too, stood motionless, aware that something had happened while unclear as to what it might be. His extended finger cast a flickering shadow on the wall of the cave where the sun's light streamed through. A sound began, low at first and then rising in volume and pitch, as the natives sounded out their awe. Then, at the rear of the cave, a shadow moved, detached itself from the general gloom. The shadow resolved into a man, naked, his skin glistening. He walked forward, stately, taller than his kind by more than a hand's span. He advanced to within a pace of El Cordobes, looking at the derisively extended finger, and then at the bloodshot eyes of a man who had for some days been suffering with a common cold, an ailment rendered more vexing by the attention of flies. The two men stared at one another. Past, present and future were focused in a single moment and in an encounter which neither could have imagined. Then the man whose body shone and smelled of the coconut fruit the sailors had seen fringing the seashore sank to his knees and bent his head. For a full minute everyone in the cave stood still as if time itself had been suspended before, slowly, the man rose and once again stared into the eyes of the stranger who had signalled with the sun and who had spoken to him with the sacred sign which was the symbol of the gods.

For his part, however, El Cordobes stared not into the eyes of the regal native but at his ear. At first it had been his nakedness that fascinated and appalled the adventurer. Now, however, he realised that this was not complete, for hanging from his left ear and shining brightly in the sunlight was an ornament. It was roughly shaped but even so clearly recognisable for what it was. It was a hand, all of whose fingers were tightly closed except the middle one which was extended and pointing down towards the ground. It was not, though, this configuration that drew the eyes of El Cordobes, but the material from which it was fashioned. As it shone and turned in the shaft of sunlight, and as all those in the cave watched, as if for permission to resume their lives, it was clear that it was made from gold. Two men, it seemed, had found their destiny.

El Cordobes was shrewd if not honest and possessed cunning if not intelligence. He realised that fate had offered him a weapon and he must use it for his own purpose. He signalled that those of his fellows who were still in bonds should be released, as much to see if his wishes would be obeyed as to offer them relief. At a wave from the chief the natives hurried to obey. Another gesture brought them food and water while the leaves of a tree were laid before them and by various theatrical antics it was made plain that these, too, were for eating.

From the moment that he espied it, however, there was only a single focus for El Cordobes. He had seen what he sought and nothing remained but for him to discover the origin of the gold which shone not only in the cave but the very heart of his being. Gold had become more than the object of his quest, more than his vindication and absolution. It had become his language. It shaped the way he saw the world. It had entered into his soul.

At first there was a risk that he would lose control over his men. When they had eaten of the leaves placed before them they lost interest in their surroundings, lying back on the rock as if it were a pillow filled with down, and when a little later women of

73

the tribe were led forward to meet their gods, those women were embraced as never before had human beings been embraced by deities outside the legends of antiquity. But when one appetite has been satisfied another will present itself, and at last he brought his men back to their true vocations.

The priest, meanwhile, harangued his new flock, though not in a language any of them could understand, and sprinkled a little water over their foreheads as token of their conversion, every drop of which had been carried in pots and leather water bags from the forest below. When once they had been summoned into God's good grace, their chief requiring, as it transpired, some little encouragement to indicate the source of their gold, the natives were pitched into the void so that they might sail towards heaven, albeit in a somewhat contrary direction. The chief, seeing he longer had any tribe to preside over, and having no inclination to serve such gods as these who required the sacrifice of life as the price of redemption, took leave to hurl himself into space, holding the golden ornament, which he understood to have provoked his doom, close to his chest. It was returned to El Cordobes by one of his soldiers. The finger had snapped in two, but this hardly mattered to one who wanted only to consign it to the crucible. What concerned him more was that he now had no guide to lead him towards his fortune.

'But we have saved many souls,' objected the priest.

'Fool. The world has an infinite supply of souls. Gold is a true rarity.'

He had the merchant's grasp of priorities and there would be few in the years to come who would contradict his judgement. It took no more than five years to bring the natives to their knees, sometimes by dint of removing their legs immediately below this joint, but more often by the expedient of shooting a few and roasting others on a spit so the air was full of the smell of human crackling. Others died of the illness which El Cordobes had introduced. It took a little longer to find the gold, though there was little enough of it to be sure when it was at last uncovered at the very heart of the forest in a decaying city presided over by a ghostly band of lepers. Thus yesterday reached out a poisoned hand towards the present.

In the end Sagrado Dios would build itself not on gold but on copper, which shone hardly less brightly but which in time turned green and seemed to return the buildings whose roofs it burnished to the world of nature that had been sacrificed to their construction. But in the years to come few forgot the cruelty of those who had travelled across the sea with no other intent, as it seemed, than to destroy everything and everyone they encountered.

The Mayor was not on good terms with his wife, except on occasions of public ceremony. She prized her public status but she prized still more the one-legged sea captain who had caught her eye at the annual seafarers' ball which all attended in fancy dress. He appeared as a pirate and it was some time before she discovered that the ivory leg on which he stumped noisily around, vaguely in time with the music, was not his own. By then she had compromised such virtue as she still retained, following many dedicated years of adultery or 'exercise', as she preferred to call it, as in her frequent remarks to her maid: 'I'm off for my exercise.'

Their passion had been satisfied on that first night in the robing room where she lay among the nest of capes laid upon a chaise-longue by their trusting owners. Discretion, and not a little anxiety, required that neither remove their clothes, at least no more than was strictly necessary to cement their new relationship. Somehow their subsequent encounters, too, occurred in circumstances which seemed to necessitate similar preventative tactics. Nor was she unwilling that this should be so, for she suffered from a complaint which had fascinated her many lovers but which had remained the cause of distress to her: she had inverted nipples. It was thus several months before she made her discovery, and that in such a way as to leave her for a moment confused and disturbed.

They lay in the darkness of his room, in a modest house overlooking one of San Marco's two canals, a feature which led a particularly undiscriminating traveller to compare the city to Venice. The shutters were closed and a fan turned slowly over a bed fashioned to resemble the prow of a ship by a carpenter whose acquaintanceship with naval architecture was on a par with the traveller's knowledge of Venice.

They had shared a glass or two, or perhaps more, of rum, the Captain's favourite drink and perfectly acceptable to his companion who had no particular favourites among the drinks she avidly imbibed. Now they were in the throes of what passed for passion with two people who were a little overweight and performed, it must be said, as if by memory rather than instinct. Lost in a reverie prompted by lust and liquor in almost equal proportions, they began to peel off one another's clothes.

The lady had bathed twice that morning in anticipation of such a procedure and had selected her underclothes with a care that made her rather regret the darkness in which she now began to unbutton her partner's jacket. Unfortunately his approach to personal cleanliness rather differed from her own, being used to the salt spray of the sea to wash away grime and regret. Happily her own perfume, applied liberally shortly before leaving the City Hall for her 'exercise', was powerful enough to suppress the rancorous odour of a regiment of horses, so the odd smell of rotting socks and tobacco laced with molasses was swiftly buried in the sea of her perfumed flesh.

The Captain made short shrift of her corsets, accustomed to the tying and untying of knots, though his seaman's touch did not go unnoticed later as her maid attempted to undo knots guaranteed against a nor'easter gale and requiring teams of boy scouts to identify let alone unravel. Her flesh relaxed like a jelly turned out of its mould and with a sound not unlike it. There was a rustle as he threw her dress unceremoniously to the floor where it joined his shirt, whose buttons had exploded one by one as she tore at them as though a group of undisciplined soldiers were discharging their weapons in a firing squad.

At last they were naked. The rhythm of the fan seemed to change as if it detected their readiness for what must follow, as lightning anticipates the thunder. So it was that he sent his hand wandering, a scouting party sent to bring back news of the lie of the land. It crept upwards over a stomach once flat and muscled and now like a sudden rounded hill, until it came to the upward slope of her breasts which, though large and shapely when confined to tightly laced clothes and when she herself was vertical, had now settled somewhat as two eggs in a pan. Nonetheless there was still a satisfying slope up which his fingers began to advance towards what he doubtless regarded as the satisfying summit, except that instead of reaching the expected pinnacle, the hand stopped, as though puzzled, and then slowly retraced its steps, as it were.

Only after a slightly frantic and undignified scrambling about did it become motionless as the Captain struggled to understand the evidence of his senses. There was no summit. The hand switched at once to the twin mountain peak, only to experience the same frustration. A moment passed as the Captain's simple brain filled with a range of possibilities, each more bizarre than the one before. Had he, perhaps, inadvertently, knocked them off (being, as it turned out, familiar with the notion of detachable appendages) and could he surreptitiously search for them amongst the bedclothes? Did she regard them as supernumerary and had she had them removed at some stage in the past?

After a moment or so, however, he ceased to worry and began to feel that the woman he embraced boasted an anatomical uniqueness which was not without its fascination. Indeed, as he probed further and discovered not a peak but an inversion, he found the idea a positive source of stimulation and immediately embarked on his voyage towards a familiar destination, doubtless anxious to see how far she carried her commitment to the radical transformation of physiognomy. But all was well and proceeded along familiar lines. It was precisely as he and, he fancied, she approached a further destination, however, that fate took another hand. With his final convulsive gasp his leg fell off.

There are women who take pride in the impact they have on their partners, and heretofore the Mayor's wife would certainly have included herself among their number, taking great pleasure in her ability to provoke changes in the bodies of those she chose to favour with her attentions. But even she had never previously succeeded in detaching entire limbs, and the sound of it hitting the floor interrupted her natural rhythm, if only temporarily, for she was not a woman who would permit the mere disassembling of her partner to prevent her enjoying a state she had worked so hard to achieve. She relented somewhat in her exertions, however, for fear that his disassembly might become more wide-spread. Indeed the thought of her shaking him into his component parts was sufficient, eventually, to override even her single-minded pursuit of ecstasy.

A moment later and they lay side by side, the air from the fan washing over them in gentle waves. She wished beyond any-thing to know which other parts of him might prove likely to detach themselves, indeed how much of him might be said to be his as opposed to the products of some foreign manufacturer. She was also in some fear that a disease of some sort might have led to such a diaspora in his body parts. For himself, he wished to ask whether her nipples had always been thus inverted or whether they had suddenly taken it into their heads to invert and dive for cover on his approach. But such enquiries coexisted uneasily with passion and so neither spoke, though the questions continued to provoke them in idle moments. Such minor concerns, however, were not sufficient to cause them to discontinue their relationship, though in future whenever the Captain undressed her he took care to detach his leg and lean it against the wall where it could await his return, while she watched to see if he would remove an eye or unscrew a hand to place beside it and gave a sharp tap to his extended organ lest it should become unattached at some future moment when she would have no power to secure it.

The fact is that we all have our needs and few of us can afford to despise those who find theirs satisfied in ways and with persons with whom we can never imagine ourselves to be content.

There was an event in the history of the country that made its way both into the official accounts of the past and into the myths celebrated in song and dance, though each interpreted the event somewhat differently. The first Governor, known for the severity with which he pursued dissenters and reduced such limited rights as were allowed to the natives, had a son, Miguel. Until his seventeenth birthday he was the mirror image of his father, echoing his words, defending him against the very few of his contemporaries who chose to criticise his methods if not his objectives. He regarded the Indians as a kind of cattle, to be used and abused at will. He had, to be sure, been nursed by one as a child, there being, as yet, few women who chose to venture to this remote and disease-ridden outpost of empire. But he had absorbed no compassion, no understanding, no sympathy from the milk with which the woman had nurtured him. Indeed, since he was born with a single tooth, he had returned pain for her gift of continued life.

Then there occurred to him what occurs to most. He fell in love. He fell in love with the daughter of that very woman, for she, her husband long before lost at sea, had been allowed to remain in a small hut in a distant part of the grounds of the palace, not because of any past services but because she continued to work in the palace kitchens. Her daughter had been in service from the moment she was old enough to polish shoes or lift a bucket. At night she would be told the stories of her tribe, learn to draw the patterns which contained their history and linked the earth to the stars. During the day she would labour to serve those who enslaved her people. But she knew no bitterness. She grew in beauty of soul as well as body. She wondered at the fate of her people and yet, like most children, accepted the way of things until an inner life began to distil, a cool pool of being, which made her feel apart from those she served, and not merely because of the fact of that service.

There came a day, however, as there comes a time for all conquerors and conquered people, when divisions were momentarily forgotten and she fell in love with the enemy and the enemy fell in love with her. Sweet betrayal.

It was one of her functions to draw water from the well in the palace courtyard, a well whose bricks were mottled with the green velvet of moss. Her muscles had grown strong, her body lithe and supple. She had accustomed herself to the rhythm of the wheel, her hands, clasped together on the metal handle, rising and falling in time to the song she sang in her mind, since she, in common with the rest of her people, was forbidden to sing or speak the language of her tribe. On this day the Governor's son had returned from riding his favourite gelding in the nearby country, a ride on which he scarcely noticed the Indians, who bowed their heads or stepped back into the shadows. He leapt from the saddle in the courtyard, leaving others to lead the animal, spittle flecked, towards the stables, and sought out the well to quench his thirst.

He barely saw her as he snatched a ladle and plunged it into the wooden bucket she had just set upon the ground. He drank, the water streaming down his face and onto his clothes. He plunged it in again and drank once more. Only then, as he dropped the ladle into the bucket, did he look up. He had seen countless servants in his life and learned that they were of no account, that they existed in some other sphere. Now, for the first time, he looked into the eyes of another person, of a despised and ignored person, and felt his soul fly out of him to meet that of another. He had no words to describe what was happening to him, no means to understand the transformations that affected him. Instead he stood as though suddenly struck dumb and deprived of all volition.

And something had happened to her, though her defences should not have been so easily breached who stood to lose so much if she allowed instinct to conquer reason. At first she had kept her eyes lowered, not so much afraid to raise them as habituated to such behaviour. But, as the silence extended, so she slowly raised her head until, with what seemed a sudden flash of brilliance, her eyes met his and her heart dissolved in that blend of need and desire, of exultance and hopeless hope, which all have experienced but which none has yet been able to explain.

I do not say that Spaniard and native had not come together before. Power will assert its privileges and women know the currency in which tribute must be paid. There were injunctions which precluded such alliances, but those who promulgated such injunctions were their principal violators. Indeed violation was itself a form of strategy. The price exacted from those native men who sought to assert their rights in this regard was simplicity itself: death. There were few men, however, who were tempted to such alliances: indeed, there were few who found themselves in propinquity with those who might otherwise be drawn to their muscular power or sad subjection.

By the side of the palace well, in the late afternoon of an April day, two people stood no more than a few feet apart for whom such histories were an irrelevance. They stood as though space and time and history were of no more account than the fall of a leaf. For a few brief moments, indeed, they were free of all prejudices, all policies, all authorities. They stared deep into one another's eyes and there found what they separately sought. They were not equal, though, not even in their love. For she was denied the right to speak her heart in the natural language of that heart, her native language being proscribed. The penalty for speaking it was death. Even in the privacies of their huts, when they sat together for meals or, indeed, embraced one another out of love, they were required to speak their lives in a language that few knew and in which virtually none was fluent. So they whispered to one another in their true language. The effect, of course, was to turn such exchanges into acts of rebellion. But rebellion could mean little when all the power was on one side and time itself seemed to have resolved the question in favour of that power.

They spoke no words that day, but words were no more than trinkets at such a time. They stood instead, as the sun moved overhead, and forged bonds in silence that words alone could never have consolidated with such force, until, at last, the girl's mother came out in search of her daughter and saw at once what peril she was in. She seized her by the arm and pulled her back to the servants' quarters. The young man did not move and, indeed, still stood there when there was no one but himself to see the sun set in a blaze of crimson fire.

That the match was doomed from the start would have been clear to anyone and was certainly clear to the girl's mother, who did everything in her power to prevent the two meeting again. But what power did she have and when did two young people ever see what others could by virtue of standing outside the magic circle of love and illusion?

They met again because he willed it to be so, and his authority was absolute. She found herself ordered to attend the young man's sister and hence to live in proximity to the young man himself. They would meet in the long corridor of the palace and in the rooms where she laid pewter plates on a great oak table. At first he was content to watch her, as one would admire the beauty of the countryside, and she could report to her mother that he had never touched her, indeed never spoken to her. And her mother, knowing her daughter to be honest, believed that there was a chance that she would survive the terrible plague of love.

It is the nature of certain illnesses, however, that once they have invaded the body they lie silently inside until suddenly, one bright day, they reach out their tendrils and close around the living heart. So, one day, as they passed each other in the cool of a corridor that connected the kitchen to the banqueting hall, a corridor where no natural light reached and the shadows leapt and jumped as candles flickered in the draught, he reached out his hand and touched hers, though with infinite gentleness as though it were no more than their shadows which brushed against one another.

Then she was gone. A door opened, a door closed, and she stood staring at her hand to see if it might bear some mark to indicate what had happened in this anteroom to tomorrow. When at last, later in the day, she returned to her room, no bigger than a cupboard and with no window to look out upon the world, she glanced down again convinced that her hand would reveal its secret. But nothing was visible to the eyes. Nonetheless she raised it to her cheek and pressed it gently to her warm skin as though he had kissed her and bade her preserve that kiss for ever.

A kiss had to follow and, in time, it did. Meanwhile, his whole demeanour seemed to change. No longer the arrogant youth who treated all with contempt, he began to show courtesies, even to his inferiors. He even challenged his father at a family meal, demanding to know why the natives were forbidden to speak their own language and protested further when told that it was a necessity decided many leagues away across the sea.

Still the two had exchanged no words. Perhaps neither could decide in what language such a relationship should be conducted. There was another language, though, in which both were fluent, a language of looks and sighs and gestures. Then, one day, he slipped her an envelope. Inside was a flower as blue as her eyes, a flower he had kept pressed in his Bible. She held it close to her heart and whispered his name to the night sky. She thought none would hear her but her mother did and cried the night away, not stopping until a cock crowed and in the distance she could hear the bell of the new cathedral striking the hour.

They kissed in the chapel. She had been ordered to take flowers and place them on the altar. He followed her in and knelt at one of the pews. He watched her move and thought how wonderful she was in all respects. She turned and saw him kneeling there, the sun's rays slanting down from a high window, illuminating him like a saint. He stood slowly so that the light flowed down his body. She watched as it moved over his clothes.

Then, as if released from a trance, he stepped into the aisle and held his arms open. She walked forward as though she had no control over her actions and, in truth, she did not. She took a last step towards him, leaving him to close the remaining gap between them. He stepped forward and closed his arms about her. The kiss lasted as long as it took for the sunlight to slide across them and leave them in the shadow, weak with passion and contained within a universe of their own construction.

It was an act that sealed their love and their doom in the same instant, though there was another act, barely a month later, that was as irrevocable as the sentence of death which is pronounced on us all at the moment of our birth. She entered his room, in the silver cool of moonlight, as he had asked, entreated, begged that she should do. For a second she stopped as though transformed by that light into a living statue, before, with a single gesture, he lifted her nightdress high above her head and sent it floating, like a dying angel, into a dark corner of the room. Her pale brown skin seemed white in the moonlight, as though by some miracle she had been transformed from despised Indian into a Spanish princess. He looked at her, aware of the miracle she had wrought. Then he removed his own clothing and closed around her quite as if he and she could be as one, as though the injunctions of kings and the rules of their tribes could be wished away in the instant.

They made love that night and the nights which followed until one night, as he reached for her, she held out her own hand, palm at right angles to her arm, and halted him. Then she took his own hand in hers and placed the flat of that hand against the soft tautness of her stomach. He looked into her eyes and she nodded gently. They had killed each other with their gentleness, become assassins of the love they bore by the bearing of its consequence.

For many weeks she held the secret in her heart as, in her imagination, she already held the baby in her arms. But some secrets betray themselves no matter how we may guard them. The sickness she had explained away, telling her mother that it was a consequence of mildewed bread, an explanation plausible enough when they were required to live off their master's leavings. Her gently swelling womb, however, could find no other explanation, though at first she had sought to blame it on an appetite she had, in truth, never had. At last her mother stood before her, tears already forming in her eyes, demanding to be told the truth, a truth which instantly bubbled to the surface like a spring which has at last forced its way into the air. Nor could there be doubt as to who might be responsible, for she had seen the glances that passed between them, hoping only that such madness must end. And so it had, but in a way which must spell her doom.

'You must leave immediately.'

'Leave? Where should I go?'

'You shall return to our village.'

'And what shall I say?'

'To whom, child?'

'To my mistress.'

'Your mistress hardly knows you live. I will give her a story.'

Her daughter hesitated. 'And him?'

'Him? Are you mad? You are a plaything, a distraction. He will be relieved that you have taken yourself away.'

'No.'

Her mother paused, yet the love she bore her daughter required the cruelty she practised. 'What will happen if you stay? Whatever he may be, his father will know how to handle you. Oh, my child, why?' she asked, who well knew the answer to such a question.

86

So the young girl was hurried on her way. Two days later a cousin arrived at the back door of the kitchen with a mule and led her from the palace, and a young boy discovered that love brings pain as much as pleasure.

Had he allowed her to become a memory, hidden somewhere deep within, all may have been well; but he believed that life itself could not be borne without her by his side. So he rode out in search of the woman who carried his child, the woman he could not marry but who he believed might live beside him all his days, so deceived was he about himself and the possibilities that confronted him. At first he rode with a sense of purpose but no sense of direction. He rode believing he must discover what he sought. But at last he realised the foolishness of this and turned to the missing girl's mother. She refused his entreaties. He cried in despair, as any young man might do, but by degrees he recalled who he was and recalled too the dependency of the woman he had thought to appeal to as her daughter's mother. So it was that entreaty turned to threat, until the love he felt itself began to be infected by his anger. By what right, he asked himself, had she abandoned him? Was the child she carried not his own?

There came a moment when the girl's mother accepted that she must give answers to his questions, as his threats began to endanger her entire family. At last, therefore, she gave directions where he should go, begging only that he should offer her protection. His manner changed at once, though his understanding did not deepen, for he reached into his purse and pulled out a golden coin which he pressed into her hand. As she turned to leave she looked down at the bright coin in her palm and knew in that instant that all was lost. The door slammed shut; she heard the sharp explosion of horse's hooves on the cobbled courtyard and his exultant cry as he commanded that the gate should be thrown open to allow him to pursue his dream.

It took him two days to reach Anzuelo, two days in which he was restored to his original feelings. He was on a quest and the mere fact of the quest made the objective glow with a pure significance. All other thoughts rushed away. When he found her, however, he found, too, the village in which she lived and the people from whom she sprang. They were poor and with poverty came, as it seemed to him, dirt and squalor. He noted that the skin of most of those he saw in the dusty streets was darker than that of the girl who had shone like bronze in his arms.

He found her at last on the very edge of the village. She was living with an uncle and aunt and was sewing a rough cloth when he entered. He looked at her and it seemed to him that she was not quite as she had been before. Nonetheless he took her by the hand and lifted her onto his horse. As they rode together his former feelings restored and he felt the warmth of her body against him in the failing light. That night they lay together. She gathered sticks while he fed the horse, and then they sat together beneath the stars as the sparks from their fire rose in a spiral of orange and red. They sat side by side but thought different thoughts. For the first time he had begun to understand the impossibility of their relationship. To have seen her in her village was to understand that she had a past which must determine her future. She knew few words in his language, beyond the commands she was required to obey, and was forbidden to speak her own. Safely to hand in the servants' quarters she had been a lover to whom he could turn at any moment. In the cramped room of a hut far from the capital she had seemed for a moment no more than one among many. Yet she carried his child, or so she insisted. For her part she felt his coldness more than that of the bitter air. Far away she heard the sound of coyotes, their cries as mournful as herself.

When they returned to the palace he was summoned by his father who, despite his spies, had been the last to learn of the situation. The young man stood in the middle of the polished floor while his father paced to and fro. He shouted so that his words could be heard well beyond the room, so that they reached even into the kitchen where the girl sat, tears tracing their way down her cheeks. He spoke of duty and betrayal, of contamination and the law. He instructed his son in the realities of power and the necessity of authority. And, finally, and more quietly now, so his words did not escape the room, he spoke of the ship on which his son would sail on the morrow, travelling to the north and east towards a new life in Madrid. And what he said now fell on receptive ears, for the young man had always yearned to go on just such a journey.

And did he enquire after the fate of his beloved? Who can know, for their voices were low now. A decision had been made and father and son were reconciled. Certainly that night was not spent in her arms but in gathering together what he might need as he set out on his great adventure.

The ship sailed at dawn and word did reach the woman he abandoned, for servants were required to accompany him even to the harbour's edge and they reported his departure to the young girl's mother, as she, in turn, when she judged the moment right, informed her daughter of his desertion.

The child was born and removed at once. She knew nothing of its fate. A woman came, accompanied by officers of the palace, and while she still bled from the tearing of the birth, they pulled the baby from her arms. A month passed and she was arrested, charged with the theft of silver knives and forks from the boxes where they were kept for official functions in the Great Hall. The charge was serious enough, but when she appeared before the Governor in the same room in which father and son had been reconciled and was asked to answer the charges put to her she answered not in Spanish, as was required by the law, but in her own tongue. The penalty for theft was severe; that for breaching the law which forbids the use of other languages than that of the conqueror, draconian. There was a silence in the room. The Governor turned first to the left and then the right, seeking the agreement of the two men who presided with him. They nodded. He turned back to face the girl, caught now in a thin beam of light where the sun penetrated even this dark place, a slant of light like a dagger. He leaned forward and spoke in the merest whisper.

'You have condemned yourself by the words you speak. You sought to take what was not yours and now are come to this retribution. There can be no other sentence than that which I now pronounce . . .' he paused, 'in the language of the angels.' She was executed that day. There were eight men in the firing squad. She refused the blindfold offered her. In the distance she could hear a coyote howling. The rifles fired. She fell. It is said that a single bullet had struck her golden body, though that stilled her gentle heart. Her body was thrown from the cliff. She flew through the air like an angel, her black hair streaming, her arms outstretched. The sea took her into its depths where, according to the custom of her people, she would live for a thousand years until the gods awoke and reclaimed the land which belonged to them alone.

And the child? The child has a history of its own and his story, too, is worth the telling.

Jacques the Navigator was the first European to negotiate the country's rivers. Like many another voyager he arrived in the country by error, having been taught his star systems by his father whose Greek mythology was stronger than his astronomy. He set himself at once to build a birch-bark canoe, difficult in a country entirely lacking in birch and in which the most common tree was covered with a bark as porous as it was difficult to work. However, what he lacked in constructive knowledge, astronomical ability and simple talent, he more than made up for in persistence. At the end of two years, in which three separate vessels had been shaped, launched and sunk, he set himself to build a raft, binding together the trunks of small trees toppled by the Tailless Poisonous Beaver which frequented the area. Distinctive creatures, they had thick black coats distinguished by a wavering yellow line which glowed in the dark and thereby made their skins of limited appeal to the fashion trade, the more so since the poison they could spit some twenty feet seemed to suffuse their whole body at death and thus those who came in contact with them were liable to develop a rash almost as yellow as the line which ran the length of their bodies.

For some few years, though, under the reign of Napoleon III, there was a vogue for such skin colour, his own being tainted by jaundice, and hence for the animal which was hunted nearly to extinction by men who had learned that, painful though the skin condition which resulted from exposure to the Poisonous Beaver might be, it had the effect of furnishing light on the darkest night since the scabs and abrasions glowed with a yellow luminescence. There were even some who sought deliberate exposure to turn themselves into temporary novelties at the palace balls which for many a year were a feature of the fashionable scene in the nation's capital.

He launched his raft on the first day of January 1642 and allowed the force of the river to carry him forward on his exploration. The river flowed from a small lake on what is now the northern border. It began then, as it begins now, as no more than a gentle stream working its way slowly down from the plateau where distinctive animals lived: the speeding sloth which captures its prey by simulating lethargy, the flying frog,

91

which blows itself up to six times its normal size and then rises on thermals until the sky can seem black with these balloon-like creatures which can catch moths and even small birds on the wing. When they attempt to eat them, however, the valve at the back of their throats is necessarily released so that the captured air rushes out and they shoot across the sky at considerable speeds. It is unwise on such days to venture out.

As the river progressed it passed through sandstone rocks, where it had worn steep gorges. There are vivid portraits of these in his notebooks, sometimes spattered with water stains, for it is here that the water began to gather speed for its descent onto the plain. Today this area is popular with sportsmen who white water raft through an area now known as the Serpent's Tail. But where they ride on flexible boats and protect themselves with helmets and life vests, he was protected only by his indomitable courage and total ignorance of what lay ahead. And what principally lay ahead was the Raft Falls, which did not, of course, at that time bear such a name, or any of which he was aware, that could forewarn him of what he was about to suffer. In many ways the country's single greatest natural attraction, the Falls mark the point at which the river launches itself into space and descends, seemingly in slow motion, to the rocks below. However, at the very centre of these rocks is a deep pool which turns, equally slowly, as though this were some giant bath from which a plug has been but recently removed. Indeed there are those who suggest that there is such a hole and that a portion of the waters does indeed descend into it, thence working its way through a series of subterranean tunnels only to rejoin the river some distance below the Falls. However, whether or not that is so, any who see the Falls must be filled with awe for their beauty and their power. Seen from a raft held together with looping vines, however, they must have looked a very frightening spectacle.

Jacques writes in his diary of a sound like a million bees buzzing in his ears (and the Giant Bee of Carenosa is a native of this region). Being close to the river's surface he could see nothing of what lay ahead, except that he was aware that the river had picked up speed and his raft begun to turn around in the eddies that seemed to spin towards him from the red sandstone walls of the gorge.

His survival of the Falls, the only one ever recorded, converted him from a studied atheist to the religion of his parents, though it would have required a God with acute hearing to distinguish his prayers, even screamed as they were at the top of his voice, against the reverberating sounds of the rushing waters. It was a conversion which affected the cartography of the whole region for hereafter, whenever he named a natural feature in his diary, he gave it a name derived from the Bible. Hence, the Shadrach Rocks, the Abednego Rapids, the Nebuchadnezzar Bluffs. His survival, however, marked the doom of many others; for though he had the luck to fall at the very edge of the turning maelstrom so that he hit neither the rocks nor the downpulling spiral, and was ejected like a cherry stone from the mouth of a baboon, no others were to prove so fortunate. Yet not a year would go by without at least one attempt (usually by a young man anxious to impress) to repeat his adventure using whatever might come to hand. So people had gone to their deaths in barrels, boxes, and even, appropriately, coffins. Some had actively sought death, shouting their explanations mutely to the world as they were swept, human flotsam, past a single looping wire (itself the remnant of a failed attempt to tightrope-walk above the relentless waters).

So regular was this madness, which accelerated in the summer months, that for some it was reason enough to visit the place. Indeed a man was employed to walk the banks a mile downstream where the bodies would normally come to rest. Strangely enough, though, and perhaps in confirmation of the theory of a subterranean sink, other corpses never did resurface, disappearing to a nether world to bob their way through eternity in barrels carrying slogans in white paint: 'THE FALLS OR BUST', 'GERONIMO!', 'DON PABLO'S PAINT IS THE BEST PAINT'.

It was thus a miracle that Jacques survived, but survive he did, though the sheer weight of the water knocked him unconscious so he drifted through the ravine now known for its Wobbly Bats, so-called because the absorbent rocks send back no echoes to the ears of the creatures which swarm above the surface hunting for the Rapid Flies (which mate where the foam-flecked rocks are green with algae), and which, hence, found themselves flying repeatedly into the canyon side, resulting in a deterioration of the brain. He came to, finally, as the river swept around a wide curve and entered the dense forest which stretched for the next twenty miles. Because he was unconscious for several miles his map of the river at this point was conjectural, a form of fiction that proved the undoing of more than one adventurer as it omitted what was later known as the Dead Man's Rapids.

It was here that he met the Indian girl who would act as his guide. Nor was their encounter without its bizarre dimension, for she was sitting on a branch when his raft passed underneath and hence tumbled on top of him, precipitating mutual terror. In the end he entranced her with a set of beads, though not, perhaps, his rendition of 'Frère Jacques', she, like the rest of her tribe, being tone deaf, indeed nearly stone deaf, the roar of the rapids doing permanent harm to the inner ear. Without her help it is doubtful whether he would have survived his encounter with the natives, one of whose less appetising habits was to attack their enemies with arrows tipped with a venom which paralysed without killing and then roast them on great fires for the general wellbeing of the tribe. In time their habit of feasting, in particular, on the brains was their undoing since they thereby ingested a particularly virulent brain disease caught from a neighbouring tribe's distasteful practice of cohabiting with monkeys. Within a matter of years most were dead, though their deaths would not have been rapid enough to save Jacques without the intervention of the young girl, who thus earned herself an honoured place in the history of the country and eternal damnation in the history of the few natives who survived only by virtue of being vegetarians.

Their culture being oral rather than written, and hence devalued and ignored, they were subsequently forced to see statues of her in many of the towns which grew from the river settlements inspired by Jacques's voyage and to suffer the frequent singing of 'Frère Jacques'. The poison with which the tribe had tipped their arrows, meanwhile, was adopted by modern medicine since, much diluted, it proved a powerful diuretic and sexual stimulant, a combination which could, on occasion, prove inconvenient.

The forest, as he noted, bred animals of a kind that no white man had ever previously encountered, from the Very Slow Worm, which rarely travelled more than twelve inches in the five years of its life, to the Soft-Shelled Armadillo which lived on an insect population as varied as it was numerous, but which frequently found itself eaten by its natural enemy, the Toothless Dringo, a wild dog later domesticated and employed to guard properties of low value. The Beaver Ant (drawn in superb detail by Jacques in notebooks which, when published, brought him instant fame and which, centuries later – when not being forged in Taiwan – were torn apart by second-hand booksellers so that the illustrations could be sold separately from a text which, even his greatest admirers were forced to admit, had a certain eccentric banality), unique to the forest, felled small trees and dammed the narrow tributaries which meandered through the thick vegetation. These remarkable insects fed on water creatures by forming themselves into a kind of fishing line, each holding its neighbour, with the final ant, adept at holding its breath, forming the hook. At that time, too, there was a forest cat whose camouflage was so complete that while it was able to feed at will on the animals that blundered unknowingly into its path, by the same token found it all but impossible to locate and breed with others of its kind and hence became extinct not long after Jacques had described it.

There were, of course, snakes of all kinds and sizes whose only real enemy, besides a quick-footed creature which Jacques called a Viteped but which, over time, proved not quite quick enough to survive, was one another. On one day he watched as no fewer than five snakes slowly devoured each other in turn, obeying an instinct so powerful that the final snake, with a girth of more than three feet, and with vivid yellow and black markings, began to devour itself. Centuries later his drawing of this serial digestion was adopted by the university's School of Postmodernism.

Some animals were harmless, going about the business of survival with admirable restraint. Such animals had their natural protections. Dung Beetles seemed to feature on no one's menu, any more than did the Vomit Toad. It was a world in natural balance as the complex miracle of reproduction, sometimes involving astonishing transformations requiring months of chemical and biological processes, resulted in the production of a living creature that seconds later found itself dissolving in the digestive juices of another animal. That other animal existed for no other purpose than to perform this action and then reproduce itself so that further generations could snap up the newly-emerged offspring of creatures who seemed not to understand that their sole function was to enhance the calorific intake of their predators. How wonderful a mechanism is nature, Jacques might have noted, were he not now suffering from a fever induced by the Dung Fly which developed inside the apparently immune Dung Beetle and which thereby carried the decayed contents of the digestive tract of the Aquaphobic Water Buffalo into the bloodstream of any warm-blooded animal unfortunate enough to stray within range of this flightless fly.

Though the forest was only some twenty miles wide at this point in his journey, it took Jacques more than a week to penetrate, for there were several tribes who inhabited it who must be persuaded, by his Indian companion, to permit him to go on his way. So ill was he with dysentery brought on by the Dung Fly Fever that in the stories told by these tribes in later years he was known as the Squatting White Man. Once the forest was left behind, however, the wide plains lay ahead and, almost immediately, the confluence with the Lonesome River, itself a natural wonder which attracts such visitors as have the perseverance to reach it, for the Lonesome River is six times wider and ten times more powerful than the Jacques River down which he had been navigating. To move from one to the other is no less daunting today than it was then and there are many who have lost their lives at this point.

The Lonesome River is dark orange-brown with mud and, at the time Jacques encountered it, dotted with massive tree trunks and the corpses of dead animals. The so-called Foolish Deer, a kind of antelope with the agility and speed of a jaguar but the instincts of a lemming, invariably tried to cross the river at the height of the rainy season and thus provided food for the Thompson's Alligators, who waited downstream and formed an almost impenetrable line across the river, mouths open.

For those who travel there today, joining the Lonesome River is like stepping from a bicycle to a speeding car, an image that, admittedly, would mean little to most people in a country in which the words 'speeding' and 'car' were seldom found in close proximity. Jacques survived; the girl did not. The raft was spun around as it hit the braided water where the two rivers met, and was partly pulled beneath the water by an undertow that was no less daunting for being invisible. When the raft bobbed back to the surface Jacques was alone and, had they but known it, the Thompson's Alligators were in for a tasty meal.

The Navigator must have been terrified at such a moment. He had lost his companion, was at risk from the tree trunks that span and dipped in their own private eddies, and was being carried at speed into the heart of the unknown, unknown at least to him. But what is life if it is not such a journey from the known into the unknown? Such, at any rate, was the essence of his philosophy when he tried to spell it out in his diaries, more admired than read but, like other such texts, influential nonetheless.

The citizens of Sagrado Dios were, they told themselves, a peaceful people. Their history may have been stained with violence, from the time of the Conquistadors through the revolutions that convulsed the country as frequently as the earthquakes which tumbled people from their beds (and other people's), but this, they told themselves, was no more than would be true of any society and a good deal less than many. It was true that slavery had left its legacy, that there were bandits of singular ferocity and, from time to time, regional conflicts which severed state from state and heads from bodies. A detached observer might also note a certain tendency to resolve family conflicts with the long curved knife more usually employed for cutting sugar cane, and the casual brutality of parents to children was no more, they insisted, than the discipline love necessitates. But if these were, indeed, a peaceful people, their neighbours were not. By repute they had been known to eat their own kind, abuse their mothers and donkeys, maim their children to hone their begging skills, eat monkey brains while the creatures still lived. All this was documented, it was said, and certainly believed (their football team was also renowned for its fouls as well as for consistently beating the Sagrado Dios team, whose health was safeguarded by the Sisters of Small Mercies and which, as a consequence, was rarely able to field eleven players). But such monstrosities would have been without meaning had they not had ambitions to conquer their pacific neighbours or at least to lay claim to some portion of the land which tradition made clear belonged to Sagrado Dios, though it had been occupied for rather longer by its claimants.

These national conflicts tended to flare into actual battles whenever presidential elections were due in either country, or shortly after the revolutions which conveniently obviated the need for such. By common agreement domestic problems of poverty or disease, of failed crops and policies, would be set aside and rallies held to denounce the people of El Colombo. Usually such declarations of solidarity proved sufficient to deter aggression, or at least no aggression took place, but occasionally actual fighting did occur, albeit sporadic and of a somewhat indefinite and undefinable kind.

The territory in dispute lay where the forest broke off for a kilometre or so and a sulphurous bog, scattered with occasional outcrops of rock, stretched over an undulating if abbreviated plain. From time to time this would belch a mixture of gases that had been known to ignite and which, in days more superstitious than these, had earned it the name of the Devil's Cauldron. To a stranger's eye it might not have been immediately obvious why either side should wish to lay claim to land where nothing grew and the incautious might have his choice between being gassed, burned or sucked down into the acid mud. But there is such a thing as symbolic value and where two states meet land acquires a significance not always apparent to the eye. Certainly both sides kept contingents of troops in the area, though a little back from the 'flaming breaths', as they were known.

All male citizens were, in theory, required to spend a year of their lives in the military and so they did, unless they did not. And many did not. Over the years so many exemptions had been introduced that only the truly poor would find themselves being initiated into the mysteries of the Lee Enfield rifle (purchased, in 1946, by a president who wished to enter his son for Eton in England, and believed that a gesture of confidence in a country with a military tradition, and a sudden excess of military equipment, might ease his way). Old Spanish forts were still to be found throughout the country, and where these had not been claimed by goats or Jackson's cows (a breed which thrived on sugar cane and produced alcoholic milk), they were turned into barracks for a military force. If such a force would have been liable to plunge a European general into despair, it nonetheless served such purposes as Sagrado Dios had, which is to say a place to send men when the jails were full, unemployment was high (or higher than usual) or when some gesture of force should prove necessary against a neighbour whose military policy was much the same as their own.

It is true that as a military force they were not as impressive as they might have been. It was not unknown for firing squads to miss their targets even when the victim was tied to a post and positioned no more than fifteen paces away, while a German commander, hired by a president to forge them into a more effective force, had been discovered one night sobbing in his room. But there was no doubt that in an emergency they would rise to the task and save the national honour.

Their commander was Generalissimo Maximillian Alexander Cabello, who preferred that people should address him by his rank and full name. 'Excuse me, Generalissimo Maximillian Alexander Cabello, could you please pass me the salt?' He had acquired his rank through a series of rapid promotions in the three weeks which had constituted the most recent revolution. But if greatness had been thrust upon him he was determined that he should master skills appropriate to his rank and which others had acquired through years of experience. Thus he studied diligently and deployed the lessons to be gleaned from military history. As a consequence his men found themselves enacting battles long since fought and concluded. Teams were sent to discover a topography similar to that at Thermopylae or Waterloo, Gettysburg or the Somme. Lacking resources, he was obliged to re-enact these within certain limitations as to numbers, uniforms and ammunition; but men could be moved about and if bullets were scarce smoke bombs were not, and a piece of coloured cloth could easily distinguish Russian from Frenchman as they sweated and swatted away mosquitoes at the gates of Moscow or waded the rivers at El Alamein.

But all was not well. Only a month ago he had received a clandestine letter from a man who it was rumoured had ambitions to rise to the presidency. 'Dear Generalissimo Maximillian Alexander Cabello,' it had said, 'I have reasons to believe that those with ambition to possess our dear country are planning an attack on our eastern borders.' 'The Devil's Cauldron,' he mouthed, finding it difficult, as ever, to move his lips in time with his thoughts.

One of the burdens of being a general in such a country as this is being sure which authority it is wisest to obey: that which emanates from those who hold the present reins of government, or those who may shortly do so. Tradition, however, suggested that some middle path was normally best, while inaction had a certain diplomatic cogency. So it was that the General decided he would hold an exercise on the eastern border and turned to his reference books to see which battle he could most usefully enact. The landscape, he knew, was unpromising, and he had by now had his men work their way back and forth across Europe and through the centuries. But as luck would have it he found the answer not in the neat drawings and succinct accounts of military manuals but in a volume of poetry, thrust into his hands by a woman of the upper class who had been seduced by his stature and his uniform, and who, with her bosom heaving and her husband in the other room, had announced, 'Generalissimo Maximillian Alexander Cabello, I love you.'

The Generalissimo was perhaps a fool but not that much of a fool. He acknowledged the power of a uniform and had indeed elaborated his own in order to heighten the effect. He thus took the poems and much more and thanked his rapid promotion for the rapid conquests which it brought in its train. By now, and for no other reason than that he picked the book up in error, he found himself reading a stirring account of the Charge of the Light Brigade. Now, dear reader, lest you are fearing that he was about to sacrifice his life and that of his men by charging non-existent Russian cannon across a bog with a tendency to blow men up or suck them down, you may be reassured to know that this army had no cavalry. It did, to be sure, have a large number of mules which carried equipment along forest paths and over mountain tracks; but a charge by these would be a long time reaching its objective unless urged on by kicks or lured forward by carrots, which under conditions of battle, with shells descending and bullets splashing mud spouts, would seem a touch implausible. What seized the General's imagination was the simple fact of direct assault, for if his country had a military tradition it had largely been built on strategic retreat, or, to be more strictly accurate, retreat.

So it was that the Third Battle of the Devil's Cauldron took place (the first two being the kinds of defeats claimed as victories which formed the basis of the country's military reputation). The General assembled a force of one hundred and fifty men, the rest of the army being required for ceremonial duties and to protect the President who had heard rumours of a potential rival. It was a battle that fell some way short of its paradigm, not least in that it lacked an actual enemy, it being Conscription Day in the neighbouring country, a day on which all recruits reported to their barracks and all those completing their military service were discharged. There was thus a twenty-four-hour period in which the enemy country was technically and actually defenceless, with the exception of a few border patrols which fell under the aegis of the Ministry of the Interior and did indeed report what they saw, though they had neither the will nor the power to intervene.

What they saw was a detachment of soldiers, mounted on mules, who set out from the far side of the cauldron with ceremonial swords drawn. Even the General recognised a certain disproportion between his own attack and that on which he sought to model it, but a little imagination was all that was required and he had such even if his men did not. So, into the valley of death rode the thirty-eight, unsure what function they were to perform but obeying orders as soldiers must no matter the stupidity of those who command them. Thankfully only six were seriously injured, and they not strictly by military action. They were hurt by sudden eruptions of hot water and overcome by sulphurous fumes. The rest were rescued by their mules who may be stubborn but, on the evidence of this day, were far from stupid. They stopped when they were no more than fifty metres from the Cauldron and the warm mud had already begun to suck at their feet. No matter how hard they were kicked, and few of the soldiers, it has to be said, felt moved to kick them with any force, they were immovable.

It should not be thought that the General was in any way depressed by the result. Had the show of force not had its effect? Did the enemy dare to show his face or offer any opposition? Did he not advance into the disputed territory even if he was forced to retire shortly afterwards?

How else may we tell a victory except by the medals that are awarded? Since it was he who was responsible for deciding on such rewards, the victory was swiftly announced and celebrated as he led thirty-eight men and accompanying mules in a victory parade down O'Grady Boulevard to an indifference as total as it was predictable.

Nor was this victory essentially different from many others celebrated by the military each year, with a special ration of rum served from a silver measure in the several barracks scattered around the country and on board the ships of the National Navy, the latter consisting of a converted minesweeper (no longer functional) that had passed through more hands than the chief whore of the Golden Slipper, itself conveniently situated in the Avenida Pamplona just off the Presidential Square where rum, incidentally, was regularly imbibed, though usually in anticipation rather than in celebration of victory.

The fact was that, the proliferation of military uniforms notwithstanding, Sagrado Dios was not a militaristic nation. This might seem a strange observation to those who have heard of its revolutions and its skirmishing with neighbouring countries, but such reports are not without a certain degree of exaggeration,

while distant countries are prone to regard with a certain con-
descension those other nations with a tendency to change their
governments with a bullet rather than a ballot.

In fact, there was little systematic violence. What there was
was a love affair with uniforms. Even the men who swept the
street, pushing small barrows up and down, collecting cigarette
packets, candy wrappers and the occasional and still illegal
condom onto a broad spade, wore peaked caps, jackets with
shoulder flashes and trousers with gold bands down the sides.
The military, meanwhile, seemed to share a tailor with the
costumers of a production of *Aida* (had such a production ever
been staged in Sagrado Dios), each regiment being permitted a
certain discretion (if that is a word to be applied to uniforms
which ran the whole spectrum from deep crimson through to a
yellow which shone in the dark, a product of the Poisonous
Beaver and something of a disadvantage on military campaigns).
And what was true of those who bore arms (when arms, as such,
were available, the budget being in a state of permanent collapse)
was true, too, of citizens.

It was not only the annual parades which found them dressed
(or undressed) in glittering costumes, for there were few who
were not members of a craft, a guild, a club or society, an
association, a lodge, a coven or chapter. Each of these in turn
wore distinctive clothes with colours that distinguished it from
all others. Indeed it was possible to overlay on a map of the city
a patchwork quilt of such, for there was a certain territory which
surrounded each group and its meeting place so that this was
acknowledged as a green area and that as a magenta one. As was
inevitable, there were frequent disputes over territory, arguments which often had their roots in history.

Usually these disagreements were no more than family
quarrels; but over the years that part of the populace which had

105

no access to such groups, being neither in trade nor adherents of any particular sect, began to develop loyalties of their own. This, though, was expressed by nothing more than a preference for clothing of a particular colour. Some would wear a red bandanna, others would paint their bicycles blue or even the curbstones yellow and green. Viewed in one way this merely brightened the city so that it was a whirl of colour. However, on occasion these loyalties, shallow-rooted though they were, would lead to acts of vandalism. The rider of a red bicycle would find that his tyres had been deflated if he left it against a wall painted turquoise. The shop painted apple green might be spotted with coral pink by those en route from a yellow bar which they had similarly defiled.

At times, however, there have been those for whom such painterly intervention was not sufficient. By some logic difficult to understand, those most excluded from organisations whose whole reason for being lies in such exclusions would come to feel the fiercest loyalties. The young, the poor, the unemployed, and even those whose skin colours were themselves an exclusive badge of consanguinity, would form into gangs that roamed the streets seeking those who announced themselves too unequivocally by the colours they wore, assaulting them with bricks, the sticks constructed for the national sport, and even with knives and machetes. It was like a disease that has its season and spreads by contagion. So, colour flowed into colour until blood flowed scarlet in the street. Then it was gone again and peace returned.

The police, who of course also had their own association, which favoured black, move swiftly and ruthlessly on such occasions, for so many are the divisions that pure anarchy is always close at hand. Question those arrested, sentence and imprison them and then ask why they attacked someone because they wore cerise rather than cobalt blue, and they would at first affect incredulity at such a question. However, as time passed, they would find it ever more difficult to explain to themselves and others why their passion had attached itself to so strange a cause. There were those who attempted to carry these passions into the prison-house itself, demanding to be placed only with those who shared their preference for aquamarine or emerald and, indeed, there were occasional injuries and even deaths which resulted from such prejudice. But for the most part other urgencies quickly replaced these, and after a time the madness passed, they having paid the price for defending, as they supposed, those with whom, in truth, they shared nothing but a nationality.

Nor were these the only distinctions, for within each sect or association there was a plethora of ranks, each one reflected by elaborate uniforms and costumes. This might be a republic, having freed itself of royalty in shaking off the shackles of imperial power in the revolution of 1908, but it had reinvented the whole panoply of regal ranks and distinctions. The country thus abounded with those who entitled themselves Grand Wizards, Dukes, Imperial Legates, Masters and much more. Men (and few in these organisations were women), who during the day dressed and behaved with perfect sobriety, would, on entering their buildings, bedeck themselves in clothes that would have struck a Turkish Emperor as garish. They would greet one another with a strange succession of winks, nods and elaborate handshakes. Anybody who happened to stray into these places, as none did unless they were colour co-ordinated, might reasonably suppose they had entered a hospital for the profoundly afflicted.

Why did they do so? Why, indeed, for it was the most conservative in views and attire who thus transformed themselves. A

107

journalist on San Marco's principal newspaper suggested in the first of what was to have been a sequence of six articles (five of which, unaccountably, failed to appear) that it was perhaps precisely because they longed for the distinctions which in public they felt constrained to decry. The title of the next article was to have been 'The Transvestite Tendency'. The reporter is now a schoolteacher in a remote village in which even school uniforms are banned.

One curious effect of this division of the country into so many different colours (and new organisations were forced into ever more subtle colour discriminations since no two could occupy the same space on the spectrum) was that the President was required in some sense to act as unifier. It was all very well for citizens to announce their loyalties but if he chose to wear, say, a blue shirt this would be to invite much of the population to whistle and boo if he should make a speech when thus attired. By the same token, though it was impossible for him to refuse requests to become Honorary Grand Vizier of this or Honorary Great Potentate of that group, he had always to be prepared to embrace a whole dictionary of other titles or risk offending those excluded.

There were some of his predecessors who had attempted to solve such problems by ensuring that they never emerged in public without a little of each colour about their person. This had proved workable enough for the first half-dozen or so and when the tendency was not so firmly established, but as the years passed, so the presidents looked more and more like clowns. Exhausting the possibility of displaying all the colours to which they had committed themselves on their clothes alone they would take to wearing hats (which got taller and taller), carrying canes, which looked like children's confectionary, striped around as they were with spirals of different colours, and small cases which got larger until it began to look as though they might be salesmen about to depart on a world cruise.

Eventually, over the decades, a compromise would be effected whereby the predominant colour which the President wore every day would reflect the most important date in the history of each group, usually the date of its founding but occasionally, and provocatively, the date of its having achieved ascendency over the colour most immediately proximate to it in the spectrum. However, so as not to offer any implied insult to those whose particular day this was not, the presidential balcony, his box in the theatre, and even the presidential car (mercifully usually not functional) were decorated with all the other colours, thereby contributing to a perpetual air of carnival, which particular could prove somewhat confusing to those from outside the country.

Thus, on the occasion of state funerals, visiting heads of state would frequently be shocked when their protocol secretaries insisted that they carry multicoloured sticks, a little like African fly whisks (and usable as such), and travel in carriages more appropriate, as several insisted, to funfairs rather than funerals and certainly not in tune with the solemn obsequies they imagined themselves to be attending. There were those, though, who saw such occasions as a challenge to discover which of them might wear the most colourful clothes. However, cultural misunderstandings being what they are, they also at times failed to perceive the reason for these colours (those new on the international scene often lacked protocol secretaries) and imagined that their very vividness must be an invitation to a general mood of festivity and hence took the licence they were not being offered to arrive at the graveside playing bizarre musical instruments and performing dances of quite extreme eroticism (life and death frequently being seen in their own countries as no more than two sides of the same coin).

This ill-judged behaviour was regarded as an insult and as a result these funerals were often followed by trade boycotts, so various items would disappear from the national diet for a while. On the other hand there were those who admired the spirit of people who chose to laugh in the face of death; and by degrees, as the decades passed, it became common practice to make death an occasion for celebration. Each grave bore a small coloured flag so that when the wind blew it was as if a shimmering rainbow had swept across the cemetery.

The tradition of the President acknowledging the special colour day ended with Pablo Escabar, who would have been perfectly happy to continue it but was disabled from doing so being colour blind. One red day he wore blue, green and yellow. And being also a little deaf he was unaware of the whistles of the crowd. He smiled and waved and though as a consequence he was shot dead by a red (happily failing to hear the shot), the point which he had inadvertently made was soon agreed by all citizens. In future, as a result, the President always appeared beneath a flag which contained so many small patches of colour that it seemed white as it flapped in the summer sun.

Justina had returned to her home with a feeling of triumph, modified only by the unfortunate affair with the bell-ringers' float and the fact that her father had shown not the slightest awareness that this was the most important day in her life. She had long since accustomed herself to his disregard, however, and, recognised that it did not signal a lack of love. Indeed, many were the occasions he encountered her in the kitchen, at the dining table, descending the stairs, and stood as though transfixed by a vision of beauty. At first she had thought she alone was the subject of his awe, if not quite his love, until on one occasion he had uttered the name of her mother (a mother who she was told

was long since dead) and she realised that he saw not one but two
people before him. She knew, too, that he was not quite as others,
but though they were inclined to see his behaviour as madness,
to her it was simply the way he was and as such infuriating and
endearing in the same instant. By degrees, indeed, she became to
him as a mother to a wayward son, taking him in hand, protecting him from alarm and seeing that he presented as ordered
a face to the world as he might and that he tucked his shirt into
his trousers.

She had presented herself to him that morning in all the
radiance of her queenly costume and saw that he was quite struck
dumb. He raised a hand towards her as though he would
embrace a phantom and a tear worked its way down his face. But
when she explained once more why she was dressed so he
merely nodded and told her that she should enjoy herself, as if
she were a child seeking permission to play outside. Justina was
used to such disappointments and found herself patting him on
the hand quite as though it were he and not she who required
consolation.

There was another, though, who watched and experienced
such a collection of contradictory feelings that he could not
entirely distinguish one from another. The Professor's student
had come early to the house merely so that he could leave a
volume of the letters which his employer had suggested he might
borrow from the library. The letters were by a traveller from
China who had crossed and recrossed the country at a time when
few of those who were native there would have chosen to stray
more than a league or two from home. Thus it was that the
earliest cartographer, naturalist and anthropologist, Jacques aside,
was a man from a country so far distant that few of those he
encountered could even envisage the existence of such a land.
How much faith, therefore, was to be placed in one such as he,

who might have had reasons of his own to falsify or invent, for who knew his motives in coming so far? Indeed, several of the animals he described had never been seen before and never been identified since, while even the outline of the coast had evidently transformed itself in the three centuries following his supposed visit. Therefore, the Professor would assert, the whole country was fictionalised from the very beginning and the letters were neither more nor less than a novel with the cartographer not a flesh and blood author but a character, a narrator, whose unreliability was an essential aspect of his role.

This, then, was the book Manuel placed on the table before suffering a kind of paralysis when Justina walked through the door, the back of her white costume not yet cross-laced, the graceful fall of her body, with its soft down golden in the morning sun, open to his vision. She had evidently forgotten her condition for she stamped her foot and turned about, still further loosening her costume so that the gentle ridges of her spine led his eye down, step by seductive step, until the shadowed cleft of her delicious behind made him feel weak in every limb. Poor boy. He knew, or thought he knew, that she despised him but could not understand why that should be so. He had what most of his kind and hormonal condition would have surrendered parts of their anatomy to acquire – access to her home. And whoever has access to the home, as all such youths know full well, may thereby have access to the body they desire, or at least that is what they tell themselves as they compose stories of mounting improbability.

He left the house and waited in the shadows with his bicycle, meaning to encounter her by accident. Feeling somewhat exposed in such a position, he took to riding up and down the street, contriving to detach his bicycle clip each time so that he might have an excuse for thus lying in wait. But he knew nothing of the tradition which attached itself to the O'Grady Day Queen.

For on the morning of the great event she is, by custom, collected from her home by car. Accordingly, at eleven, a shining black hearse drew up outside the Professor's house and two pallbearers, with black ribbons in their hair, descended. There was no particular symbolism in the hearse, which was used for weddings as well as burials so was functional. As has been suggested before, the general standard of mechanics in Sagrado Dios was not overly impressive. When spare parts were needed, they were more often manufactured in the rear of tumbling sheds than ordered from distant manufacturers. Those manufacturers would be unaware that a finely engineered component would be inserted into an engine which itself had been reconstructed several times in workshops whose engineering tolerances were greater than a manufacturer could imagine possible.

The hearse was convenient because it was seldom required to progress at much more than walking pace and hence, aside from quantities of oil that were poured in at one point only to gush out at another, never suffered from the diseases which afflicted most machinery in a country whose climate and topography seemed designed to frustrate the logic of the industrial revolution along with communication of every kind.

Justina appeared at the doorway, her dress shining the brighter through contrast with the funereal assistants, one of whom courteously opened the door and invited her to sit beside the coffin which they were required to drop off, as it were, at the cemetery on their way to the parade, time being short for a body in a climate that can make the meat on your plate decay before your eyes if you delay too long. The coffin did not bother her, for it was covered with a mass of flowers whose perfume made her feel even more light-headed than before.

Once again the student detached his bicycle clip. It rolled under the hearse. She looked at him but apparently saw nothing.

113

The doors banged and in a cloud of blue smoke (it was ten years overdue for its service) the vehicle pulled away, leaving behind a black snake of oil and a bicycle clip squashed flat by its tyres. He climbed on the bicycle and rode after the hearse; but each time his feet went round his trousers caught in the chain until the trouser leg was frayed at the bottom, eventually catching and stopping his progress entirely, in fact pitching him face down in the gutter on which someone had sprayed the insignia of the Thousand Points of Light.

Manolo Fraga had been the despair of his mother. When other mothers spoke of their children falling into bad company he was the bad company they had in mind. He smoked at five, drank at six and ran a protection racket at ten. He was therefore, by general agreement, a natural to become Chief of Police when his immediate predecessor had been sentenced to the traditional five years in prison. He knew every racket, broke every law, understood how to hasten the corruption of the apple on the tree. Not that such people can be bought off with the gift of a little authority. At school, which he briefly attended, they gave him a badge and even allowed him to discipline those who broke the petty regulations all schools institute in order to inoculate the citizenry with a tincture of arbitrary rules before they encounter the like in later life. He used his new-found authority, however, to turn his whole class into a gang whose effectiveness was admired even by the professionals to whom they turned in order to fence the objects they stole.

At the age of sixteen he was one of five who raided the home of a member of the opposition party, stealing not money but documents, when he was caught by an officious policeman who had failed to understand the nature of his orders. Unfortunately for Manolo Fraga the local magistrate was equally uninformed and sentenced him to two years in the city prison before correcting his mistake the following day. Never again did he find himself in court except to give evidence against those he arrested as a policeman, a job he was given on his birthday almost as if it were a present.

Manolo thrived on power, but unlike many of his kind understood that knowledge, rather than a club, may be the source of what he sought. And so he was respected in the poorer sections of town because he punished those of his officers who practised random violence, as opposed to chastising those who failed to pay such debts as are inevitable if one wishes to engage in certain transactions not altogether favoured by the law. He was respected in the wealthier parts of town because it was suspected that he must know a deal more than he admitted about affairs best kept in the shadows where for the most part they were conducted.

He had two wives and seven children. One wife he lived with on weekdays; the second was available only at weekends. The former was deeply religious, the latter a reformed prostitute, which is to say that she no longer regarded as a profession what she continued to practise as a weakness. It was as though he could not satisfy himself as to what he looked for in a wife and hence sought to constitute one for himself made up of the parts he favoured most. The first wife had mothered all seven children and took pride in pointing out her husband when she took them down the street like a duck leading her ducklings across a road. She knew of the woman who lived in another part of town but understood that a man must have his necessities, no matter how comforting his home or companion in that home.

He was a large man in every way and his colouring suggested that he might have some connection with Seamus O'Grady, who had scattered his seed if not with abandon then with a

115

certain generosity. His skin was pale except when he had a little to drink when it would move from pink to puce to purple like a cuttlefish on heat. He was a deal taller than any of his men, though there were those who, from time to time, were unwise enough to challenge him. He found nothing strange in his double life nor in his promotion from small-time crook to Chief of Police, a transformation which in fact was not as great as it might seem. Life is too short not to be lived to the full. The candle burned at only one end gives out only half the light and warmth; so what if it be for twice the time?

He took perverse pride in being an honest man, taking less than half the bribes of his predecessors and then not permitting them to influence his behaviour more than a change in the weather might do. Indeed he took such pains to stamp out corruption of the more obvious kind that he established a reputation as a man of complete integrity, so long as the word 'complete' should be defined with the generosity expected in a country where little happened unless lubricated with the grease of what was everywhere known as 'a little chicken', presumably because it would thereafter lay the required egg.

His domestic wife was a woman of deep feeling who loved him nearly as passionately as she did God, to whom she longed to cede her children as soon as they should be old enough to prostrate themselves in the aisle of the cathedral or wall them-selves up in silence to become brides of Christ. Unsurprisingly they entered into a conspiracy with their father to ensure that this would never occur. Each day, however, she would disappear at dawn to offer prayers in a chapel in the cathedral, a chapel dedicated to Saint Geronimo the Just, a saint not recognised by the overly punctilious canon acknowledged by the Church of Rome but sanctified in the hearts of all those who worked in the great basilica of San Marco.

Geronimo, as befitted his name, was an Indian, albeit one who for much of his life had masqueraded, if somewhat unconvincingly, as a Spanish duke. How he had come to do so was lost to all, but this was not what had led the city fathers to undertake a papal function and dedicate a chapel.

In 1776, while Americans were busy throwing what they would later delight in calling beverages into Boston harbour as a symbol of their desire to live as free men and women, Geronimo had performed much the same function for his country. The Spanish were still in power, as they would continue to be. The Governor at the time was a man of jet-black hair and jet-black heart by the name of Gomez and he made a habit of exercising what he insisted was his right, namely to deflower whatsoever virgin he might wish on the night of her wedding. Now it so happened that Geronimo's sister was to be married and the Governor had already indicated his intention to exercise his right, though he was married to a woman who was as beautiful as she was virtuous. The day came and the wedding took place. The air was full of coloured paper and good will when a detachment of guards presented itself at the villa where the bride and groom were gathered with family and friends.

The peremptory demand was made and after a long period in which it seemed that a rebellion might spring from such an importunate demand, the bride emerged, still wearing her elaborate gown. She was placed in an open carriage and paraded through the town, for beyond the pleasure he sought the Governor was about the business of reminding the citizens of the absolute nature of his power. The carriage passed through the streets and the citizens turned their faces away, ashamed for the young woman, for her new husband and for themselves, for they knew that the crime the Governor was about to perform on the new bride was but a symbol of that which he performed daily on their country.

And so she was delivered to the palace and led inside by the guards, who themselves smiled for they believed that their own status must be enhanced by the humiliation of those they ruled, a familiar enough illusion through the centuries. They stopped, finally, in front of the double doors of the bedroom. The Captain knocked sharply and then withdrew his men, leaving the girl to her fate.

It was, of course, not the girl at all but Geronimo. According to the Church he was canonised because he was executed for his crime of protecting virginity, for the real young couple disappeared into the interior and there raised a family who gave God two priests and three nuns. According to a story widely believed on the streets, however, the reason for his execution was quite different. He had entered through the double doors and there discovered the Governor naked on his bed. With various gestures the young bride, still dressed all in white and with a veil over her face, indicated that he should turn his back on her. Prepared to tolerate her modesty in the knowledge that he was about to violate it, he complied. Whereupon Geronimo threw off his disguise and sodomised the Governor before running into the next room and raping his wife, such was his potency. And though he died for his double insemination, nine months later the Governor's wife bore a young son who looked not at all like her husband, who never again exercised his presumed rights over the virtuous on the night of their union. Of course the wife of the Chief of Police knew nothing of this. She visited the chapel out of simple piety.

The other wife never went to the cathedral. She spent part of her day visiting the stores along the Boulevard O'Grady. For the most part she bought nothing, being in need of nothing that clothes or jewellery could satisfy. What she primarily bought was food. She who had spent a lifetime indulging others now indulged herself. She purchased chocolates made by a Belgian exile from an African colony. She bought cakes from a café which called itself after Mozart, though nobody who worked there would have recognised his music had they heard it. To be fair she also wandered in the fruit market and selected the most luscious of passion fruits, guava and melons, holding each in her hand as she had held other objects testing if they be ready. But mostly she chose food whose sweetness added to her already considerable girth. She poured cream on gateaux already piled high with the same and sprinkled sugar on the richest of desserts. Because her weekend husband loved her she no longer felt the need to retain her attractiveness. To be sure she had never exactly been thin and many a man sought her out precisely because of her ample body, which offered comfort and enfolding pleasures where others could render only a swift and muscular quietus. Working in a profession where no pleasure is deferred she saw no reason to delay the satisfaction of her own.

The Chief of Police watched her steady growth in size, grateful only, at first, that such expansiveness owed nothing to the threatened arrival of yet further children. What he did not know and would never have understood had he done so, was that it was pregnancy she had longed for more than anything in her life while knowing that it was not to be, for a disease picked up when she had worked for Madame Blavatsky had ended any possibility of that for the rest of her life. At the time she was not ungrateful, for it meant that she did not run the risk that the others did, fervent Catholics all and hence denying themselves the one way to protect themselves from the inevitable consequences of their trade. But as the years passed and as the men left her bedroom, placing a few notes beside the photograph of her sister's brood of two girls and a boy, she would find herself staring at the wall with tears tumbling down her cheeks.

119

She had long since learned to relegate this to some distant part of her mind; yet what the mind may not know the heart will recall and she still woke in the still of the night and listened for the cry of a child that never came. In a sense the men were the children she could not bear and the Chief, especially, whom she treasured not so much for himself as for those others she would have embraced had she ever been permitted to do so.

After a time, however, she began to grow so large that even as great a man as the Chief of Police felt that to embrace her was to engage in a struggle rather than a tryst. Accordingly, he confronted her with his alarm, positioning her in front of a mirror until at last she realised of a sudden what indeed she had become. She who had depended on beauty now saw that beauty had fled away.

She knew, of course, of her rival but had never regarded her as such. Though they had never met she felt they were in some way distantly related. To whom, then, should she turn in her distress but to that other woman with whom she could speak of the man they shared in common? Accordingly, and breaking a lifetime habit, she rose early one day and went to the great square before the cathedral. She stood there and, as the first rays of the sun shone between the buildings to the east, sending bright fingers of light reaching across the grey stones, waited for her fellow wife to emerge from the morning mass. She knew her from a photograph she had found in her demi-husband's wallet and thus recognised her immediately as she emerged from the cathedral, throwing off the lace shawl which covered her head and face. Standing in the orange light of the sun she seemed surrounded by a halo and for a moment the weekend wife felt a wash of shame pass over her. And yet did she not love, too? And if she did not venture through the great wooden doors banded with black iron did this make her love less sacred?

120

She moved forward and stood where she knew that her rival, and she hoped her friend, must pass. The shopkeeper, outside whose window she waited, had just opened, rolling up a slatted wooden shutter to reveal a window full of religious objects: pictures of the Virgin, candles of every size, and an effigy of St Geronimo in the whitest of wedding dresses. As the woman she sought was about to pass she stepped away from the window and laid a finger on her arm.

'Donna Maria,' she said, and then hesitated, unsure how she should begin the conversation, unsure, indeed, how to continue and conclude it as well.

Donna Maria looked at her and then started.

'Pasionaria,' she said, before she could stop herself, for she had found a letter once in which her husband had so addressed her.

For a second they stood and stared at one another in the chill of the morning as the shopkeeper lit the tallest of his candles with a long taper and offered a confederate wink to St Geronimo. Then they fell about one another's necks as though reunited after many years. They stood thus for a minute and looked at one another seeking, no doubt, human nature being what it is, for what their joint husband might find in the charms of the other. Then Donna Maria took her new-found friend by the arm and led her back to her house, her husband, by now, being safely in his office with a coffee in front of him and what was vulgarly known as a St Geronimo biscuit (circular and with a hole in the middle) by the saucer's edge.

The two women sat that morning and drank herbal tea. The secondary wife, for that was how she had always regarded herself, explained the reason for her distress so Donna Maria, as subtly as she might, withdrew the plate of biscuits (not St Geronimos) she had placed at the centre of the table. They exchanged notes on their common husband, though careful, of course, to reveal no

121

intimacies, spoke of his career and dedication. The underwife enquired after the children and Donna Maria detected the hidden softness in her voice. Though she had many photographs, therefore, she was careful not to draw attention to them and as the morning progressed so they grew to like one another more, as should they not, both having been chosen by the same man.

So it was that Donna Maria assumed responsibility for assisting Pasionaria slowly to shed her weight, even cooking little delights that would give pleasure without adding to her girth. And in return she would look after the children when Donna Maria wished to go on an errand or visit a relative to whom the presence of seven children might not be regarded as a boon. She became a kind of aunt and when she went shopping it was no longer to the food stores on the Boulevard O'Grady that she would direct her steps but to the toy shops, where she would linger for many an hour to select just the object that would give the greatest pleasure.

Meanwhile, Donna Maria, whose time had been full but whose life perhaps was not, consisting largely of children and the work they have the power to generate, began to discover that there was more to life than pregnancy. She joined a group of would-be artists and sat with them one afternoon a week as they set their easels before a church or placed a pile of fruit in a basket to see if they could do justice to its subtle beauty. She also offered her services in arranging flowers on the high altar and grew to know the other women who shared the task. So her world expanded as the girth of her fellow wife contracted.

By degrees, therefore, the one who had begun to lose her beauty recovered it and the one whose domesticity had begun to swallow her emerged into a fuller life. The Chief of Police, meanwhile, was aware that his existence was happier than it had been before and passed that contentment onto others in the way he treated those who crossed his path. He recognised, of course, that one woman was slimmer than she had been before, and hence, as it seemed to him, more beautiful, and, to his evident surprise, encountered the other in the square painting a picture that amazed him with its veracity and, as it seemed to him, its beauty. But he never discovered that the two parts of his life had been put together, that the weekdays had joined up with the weekend. So they betrayed him by sharing the knowledge of his infidelity, thus stripping it, in some degree, of its sin. Perhaps had he known of their confederacy some element of illicit pleasure would have gone out of his life; but since he did not, the three of them lived in perfect amity, though they never found themselves together in one place.

There will be those who question the morality of this. Was not Donna Maria a religious woman? Was he not an upholder of the law? In truth that is so, but while there is religion and there is law and there is goodness, these are not all one thing. Doubtless harm was done and certainly there were times when Donna Maria stared long and hard into her heart, but she never felt the need to mention any of this in the confession box. Her sins were many, as she thought, but this was not one of them. And so this three-cornered marriage continued and like a three-cornered stool it sat securely on the ground and bore the shifting weight put upon it. The Chief of Police thought that he was the main beneficiary but this was because, being a man, he thought mainly of himself. In fact two women and seven children had their share of benefit, along with the occasional pickpocket summoned into the great office of the Chief only to find this towering man looking at a row of photographs with tears in his eyes and stirring a cup of coffee with a St Geronimo's biscuit before telling him to go away and sin no more.

★

They did not kill the child of the woman they did kill. She flew to her distant tomorrow; they retreated to their stunted present. Why did they not kill him? Why did the man who banished his son and destroyed the woman who made such banishment necessary not step on his body as he would on a beetle? Because it carried his blood and he came from people for whom blood was everything. And if it also carried the blood of that other, if it was corrupted by an alien heritage, well that might be bred out of him and if not out of him then out of those who might follow. Generation on generation might yet expiate the crime. Whatever the reason, whatever necessity drove him, he stayed his hand. The mother was sent flying from the cliff-top but the child was permitted to live, perhaps because he had no choice but to play his part in a myth that would ensnare if not him then others in the times that lay ahead.

The boy was not banished to the countryside, given to a stranger, substituted for another; he was raised in a remote part of the palace where he could be watched, where all aspects of his education could be overseen, where he could be shaped and formed as you would make a shoe for a particular foot, or throw a pot, never lifting your shaping hand, ever turning, ever smoothing, drawing up, until at last you could bake it hard so that it would change no more and then bake it again so that the glaze became part of its structure. But this is a simile and the boy was not.

The boy was taught his Spanish heritage, not that other, of course, for what is to be said for a culture which has no books, no history independent of myth, no victories that mattered beyond the tangled jungles that were their setting? To be sure there were stone structures, far from the coast, along rivers now silted and returned to the land. These structures suggested that there had indeed been those who linked heaven to earth and were familiar with the principles of mathematics or the principles of principals. But these were now lost and could have had no connection with those who planted fields and carried burdens and wore feathers in their hair at festivals they celebrated without knowing of their origins. And which civilised people would paint their faces except perhaps the ladies of the palace who painted their faces and fixed feathers in their hair, but did so because they thought that to do so would please men and not the gods? At best such people were corrupt descendants of some long-lost world, though more likely they were related to the savages who over-threw a once glorious but now irrelevant civilisation. So he learnt of Spain and England and France and a little of neigh-bouring countries, though not to their credit. They were no more than coloured shapes on a map whose names were inscribed in the language of the gods.

He was tutored in theology and the classics and taught to ride and fence and dance. But one question was never answered, no matter whom he might ask. Where is my mother? The Duke, who visited him from time to time, and who he believed must know the truth of this, as he was told he knew the truth of all things, frowned, turned away, and left the room when he ventured to enquire. His tutor instructed him the very next day not to repeat his question. Nor did he do so. Others shrugged or shook their heads or stared past him at the sea which shimmered in the sun so that after a while he directed his question to no one but himself. But he asked it just the same and prayed for her even as the potter spun his wheel and endeavoured to shape him to his will.

At eighteen the young man, by the name of Tomas, was summoned by the Duke and invited to sit in a chair and take a glass of wine. The summons and the invitation alike made him nervous, for what connection could he have to such a man? In idle moments he had thought that he might be his son, for how else to account for those visits, but saw the foolishness of this for were he such why would he be raised so far from his father's side? Besides, he had a father of a kind, the man who had raised him, though that father had indicated to him that, while they shared much, blood was not included in the bargain.

The Duke stood up and looked at the young man who, though the lightest brown, could easily pass as a natural and uncontaminated descendant of the original settlers. His eyes were dark, the colour of the soil, and his hair smooth and black. He carried himself with confidence and was as handsome as the offspring of such a union was fated to be.

'Boy,' said the Duke, who had never been able to utter the name given to him by his fated mother, a name which super-stition prevented him from repealing, for it was under that name that his soul was secured for Christ, 'I have an interest in your career, as you will know. I had knowledge of your father, who is no longer with us.' He paused and watched the young man to see if he might betray any knowledge of his origins. But the boy stared back at him, the glass of wine untouched in his hand.

'He was a good man and I would stand in his place and assist you as I may.' He paused again. His own son, in truth, had proved anything but a good man. The killing of the woman had cut a deal deeper than he had supposed it could, so that none of the young ladies presented to him could please his eye. Many others did, but these were not presented to him for marriage. He grew older and stouter, drinking and despairing more, never quite able to drive out memories that bled into his dreams and disturbed his days. He replayed his part in the death of a girl who had done no wrong except to love unwisely and live to bear the consequence of that love before dying the death required of such a consequence.

No event, no person, no pastimes could distract him from an obsession which slowly corroded his soul. Nor had the Duke used the past tense inadvertently, for his son was indeed dead, throwing himself into the sea at Cartagena, falling not as an angel but a broken doll. The bastard child was thus the Duke's only link to that son, as that son had been the only fruit of his loins.

'I have decided that you are to serve in the army,' he said. 'Accordingly, you will be given the rank of lieutenant.'

The boy had had many ambitions, but this was not one of them. Though he had been tutored in the glorious history of his country, in truth he had seen little to glory in; while the life of a soldier did not recommend itself to someone drawn to the natural world, who took pleasure in drawing and walking by the edge of the ocean, feeling the pull of the shoreline as though his destiny might perhaps lie on the margin. For a time, indeed, he had suspected that his very being might reflect some such ambiguous division, for he had felt a momentary attraction for a young boy whom he saw once from his tutor's room, a young boy who stripped to the waist each day and poured a bucket of water over his head and then sat in the sun to dry.

It was a passion that passed, however, as his body settled on what path he should tread, and soon it was the girls he watched and the glimpse of a bronzed thigh would set his blood pulsing in his ears. Indeed there was one girl in particular, a native girl who carried water and laundry and whose dark hair glistened in the sun. For week after week and then month after month he did no more than watch her until, one day, he encountered her by the well and reached out for the pail she carried. She jerked away from him, anger flaring in her eyes. She well knew that she must keep herself apart from one dressed as he, from those who oppressed them and forbade them the use of their language, though in truth that language was no longer fully hers to command. Each generation resisted the power and authority of Spanish with less conviction and retained its hold on the ancient tongue with a grasp which slackened with the years.

She walked away, barefoot and proud, and he watched as her hips swayed and her simple dress flared out in the breeze that blew from the sea into which his mother had once plunged. But to come even that close to her fixed her in his mind. Nor was this unobserved, for there had long been those employed to watch him and report back whom he might speak to and what he might be doing, for the Duke was alert for the first sign that he had inherited his mother's spirit as he had his father's looks. Though he had stayed his hand those years before, he had never convinced himself of the wisdom of this. Calculation and sentiment were kept in almost perfect balance. Or they were until the death of his son. Since that time, and by an irony of which he was too well aware, he had grown to look on this alien young man as truly flesh of his flesh. He was all that remained to him, his sole claim on the future, for no woman had borne him a child since that first child who had chosen a watery grave to mimic that of the woman he loved. Now, on receipt of the new intelligence, he decided to act with speed. The lieutenant reported for duty and found himself riding out of the city towards the north where there were those who disturbed the equanimity of the nation. He had been trained in swordcraft and military tactics and was better educated than those who rode beside him and carried superior rank. But it was clear from his bearing that he outranked them in terms of his connections, so there was a deference to their manner that he found distressing.

They rode for three days, camping each night under a mist of stars. Nor, once he had overcome his regret at leaving a girl who he knew could feel no regret at his leaving of her, was he as displeased as he had thought he must be. He was in the natural world he loved. He rode across a plain and through a forest that teemed with life and, despite the heat and the annoyance of flies which blackened the eyes of his horse and stung him about the neck and wrists, breathed freely for the first time in his life.

For the most part he felt nothing in common with those he rode beside. They were products of the Military Academy and seemed little more than children given leave to play the role of men. Each night they drank heavily, at first from the bottles of wine they had brought with them and then from liquor they acquired from the peasants, liquor so cheap they had no need to steal it. But there was one man, a captain, older than them by some twenty years, whom he did admire. He kept discipline and enforced a degree of justice when his men sought to exploit those they might be presumed to protect, and though he drank as heavily as them, and perhaps more, he kept apart from them as if he shared nothing with them but the assignment on which they found themselves temporary comrades. And this man seemed to recognise that the young lieutenant had more in common with him than he had with any of his fellow officers. After the first two days, accordingly, he invited him to take supper and thereafter to drink with him, for though the lieutenant took no pleasure in this yet for company's sake he drank the sugar alcohol as the captain reminisced about his youth.

So it was that in the disinterested light of a million stars the captain told a story that turned the wheel full circle. Opening a second bottle of wine and slapping at the insects drawn to the lamp which roared away on the tent pole behind them, casting their shadows on the canvas, he recalled his first task on being called to the flag. The Duke, he recounted, had a son, a boy of mixed virtues but striking appearance. And he had loved unwisely, as many another had done. He fell in love with a native woman who in time had delivered a child. And there the

129

story might have ended were it not for the fact that instead of abandoning her, as any other in his position would have done, he had gone in search of her in a distant village. And finding her, he had returned to the palace. Thereafter things had taken the course they must, bearing in mind the severity of the father and his concern with the purity of blood. So it was that he – not then, as later, a captain – had found himself a member of the company charged to carry out the sentence of the court before which she had appeared. He and some five others had been required to take her from her cell to the cliff's edge and, after a priest had whispered a few verses of scripture in her ear, send her out into the void. None of the six had wished to do this duty and only one had done so. Himself. He alone had obeyed the order. He alone bore the guilt. Now was the time for confession.

The woman was beautiful and her offence seemed no great threat to an empire as vast as theirs, but it was his first lesson in the trade he had chosen. Each placed a hand on the woman's body and each together pressed her to the cliff's edge, but when the guns were fired, all but he had aimed at a sullen sky. He had sought her beating heart, knowing what otherwise might be her fate. He stopped speaking and poured the sugar alcohol to the very brim of his new friend's glass. The young man sat, unspeaking. 'Drink,' said the captain. The young man remained motionless. 'Drink. That is an order.' He did not smile, and the young man did as he was bid, swallowing the tepid liquid and feeling it burn its way down his throat.

'But there is more,' said the captain, lost now to time and place, the alcohol having betrayed him into betrayal. 'There is a reason I tell you this story.' He leaned forward and placed a hand on the sleeve of a young lieutenant who listened intently to the words of a man of whose existence he had known nothing only days before. 'The woman died. The child lived on. I know, because I was charged with placing him with one who would watch over him. I was charged to keep watch and make report. They no doubt thought me so contaminated with the guilt of what I had done, though it was an order that I must obey, that they thought me safe, and so I have been until this moment. But you have a right to know.'

'I?'

'Yes. For who are you but the one of whom I speak?'

In placing him with the captain, over whom he presumed himself to have total control, the Duke had thought he was secure. But guilt will lead to confession. There is no one who will not one day wish to purge his soul, especially, perhaps, one who may have to ride into battle and perhaps thereby go to his own death. So now the young man knew his origin and knew, too, to whom he owed his privileges and why.

He left that same night (when the captain lay on his canvas bed, his blood running into the ready soil, free at last) and rode under those selfsame disinterested stars. He rode through that night and two more, until at last he came to the palace. Leaping from the horse, he ran up the marble staircase and along the corridor until he came to the Duke's chamber, striking the single guard with the hilt of his sword so that he collapsed and lay still in the wavering light of candles. He threw the door open. It crashed against the wall and in a few steps he was at the Duke's bedside before he could do more than raise himself up.

He did not kill the Duke, though it was that which he had returned to do, but forced him to dress and accompany him to the cliff's edge. The guards had moved to stop them, but were waved away by a man who could feel the point of a dagger at his back. Together they stopped and looked down at the rocks below. A wind had risen and seemed to urge them further.

'Tell me again. Why did you kill her?'

131

'She had broken the law.'

'In giving me birth?'

'In speaking a forbidden tongue. In seducing . . .'

'Take care.'

'It was a necessity.'

'And now?'

'Now?'

'What should I do now? Avenge my mother's death?'

'You are not your mother's child. You are my son's.'

'Indeed?'

'I have plans for you.'

'You had plans for my mother.'

'Think of the future, not the past.'

'I do. It is a future in which I see neither of us.'

He pressed another step forward until a further step would send them both flying.

'Do you have no regrets?'

'I regret nothing.'

'Nothing?'

The man faltered, for in truth he regretted everything. What he had sought to gain he had lost. All his certainties had fled away. If this was to be his fate then he would accept it for what it was. It had been a mistake, all a mistake. He should have stayed in Madrid or Salamanca.

'Shall we fly?' asked the young man whom he had almost begun to think of as his son. 'Blood is important, is it not? Mother and father were both flyers. Shall we step into the air?'

They did not step into the air. The dagger was returned to its sheath. The young man left the palace, never to return. And the Duke? He lived until he died, being, whatever his rank, his blood or his nationality, a man like other men.

★

Sagrado Dios is shaped a little like an exclamation mark. It is long and narrow, with an island a hundred miles or so from its southern extremity, an island claimed by a European power whose citizens could no more identify it on a map than they would willingly travel there even if bribed to do so. It was defended by troops whose function it was to raise their national flag and who cursed their luck that they should be relegated to an island known only for its penguins and then only to those with an interest in such. It was the last vestige of a once great empire which saw itself as a standard-bearer for a civilisation whose virtues were demonstrated by a series of wars against those too backward to understand the value of what they were being offered. Now the empire was represented by this place as if the universe were retreating to its original compacted atom. It was a gesture of such hubris as to expose an ineluctable weakness, power ever revealing its fragility at the margin of its reach.

The north of Sagrado Dios is tropical; the south not unfamiliar with ice and snow. Those in the south tend to be of a puritanical frame of mind, being suspicious of their body and its snares and dressing accordingly. They are by nature radical in their politics, allowing their passions to be directed into schemes to transform their lot. In the north, closer to the equator, they are more volatile but also more conservative. There the body inscribes its own needs, insults are swiftly avenged, lusts consummated; but they are content for the social world to be as it is. There are revolutions, to be sure, in which peasants rise against their masters, but they never do so expecting change to be radical, or if so expecting never feeling a sharp disappointment if this does not turn out to be their fate. Life is leisurely, duty undemanding, licence permitted, politics corrupt, business unhurried, love a necessity.

In the south love is a burden, business a vocation, politics a branch of philosophy and economics, licence the spawn of the devil, duty a genetic compulsion, life a sentence to be served. This in part explains the Civil War of 1860 in which the south sought to liberate itself from the libertine north. It was a war it should have won, showing all the discipline and military rigour lacking in its northern neighbour, organising its logistics with admirable efficiency and rigour and issuing manifestos of ringing clarity and daunting rhetoric. It lost not because of any deficiency of logic or failure of manufacture, of strategy or tactics. It lost because its citizens lacked imagination, a certain anarchic flare, a subversive and random brilliance and the ability, finally, to accept the casualties they suffered and which provoked their honest citizenry, their businessmen and their politicians, to engage in the kind of cost analysis of which their northern counterparts were incapable by nature. They failed because they could not endure. What linked these two, then? A history and a river system, a river system described and first travelled by an eccentric Frenchman of masochistic tendencies.

From this voyage, too, came many of the foods which, if not exactly commonplace, are still to be found. At the time of Jacques they were the necessities of native tribes. Now they are luxuries served in only the most expensive of restaurants, or in fast food outlets, somewhat slower in Sagrado Dios than elsewhere in the world. Here the favourites are made from cow's udder and pig's intestines, known locally as Milkies and Silkies. In the days of Jacques the Navigator, however, the food was rather different and, after the loss of his supplies in his miraculous descent of the Falls, he was obliged to be tutored by his native guide in the cuisine of the forest before her unfortunate trans-formation into food for the Thompson's Alligators. Thus had he been introduced to bat on a stick.

The Wobbly Bats were so unstable that it was possible to catch them by whistling so that their acoustic negotiation of the gorge became further confused and they flew directly into the walls of the ravine and dropped into the river. While still stunned they were scooped up and later roasted, their wings becoming brittle like a thin parchment bread, their bodies producing meat not unlike that of a rat, though rather less substantial. Dung Beetles, too, could be eaten provided they were carefully prepared. They were wrapped in leaves, and cooked in a fire lit in a small pit before being covered over with earth. Thus baked, they were served with strong herbs to counteract an odour which the cooking process did not entirely purge. His Indian guide gave every appearance of relishing these as delicacies; he, however, never acquired the taste and was sick more than once because of the richness of their flesh. He had difficulty, too, with the Mountain Death Worm, whose natural poisons had to be steamed out of it. Indeed so many of the creatures he encountered were poisonous that cookery was quickly revealed to require the skills of the surgeon and the pharmacist. The Hopping Spider was a kind of inland baby squid but its poison sack had to be removed with care since its venom, to this day, has no antidote. Customers, in the few restaurants licensed to serve this delicacy, are required to sign a form absolving the chef and proprietor of any responsibility should they die as a consequence of eating it. Frogs, of course, were consumed and here Jacques could teach his guide a thing or two, though he had never previously eaten their spawn which the natives consumed as a kind of dessert, like a grey-green tapioca pudding.

Jacques, of course, was sick almost as many times as he ate, whether it be the Soft-Shelled Armadillo or the penis of the slide lizard, which resembled a snake, having no legs, but which exhibited such a voracious sexual appetite as to attempt mating with anything it encountered that showed signs of animation, thus posing a problem for those who hunted it.

From this point on, the river, which Jacques had been following, meandered slowly towards the south, gathering strength as it
went. The raft by now was showing signs of its encounters with
rocks and debris, and a certain jostling of the tree trunks which
formed it made moving around without nipping his feet or
pinching his hand increasingly difficult. But at least on the open
plain the oppressive heat began to dissipate as he watched great
herds of striped buffalo graze the spindly grass. The birds of the
forest had been brilliantly coloured – reds and purples, yellow and
orange – but here they seemed drab as though the sheer
uniformity of the scene encouraged little in the way of
individuality. Indeed what struck him more than anything was the
profusion of animals. It was, of course, his diaries which, when
published, finally encouraged first hunters and trappers and then
settlers to move into this territory, killing all that passed before
them. He saw evidence, too, of the tribes of the plain, drawn to
the river both for water and for the richness of the soil on either
side. Today these plains are covered with conical mountains of
crushed rock from the mines sunk to recover copper. The fields
may no longer be green but the river is, as chemicals are discharged
into it to be swept southwards and then eventually east where it
discharges into a sea now discoloured a mile from the coast.

Jacques saw the country when it was still pure. All was
potential and promise. The distant mountains, tipped with white
as though to signify their age, were nonetheless unsullied,
reaching up into air as clean and clear as if creation lay no more
than a day away. Today, though little remains of a once
considerable industry, a thin mist of orange and grey still floats
above plain and mountain alike as smoke from the processing
plants drifts with the ever-changing wind.

He was alone now, his native help having sunk deep into the
never-resting waters of a river which gave and took with equal

disdain, or perhaps deep inside an equally disinterested Thompson's Alligator. Like all others he sought to understand his new life in terms of his old, to reconcile the world that now presented itself to all his senses with the world he remembered and hence by which all else must be judged. There were moments, indeed, when he could imagine himself in Provence or Normandy, perhaps, or even the Loire, but it was an illusion invariably broken by the intrusion of an alien creature or the sound of cries both unfamiliar and disturbing.

It takes courage to enter an unmapped world with no destination but a knowledge that destiny must have its purpose and necessity. It is a journey, however, on which we all must go, so there is a sense in which Jacques the Navigator navigates on behalf of us all, provided that his representative nature be restricted to this one respect, for in truth his personal habits left something to be desired. A man who lives and travels alone still feels the same passions as those who may find companionship in the arms of another, but companionship in the land through which he passed being difficult to come by he was forced to seek other solace of which, in truth, he left no record. Not all stories which pass down through the generations are true, however, and there are those who still maintain that he remained the original Adam, untainted by intercourse of any kind. But the citizens of this country are known for their ribaldry. Indeed the very folk song played by the bell-ringers before their accident had celebrated one of the rumoured romances of the early traveller. It was called 'The Ballad of Jacques's Chicken'.

The final part of his journey was a painful one because by this time he had sustained a number of injuries, and though he endeavoured to cure himself of his suppurating wounds by applying the leaves of plants, as he had seen the Indians do, and swallowing the berries to be found along the river bank, he seems to have chosen unwisely and as a result suffered many days and nights of pain and even unconsciousness. His skin turned grey and his hair green, there being natural deposits of bauxite in the soil (later exploited by the American Bauxite Company). By degrees his extremities began to suffer from a damaged circulation system. His fingers and toes first blackened and then dropped off, making it difficult to navigate and still more difficult to write his journal and draw his pictures. Eventually he was reduced to holding his paintbrush in his mouth. The resulting sketches are therefore doubly affecting. The last leg of his journey was thus aptly named, for by the time he had entered the Cold Zone, where winds rushed up from the Antarctic, he had lost one leg and a hand.

Most men would have surrendered to despair if not to pain; but Jacques existed to travel. For him death was not only stasis in itself, it was provoked by stasis. So, in the face of winds that stripped the remaining clothes from his body and exposed him more completely to the ice lice of the Southern Tundra, he struggled on, telling himself that each finger lost was one fewer still to lose, that two limbs were excessive when he was required to do nothing but sit on an admittedly fast disintegrating raft. And in truth little effort was required, for the river carried him onwards to its mating with the sea and his encounter with his destiny.

Little would have been known of Jacques and his fate had another expedition not found his record nearly a century later. Because of the cold he had been preserved where he had come to rest. At first the explorers believed they might have stumbled on a novel species, for at the last he had lost both legs and both arms and the leathery carcass gave him the appearance of anything but a human being. But they discovered his oilskin-wrapped journals and, on their return, ensured that they would be published. Today they are the prize exhibit of the National Museum, where they celebrate the life of the man who in discovering so much that was new both described and in part invented a land that had always been the product of myth and legend as much as of tangible realities.

His body, meanwhile, or such of it as remained, was kept in a glass case in the entrance to the Explorers Guild, a gentlemen's club whose members qualify for membership by venturing on at least one journey of exploration and by losing at least one portion of their anatomy, the parts authorised being indicated on a list maintained by the Inspecting Committee. Once a year, on the anniversary of his death, the case is opened and each member, in turn, reaches in a hand (supposing that not to be the part of the body which secured membership) and touches the parchment-like skin. The body is then removed and placed at the head of the dining table for the annual dinner, glasses being raised to the man who first mapped this varied and magical country and who discovered and described its remarkable flora and fauna at so great a price.

It might be thought that I have been drawing too sanguine a portrait of the capital of a disregarded country, and it is true that besides its cathedral square there were slums and despite the occasional (even frequent) festivals there was much poverty and pain and distress. That this was borne with an acquiescence which verged at times on masochism rather than mere passivity made it seem no more than the natural order of things. But pain is not lessened because it is felt by those who live amidst squalor; a child lost to disease is mourned no less keenly by those who cannot record their grief with their own hands. Few in this country were rich by the standards of other lands, but we do not judge by comparisons of this kind. We live in one place, after all,

139

or at least we do if we are citizens of Sagrado Dios whose government is as loath to let its people out as it is to allow other people in.

The country had a single crop, a crop in much demand around the world its people did not see. But that demand did not result in high prices to those who grew it on the hillsides or packed it to be sent overseas. Its value accumulated as it made its way to the distant markets until at last, in North America or Europe, people who bought it would shake their heads at how simple a product could cost so much.

There had been a lumber industry in Sagrado Dios. In the north there was once a forest the size of several European countries put together, a fact that Europeans had noted in the early part of the last century arriving with bright smiles and heavy equipment. They did no more than set the example, however, swiftly falling victim to a number of diseases of considerable interest to scientists but of no interest to those who succumbed to them. For many years nothing was heard but the sound of animals offering loud invitations to breed or registering their objections to being eaten. Then a consortium of businessmen, connected to the construction industry and farming, as well as by their mutual interest in money, decided to drive dust roads into the interior, relocate (kill) the Indians, utilise (steal) the land and realise its potential (cut, slash, burn, plant).

At the centre was a mill and from this they radiated out, destroying in minutes what had taken centuries to grow. Then they prepared the land and planted peanuts. To this day it is possible to buy peanut soup in the country's co-operative stores. Demand, however, proving somewhat disappointing, the tins are still to be seen on the shelves, a little rusting to be sure but brightened by colourful labels added from time to time saying 'Now with Added Peanuts' or 'May Contain Nuts'. The fields, meanwhile, are overgrown and a few saplings have begun their upward climb, so in a hundred years or so the forest will have returned to its full height, though without the animals once so committed to breeding and dying. Meanwhile, those who made money from selling the timber are the most respected of citizens, always visible on public occasions, ready to endow scholarships, dispense advice and insist that they are evidence that there is a Sagrado Dios dream and that anyone, no matter how poor, can make his or her (to be honest, his) fortune provided that he is ready to recognise an opportunity should it present itself.

Fernando Jones, descendant of a British soldier and a San Marco woman of high expectations and low morals, the latter to ensure the former, was the managing director of a company which manufactured plastic flags, plastic knives and forks and plastic sheets for the incontinent, a process which, on certain days, filled the air above with a haze of fumes that would have disturbed any health and safety inspector had such an innovation been introduced to Sagrado Dios. Besides, to manufacture the national flag was a patriotic act and who could object to breathing the air of patriotism? But should they think to do so, how were they to express their objections when Fernando Jones controlled many of the nation's principal newspapers? Beyond that, did his works not employ those who might otherwise swell the ranks of the unemployed (though unemployment, those same newspapers explained, was virtually non-existent)?

Employees of the Plastic Utensils and Incontinence Products (PUIP) were not hard to detect. They all had wheezing coughs and large stocks of plastic cutlery, illicitly obtained, and used for a variety of household chores, though seldom to eat since they had a tendency to snap if applied to anything denser than an over-ripe tomato. Many a child also blissfully emptied its bladder on black market sheets which had dropped off the back of a donkey.

Fernando Jones's daughter, of course, was ashamed of her father's profession, in part because she was known at school as 'Piss-Sheet Pilar', which did little for the confidence of a teenage girl, though there was some compensation in the clothes she wore, designed by Pablo of San Marco, who was inspired by the young boys about whom he dreamed but settled for the flat-chested models on whom he draped his creations.

If little left Sagrado Dios, little entered. The currency was a problem. Nobody wanted it. In the countryside, barter still prevailed; but international bankers are seldom interested in having their debts paid in live chickens or hand-embroidered funeral shrouds (the latter a local tradition). Despite the govern-ment's lack of enthusiasm for people either entering or leaving the country it felt obliged, for political reasons, to establish a Tourist Board, though it was said to be well-named since the singular form of the title came close to matching the number of annual visitors. Every now and then, it must be admitted, a trickle of foreigners would succeed in making their way past the immigration official, who took great delight in asking them whether their visit was for business or pleasure, always laughing at the reply since neither was likely. The souvenir stand, how-ever, with its embroidered funeral shrouds and embossed plastic cutlery, was perpetually closed, though the bat on a stick concession thrived, drawing on sufficient customers from the nearby college of mortuary science (run, in a former tanning works, by a one-time priest defrocked for doing much the same to a number of young girls).

Should visitors have succeeded in visiting San Marco they would have found a deal of poverty, and where this exists there is also a church which teaches the poor to reconcile themselves to their poverty. Just as the Spaniards had carried a Bible to teach those they conquered the boon of their defeat, so there were those now who taught the special virtue of the poor. It is not surprising, therefore, that there were far more churches in the poorest part of town than in the richest. Those who ministered to them, meanwhile, had a harder task to perform and, due to the obedience of their congregations to obscurely argued theological views on population control, there were many more sheep in these flocks than among the more worldly wise and careful members of the upper classes. It is true that the churches reflected the poverty of those who worshipped in them – their white-painted walls were streaked here and there with rust where iron bolts connected two beams and where the rain found its way through a maze of broken tiles – just as other churches reflected the wealth of their worshippers, with gold leaf arching over the heads of those who knelt on embroidered hassocks and priests who, in gratitude for the financial support of their congregations, enquired rather less actively of their confessants the nature of their more intimate moments.

There was one priest, however, who despaired of the creed of his church, who saw that resignation and obedience did no more than ensure the continuance of grief. He had studied in Rome, and had heard the arguments he was expected to pass on to his flock. His education must have been faulty, for his own instincts were not sufficiently suppressed. He wanted nothing more than to change things and was so misguided as to believe that the church itself might prove an agency of such change. He wandered his parish and took note of the decayed buildings and decaying lives. He recorded the details of infant mortality and the rates of the various diseases. He saw the rats and the cock-roaches and watched as the children played barefoot where all must do their toilet every day. He watched and he pondered and one day he acted by preaching in his church about poverty and disease and the disregarded. But instead of speaking of the need for submission and faith, of the justice that must come in the next life and of the beauty of living without the corruption of wealth, he spoke of the need for action. He called on the rich to acknowledge their debt and, having acknowledged, to pay it. He called on the company whose smoke turned the noon-day sun black and the blue skies a swirling orange to cease discharging the by-products of its manufacture into the sky and the rivers, now flecked a mildewed yellow and green and topped with white foam. He called on the politicians to serve their electorates, pull down the slums and create new jobs for the unemployed. He behaved, in short, as Christ might have behaved and received in return what Christ might have received had he chosen this place and this time to return to his ministry.

It began with a letter from his bishop and another from the politician who came once a year to this poor parish and shook the hands of those tradesmen who were of his party. An article appeared in the newspaper owned by the man who also owned shares in the factory the priest had accused of polluting the land, reminding him that his function was to save souls and not to deprive the poor of what labour was available. 'The Priest of Unemployment' they called him in a headline. 'The Religion of Envy' echoed another newspaper, whose newsprint was supplied by a man whose brother ran the factory owned by Fernando Jones who also owned the city's other newspaper.

But the people came to his sermons in ever greater numbers until the Bishop, alarmed at the sudden popularity of this humble but troublesome priest, called him to a meeting in his palace in the city centre. The priest looked up at the chandelier in the entrance hall. It glittered as its crystals were stirred by the air from the golden fans which turned slowly above him. The floor was made of marble and was a relief from the heat of the street. On the wall was a painting of Christ, washing the feet of the poor. A door opened and the Bishop's secretary glided through, his hands rubbing together as though in anticipation of some spectacle or other. He beckoned the priest forward.

The Bishop sat at a mahogany desk. To his left was a tray filled with letters; to his right was another tray, though with a rather smaller pile. The priest stood before him, uncertain what to do or say. The Bishop signed the document in front of him, took a blotter and dried the purple ink. Then he placed the letter in the tray to his right, screwed the cap back on his pen and placed it carefully in the grooved holder on the table top. Only then did he look up and, effecting surprise, say, 'Father Jacomo, welcome. Sit yourself down. A little refreshment?'

The priest was unused to such splendour, though he had seen a deal of it those years before in Rome when he and others, mostly Irish as it seemed to him, had been inducted into the mysteries of the faith.

'Sit, sit,' said the Bishop brightly, as though speaking to a favourite dog. 'Angelo!' He gestured to his secretary, dressed in black and enfolded in himself. 'Coffee. Iced lime. Petits fours.'

Angelo bowed a little and then turned, his black robe flaring out like the skirts of a courtesan at a funeral. He was back a few moments later with a tray on which was a jug of lime cordial, frosted where the air condensed on its side. With this were two crystal glasses, two cups of coffee and a plate of biscuits, though no St Geronimos.

'Now,' said the Bishop getting up from his chair and sailing around the end of the table, 'help yourself.' He sat down on the other side of the low table.

The priest was so overawed that he could not bring himself to reach out for the drink, though, to be truthful, he was a little dry and hot, black clothes being ill-suited for the heat. He shook his head.

'Nonsense, nonsense. Permit me.' And so he ministered to his priest, as Christ had washed the feet of the poor. Indeed, he permitted himself a glance up at the painting through the open door as though in humble recognition of the parallel. When at last he had finished and they both had a glass, a cup and a biscuit in front of them, he took out a pair of spectacles and balanced them on the end of his nose.

'Now let me see,' he said, 'it is some time since you and I had a chat.'

Indeed it was. In fact, to be accurate, they had never had one.

'St Anthony's is a demanding parish,' he observed.

The priest raised a hesitant finger. 'St Andrew's.'

'To be sure,' replied the Bishop, with some irritation, 'but that, of course, is our calling. And I am glad to see that you are concerned with the condition of your parishioners.'

The priest lifted a glass of lime, cold against his hand.

'Though it is the condition of their souls that is our primary concern, as you know. Not all is perhaps as it should be. In my experience it seldom is, but there is a division of labour in these as in all things. Our care is for their souls and for the dispensing of charity. Others must bear the burden of deciding the priorities of the state, though I scarcely breach a confidence if I say that the word of your Bishop carries a deal of weight. Indeed I can tell you what others will not know for some considerable time: that I have secured an agreement that there should be an enquiry into the conditions of the river in your parish, as part of a general report which will cover the rest of the country with a view to formulating a policy with respect to the, er' – he paused –

'environment. Also I am of a mind to list your parish as a beneficiary of funds which from time to time I receive from the Holy Father in order to address just such a situation as this.' He smiled. 'So,' he said, getting to his feet, 'it has been good to have this chat.'

The priest found himself outside in the sun without ever having quite noticed that he had left. He held a biscuit in one hand and in the other a signed photograph of the Bishop, this having been pressed upon him by the Secretary, who smelled of eau de cologne, as he was led towards the ornate doors, before being eased back onto the street.

Father Jacomo walked back through the city, past the opulent shops and the bus station, through the Old Town and across the railway track to the dirt roads that defined his parish. And as he walked he replayed the Bishop's speech in his mind. It seemed to him that he was being told that he need worry no more, that the Church had listened and that he should have no further concern. He recalled the Bishop's worried face and serious tone and was sure that he would now see the transformation for which he had prayed. Accordingly, in his next sermon he gave what seemed to him to be the good news to his flock: 'No more pollution,' he assured them, 'money from the Church. Assurances from your Bishop.'

He sat opposite the Bishop and stirred the coffee with a silver spoon. There was no lime cordial this time and the Bishop stood up as soon as he came into the room.

'A misunderstanding, I fear,' he said. 'What I told you was not for the public ear, nor will you see a noticeable difference for some time.' He was not used to observing his own name in the headlines of the newspaper, albeit the one remaining radical newspaper (shortly to be closed for the third time in a month), or reading of his supposedly reckless and radical promises, and though a telephone call had sufficed to stop the further revelations of his supposed radical connections with something called the Thousand Points of Light, an organisation of which he had never heard, nonetheless it had come as something of a shock to feel the solid rock beneath his feet begin to tremble.

'These things take time and must be conducted out of the public eye. Meanwhile I entreat you to desist from turning your sermons into attacks upon the government and the solid citizens of San Marco, who do so much for the Church and the people.'

The priest stood outside the Bishop's house and looked up at its splendour. It was a sign of the Church's power; yet he had begun to doubt that it truly possessed such if it could not address even the modest requirements of a people who had been patient for so long. However he had been trained to obedience and in his next sermon he said nothing of the government or the rich industrialists. He turned his attention instead to the Church itself.

'Christ himself was poor,' he said, looking down at his congregation, which now and ever since word of his sermons had got around was packed into the church and even the small chapel dedicated to the city's cobblers. 'Shall the Church, then, be rich? Rome, my friends, and I have been there, has domes covered with gold. It has great silver and gold goblets from which Christ's blood is drunk. Even here in San Marco silver and gold are to be found. I know that the Bishop cares for you for he has told me so. Will he, then, refuse to help? No, my friends. You have found a friend at last.'

'Are you a fool or a knave?' the Bishop asked, looking at the priest before him, bereft of coffee, cordial and biscuits.

'I do not understand.'

148

'Have you seen this?' He held up a newspaper, somewhat crumpled as though it had been screwed up into a ball and then straightened out. The headline was large and black: 'BISHOP GIVES CASH TO POOR; AGREES TO MELT DOWN CHURCH SILVER.'

The priest had not. 'Praise God,' he said.

The Bishop looked up at the ceiling as if God might reciprocate. There was silence.

The downfall of the priest owed nothing, however, to the Bishop or the Church. There were other forces than those acknowledged by him or the hierarchy. The fact is that on that Sunday the priest once more stood in the pulpit and gave his parishioners the benefit of his views on the world as he saw it. For there were other problems which gave him pause. In going about his parish he had noted that among the poor there were others poorer still. Where many worked at the humblest jobs, others did not work at all. Those who were despised, themselves despised others in turn. Several centuries before, when the Spaniards found that the natives were not as tractable as they wished, they had turned to Africa, bringing from that despised country many hundreds and thousands who travelled in horror and arrived in despair. Over the years the virtue of the women had been abused by those who claimed to have ownership of them. The result was that a whole spectrum of colours was painted over the country, their gradations according to the social role they were obliged to assume. Each subtle shift of skin tone was accorded a name. One was a pecan, another a copper, a third a jet. These last, as the priest had discovered, were at the bottom of both the colour chart and the social scheme.

'Should we not embrace our black brothers?' he asked. 'Are we not all God's children? Should not even the poor give to the poorest?' He looked around the packed interior of the church

149

and realised what he had known but never allowed to enter his consciousness. The black faces were all gathered in one part of the building, as though clinging together for comfort. 'Now, let us do it now. Let us embrace them.'

As he looked back at the dwindling shoreline, he could still not understand what had led his parishioners to petition for his removal. The Bishop had been kindness itself when informing him that he was required by the Holy Father who wished to learn of so distant a land and of the problems of the spirit that concerned the poorest of its citizens.

The old man sat in the alcove of the cathedral, as he had for more than thirty years, hand extended, foot underneath his body, eyes uplifted plaintively. He was there from the first mass of the day through to the moment when the great doors were swung shut, with a sound that reverberated around the limestone walls and against the vaulted roof, sending explosions of pigeons into the night sky. Few days passed without someone pressing a coin into his hand and few with more than half a dozen. One might think that piety and charity would be natural bedfellows, that those who knelt on the scalloped stone and looked up at the plaster eyes of the virgin would offer a little to those in need. You would think that those who had gazed on the jewel-encrusted bones of the saints, interred in once fine cloth, now faded to gossamer, would be reminded of their own mortality and guard against the torment to come by buying their way through Heaven's gate. But, in truth, there were few who did so.

Perhaps he was so familiar a sight that he had become a part of the cathedral, a gargoyle leering at them from the shaded stone. Strangers would see him as they entered and again when they left before turning round as they stepped into the square as if unsure whether local custom might not require some payment for their visit. But citizens of San Marco seldom pressed a coin into his hand, unless, that is, they had special needs: sickness to be cured, lovers to find, examinations to pass.

Those that did have such needs would enter the small chapel of Saint Aleppo, a saint not known to the Roman calendar but respected through Sagrado Dios for living six years at the top of a pole mounted in the cathedral square, fed from buckets raised on long sticks, and urinating and otherwise exercising his bodily functions only at night-time when his followers would clean the products from the ground and carry them away to fertilise a garden whose giant leeks were sold to anyone who wished to cure their bodies of aches and their souls of despair. In the chapel people would write out their secret requests, (Please cure me of my piles. Pablo. Please let Maria fall in love with me. Paulo. Please remove the unsightly spot from my upper lip. Dorothea). Those that were not literate would take the precaution of employing the scribes who sat each day at folding tables in the square, ink pots and perfumed paper before them. These pieces of paper were then entwined in some part of the chapel. Some preferred to put them as close to the figure of the saint as possible, though this was difficult since, appropriately, his effigy was mounted on the top of a pole. Others favoured the paintings which adorned the small chapel, paintings that depicted the many sufferings with which the human race can be afflicted. Indeed from time to time medical historians had been known to visit this place to see what diseases might have flourished once in Sagrado Dios.

The rear wall, meanwhile, was reserved for objects placed there by those whose prayers had been answered. Here were to be found, often covered with the dust of centuries, artificial limbs, examination certificates, simple poems, small cakes covered with

151

varnish to discourage the mice, and more private things, contained in small packages and sealed with wax.

There were occasions, though, when even the offerings left for Saint Aleppo were not thought sufficient and so, to add to their chances, people would press a small coin into the hands of the beggars who many thought defiled the entrance to the cathedral built to raise the spirits and not feed the feckless.

It was a strange and lonely life and not one he could ever have anticipated when he grew up in Anzuelo. As a boy he had thought he might become a lawyer or a soldier. His parents hoped that he might become a carpenter. He became neither because one day, when he dived from the headland where the one-time mistress of the country's most famous author was believed to live, he struck his leg on a rock, wedging it in the space between that and the next. He fought a battle there under the sea, pulling with both hands, his lungs aching, his head bursting, until he passed out as a sudden and relieving flood of water entered his lungs. He was thrown free by a wave and rescued by his friends, but his leg was damaged beyond repair and his mind was cloudy and had never become clear.

When his parents died, as the earth moved and their house crumbled about them, he was placed in a Catholic orphanage. Here he was beaten regularly to teach him gratitude and because he could not perform even the simplest task they set him to do. He lived there until he was sixteen, at which time he was shown the door. They had their rules and he had broken one of them. He had grown up. A charitable trust, established a century before by a poor boy grown rich by such means as required atonement, gave him a roof over his head but nothing more, and that roof was over a single room in a house which echoed the original poverty of the subsequently rich donor. For a year or more he sat in doorways with a single message written in charcoal on a piece of cardboard (which he had to tuck inside his shirt whenever it rained) by a woman who took pity on him one day. Then he discovered the cathedral. At first those already there had fought him with flailing hands and jagged nails; but he was young and strong, if simple and crippled, and at last they left him alone.

And so for years he had watched those who visited the church and learned to read the code of what he saw: the pious poor who came each morning at dawn, tired and determined, observing an obligation they never questioned; the public official who wished all to see his observances; the pregnant girl, looking about her and heading for the pain of confession or the desperate hope of the chapel of dreams. He watched the young grow older and the old disappear suddenly, never again to cross the great square with its nodding pigeons. He saw brides clouded in white, their veils flying in the wind which scattered dust and coloured paper like the petals of summer flowers. He saw mourners in black, as though death had drained all life of its colour and not claimed only this single soul. And each time he was sure to have coins pressed into his hands: coins for joy, coins for good luck, coins in hope of an extra blessing; coins for fear that death would also reach out to claim those who carried the coffin and those who walked with heads bowed in its wake.

He was sitting at his accustomed place, his leg beneath him, his hand extended, staring up at the grey ceiling of the alcove through which people came and went, when a young woman, beautiful and alarmingly fair, slipped out of the dark cathedral and paused a moment, blinded by the morning sun. He had seen her many times before and awaited her return as though she were the sun or the seasons. She stood now, dressed in white, like a young girl coming to mass or a bride on the threshold of life, and he sat and looked up at her as a dog will stare at the moon. And then, as though suddenly recalling his presence, she

153

opened her purse, took several coins and pressed them gently into his hands, being careful, as it seemed to him, not to touch them as if she feared she might injure him. Then she paused a second before striding out into the brightness of the day. He leaned forward to see her go, her dress fanning out behind her. He saw her encounter with a young man and saw, too, another young man standing on a box saying something he could not catch. Then he withdrew himself into the shade and looked to see what she might have placed in his hands.

They were coins of such value that they were of little use, even to him. But he smiled just the same and pressed them to his lips. He knew that later that day he would need to enter the House of God and visit the chapel of dreams, for had his prayer to Saint Aleppo not been answered? The girl he had watched for many a year had indeed looked in his eyes and touched, or almost touched, his hands. It was what he had asked, what he had hoped for, what he dreamed of whenever he could shape his dreams to his needs. Who, now, could say that prayers go unanswered, he told himself.

Whatever the events in the world at large, for most of us each day comes and goes and we have concerns enough to fill each minute and each hour. Certainly this was true of a young man for whom the world revolved around a girl with whom he had never exchanged a single word. This changed, however, when he was walking home from work, his fingernails dirty, his trousers scattered with burn holes from a hundred sparks. As he passed the Café La Mancha he saw her: the once glorious Carnival Queen. She was sitting alone with a cup of coffee, or what passed for coffee in Sagrado Dios, in front of her a magazine lying open on the table. He stopped and stared. We do not, after all, expect our dreams to materialise before our eyes, and when they do we must be forgiven if we are disbelieving. His last sight of her had been on a retreating truck, a view obscured when a cardboard bell fell on top of him. He checked his pocket to see if he had the price of a coffee.

'Do you mind if I sit here?' he asked.

She waved her hand without looking up. She was as beautiful as he remembered, imperious, distant yet perfect. He sat down, aware, suddenly, of his shabby clothes. A waiter appeared before him, clutching a silver tray to his chest like a shield.

'Coffee,' he said, barely looking at the man who continued to stand beside him. 'Coffee,' he repeated.

'And?'

'Just a coffee.'

'Patrons are reminded that between the hours of six and midnight drinks may only be served with food.'

He felt in his pocket, but already knew that there was nothing beyond a few coins.

'I only want a coffee.'

The waiter shrugged. 'Patrons are reminded . . .'

'He's with me,' said the girl like a saint offering a blessing to a sinner. The waiter stood a moment longer and then shrugged before disappearing into the café. Still the girl had not looked up. He stared at her as one would at a precious work of art. But, then, of course she was a precious work of art to the young bell maker.

'He's a prick,' the Saint remarked.

The boy stared, as his universe shifted a degree or two from its true course.

'Thank you,' he said at last.

'They're all pricks.'

'Yes,' he replied, unsure who they might be and uncertain how such words could come from so beautiful a mouth. Still she read her magazine as if he were no more than a fly who had chosen this moment to settle close to hand. The waiter returned and placed a cup of coffee in front of him, spilling a good deal into the saucer.

'Prick.'

The waiter pushed his head back, lifting his nose into the air as if detecting some acrid smell, and spun on his heel.

Then, as if by chance, she glanced up and their eyes met, as they had once before in the cathedral square, and the universe adjusted itself again. They sat in silence. The cathedral bell chimed, the sound floating through him.

'Could you pass me the sugar, please?'

She nodded but made no move. He smiled. She smiled. The universe doubtless smiled, or would have done if the results of an ancient explosion were capable of this.

'Thank you,' he said, who had received nothing but that smile. She nodded. 'My name is Federico,' he said.

'Justina.'

They sat in silence again.

'Your father is a professor,' he said, anxious to keep what passed as a conversation going.

'Yes.'

'I've seen him.'

'Yes.'

'You were the Carnival Queen.'

She seemed to come to her senses at this remark, to recall where she was and what she was. 'Were you in the parade?' she asked.

He was about to reply when the memory of that day rose up before him like an accusation. He nodded.

'Which float were you on?'

'You looked beautiful,' he replied, and then blushed at his temerity.

'What do you do?' she asked, the memory of their encounter in the cathedral square now coming into sharper focus.

'I make things.'

'What things?'

He paused. 'Bells.'

'Bells?'

'Yes. I make bells.'

'Ah. What kind of bells?'

'All kinds. Great bells, small bells . . .'

'There was a float in the parade.'

'Bells of all kinds.'

'Were you . . .'

'Doorbells, hand bells, church bells . . .'

She stared at him and he could see that the pieces were coming together in her mind. Then she seemed to collect herself. 'I must go,' she said, closing her magazine. On the front he recognised the picture of Montezuma, a pop star who had just died of drugs or a broken neck (you could take your choice since, having sniffed a deal of white powder, he had tried his hand at flying, and even managed it for a second or two before impacting on a statue of Seamus O'Grady and breaking his arm, the statue's, that is, Montezuma breaking a good deal more than a marble tibia). 'I'm late,' she said.

'May I walk with you?' he asked.

'Your coffee.'

He swallowed it in a single gulp and put coins in his saucer.

They walked side by side. He could not believe that he was alone with her. For her part, she saw again a young man fall from a truck and a large cardboard bell descend on top of him. She smiled at the memory, the bitterness of the day having faded quickly. Besides, he was good-looking, not as good-looking as

157

Montezuma, but he had the advantage of being alive. A church bell struck.

'That is one of mine,' he said.

It had a silver sound, it seemed to her, as she walked beside the person who had forged it. Somewhere inside her a chemical switch had been thrown. She had been asleep and was awake and the first face she saw was bound to be that of the one she was fated to love.

Sagrado Dios has long been a country of some fascination for those who study flora and fauna. There are plants and animals here that are unknown anywhere else on the continent. But if the animals and plants are exotic so, too, are those drawn to study them. Perhaps the strangest of them was Señora Smith from Littlehampton. She arrived shortly after the swarming of the mouth fleas in 1828. She came directly from England with boxes of equipment that were carried through San Marco by a gang of men recruited by her at the harbourside, and hence not the most reliable of people. She made her home in the San Isidro Hotel, a place where rooms were rented by the hour. She wore a sand-coloured skirt, a long-sleeved shirt of comparable hue and a stiff hat to protect her from falling rock. The ensemble also served to protect her against the more usual assaults of the San Isidro Hotel.

She had large nets and small crates and bottles stored in straw and sawdust. She also carried a particularly inaccurate book based on the supposed observations of Captain Alexander Forsyth Hughes, who had spent some weeks in Sagrado Dios while his ship was being repaired. Equipped with this, ten mules and a Butting Llama, she set out for the interior. To command the men, she employed a black man she called Mr Timothy, being unable or unwilling to pronounce his name and yearning, in her heart, for the actual Mr Timothy, still in England, whose physique differed somewhat but for whom she had held a life-long affection. He was to be her guide and mentor as she explored the interior and collected her specimens. By the year's end she had a wide array of these, both alive and dead, had been bitten by a Timid Spider and stung by a dozen Bat Dung Wasps, but had survived all with fortitude. She took tea each day at three and grew to like the poppy cakes Mr Timothy prepared for her. And by degrees a certain affection grew between the two of them, based, no doubt, on mutual respect but consolidated each day, after tea and poppy cake, by lying together in the tropical heat and conjugating, for she was determined that they should learn one another's language.

Somehow they never acquired this linguistic facility, but grew together in many respects and finally married in a crumbling church in a village called Los Esperos. It was a marriage that seemed no stranger than anything else in the world to the villagers who attended the ceremony and listened as she recited the Dunciad to the assembled crowd. Whether the same responses typified the citizens of Littlehampton whither she now journeyed with her collection of animals and specimens is perhaps doubtful, for we are ever suspicious of the unfamiliar, but of their devotion there can be no doubt. Little trace of her adventure now remains, however, with the exception of her diary, which recorded the various animals she had captured and the love lore Mr Timothy had taught her on many an afternoon once their enthusiasm for foreign languages had relented; that, and the descendants of the Chattering Hare which escaped their enclosure and interbred with the native breed, thus destroying the peace of the countryside in the vicinity of the house where she lived and the graveyard where she and her native guide lie to this day.

★

Sagrado Dios's most famous author was also its most elusive. Antonio Gabriel Santiago had acquired a cult following the publication of his second novel, *One Hundred Days: One Hundred Nights*. For several years no student would be seen without it. It won the country's only literary award, but to everyone's surprise he did not appear at the award ceremony in the City Hall. It was said that he was ill or abroad. His publisher confessed to never having met him but conducting all business by letter. Nor did he offer a return address. All mail was dispatched to a box number. When the novel proved so successful journalists were sent to research his life but could find nothing but a school photograph in which he appeared, ears sticking out, dark hair smarmed down, beside his fellow pupils as they balanced themselves on school benches or sat cross-legged in the schoolyard for the photographer. Indeed he had framed this photograph, having, it seemed, run from one side of the group to the other as the image was exposed, thus doubling himself as if this early devoting himself to legerdemain.

There were, of course, those who remembered him, school friends whose own images were circled in the newspapers, but none could offer anything besides saying that he was 'good at football' or 'a poor speller'. After that, the trail went cold.

One article, however, seemed to offer rather more. A Sancho Domingo claimed to have known him as a student and had gone walking with him in the mountains. He also claimed that he had once shared a girl who could not choose between them and therefore declined to do so. The article talked of Antonio Gabriel eating wild mushrooms, known for their hallucinogenic power, and staring about him saying 'miraculous' a hundred times or more. There was much more besides. In the next edition of the newspaper, however, there was a letter, signed by

Antonio Gabriel Santiago, a mere sentence long, which read: 'Every word of the newspaper article published in yesterday's *Tempo* was a lie.' The paper printed the letter but indicated that it could have no way of verifying its authenticity. The reader thus had a choice. He was certainly being told a lie, but by whom?

Since then there had been three more novels, each one causing a sensation. They were not easy to read. They teemed with stories and characters which flowed through books seven or eight hundred pages long. In each work there were overlapping conspiracies, shadowy organisations whose original purpose remained obscure. These stretched over time, flowed over boundaries, had languages of their own. And through all there threaded, like stitches through a multicoloured quilt, characters who understood nothing of the world in which they moved but struggled on, so for some critics they became symbols of a resurgent human spirit and for others of an absurd universe which seemed to obey some hidden precept, or to assume momentary shape and form only to resolve into chaos.

These books were particularly popular in Germany, academic assistants lining up at booksellers for works which would become the basis of their second doctorate and eventually qualify them to exercise that absolute authority over their own assistants that professors had exercised on them. They prepared to subject the novels to hermeneutic examination, hermeneutics – from which the German name Hermann is generated – being a science only properly practised in a country with a fondness for abstract nouns and words which resemble sentences, a language in which meaning is tantalisingly deferred until at last a verb condescends to float down from Babel's tower, a belated signifier. Otherwise, it was the agents of Japanese and Korean publishers who rushed to secure translation rights, being under the impression that his books – which he had cunningly subtitled 'A Romance' – were works of a kind that would appeal to middle-aged women who looked for stories about bronzed young men with Swiss accents.

Several organisations were formed which assumed the names of the conspiratorial groups in Antonio Gabriel's books. They met regularly and, where there were insufficient details in the books themselves, created new codes, regulations and objectives of their own. They could not exactly be said to serve any particular purpose beyond the administration of their own procedures, but they evidently found much satisfaction from elaborating and policing them.

In a rather more serious development, however, the Thousand Points of Light began to model itself on a conspiratorial organisation that appeared in the fourth novel, *See the Light, How it Shines*. The Luminosi, it seemed, first manifested themselves in Florence in the fifteenth century, resurfacing in various Mediterranean countries in succeeding centuries. They seemed to have a certain interest in what would later have been called science, but this was not to say that they worshipped rationality. They trod every path, pursued every idea, whether it required the mind or the body to go on these journeys. And since such enquiries often brought them into conflict with those who sought to keep all knowledge to themselves, they developed an elite group whose function was to assassinate those who sought to oppress them or even enquire too closely into their identities.

It is not hard to see, therefore, what the Thousand Points of Light saw in them, nor difficult to understand why critics saw the book as reflecting the life of its author, especially when one of their own fraternity, who had denounced that author, was found dead with a fish in his mouth and an orange in his navel, for the fact was that this was how the Luminosi in Antonio Gabriel

Santiago's book liked to leave their own victims. So fiction, for a second, seemed to leap the void, if void there truly is, between the imagined and the real. And for three months the book was banned, but in that time became so popular that the authorities, believing that its popularity might spring from the ban, relented and once again people could officially read of the assassins of the Luminosi.

Then, to everyone's surprise, except that of the Swedish Academy, and to the surprise of many of its own members, Antonio Gabriel Santiago was awarded the Nobel Prize for literature. The Academy, seldom well-informed on the subject of literature but anxious to be seen to spread the benefits of its generosity to countries of which few people (especially members of the Academy) had heard, saw the ban as its chance to underline its own liberal principles. So it alighted on a writer who at the time was seldom read outside his own country, except by those German research students and the bewildered Korean and Japanese housewives mentioned above. Immediately the press of the world dispatched reporters who cared nothing for literature but who thought, unwisely as it turned out, that a trip to South America would be something of a jaunt. Literary reviewers, meanwhile, hastily acquired copies of his work (published in English only by a small press in Scotland which had convinced the Scottish Arts Council that Antonio Gabriel Santiago had been born in Dundee) and read them at great speed before writing columns in which they sought to give the impression that he had always been a personal favourite of theirs.

Not unnaturally the reporters, on their arrival in Sagrado Dios, and following swiftly on their disappointment at finding no hotels of international quality (or, indeed, of any quality at all), and hence no minibars or young hostesses, enquired where this now famous writer was to be found so that they could interview him

163

and return to civilisation as soon as a business-class ticket became available on the only airline to fly out of the neighbouring country, Sagrado Dios itself having no airport since it had no planes, a fact for which the journalists would have been gratified had they known of the improvisational nature of its engineering.

They were, of course, told that no one knew the whereabouts of the country's most famous author. It was even hinted to them that there might be no such person and that the conspiracies in his books (which none of the reporters had read since reporters are allergic to reading other people's prose) might reflect a still greater conspiracy by those who came together to create novels of inordinate length and bewildering complexity. Their very complexity, it was hinted, indeed reflected the many different hands that were perhaps at work.

The reporters did their best to locate if not the man himself then those who might have known him over the years, as if he might be found at the intersecting points of their accounts, but the few they did locate had nothing but distant memories modified by those stories about him that had appeared from time to time and which had been denied by letters to the press. Then, when all but a single reporter had returned to their own countries to write pieces called, 'The Man Who Was Nobody', and 'Invisible Man Wins Nobel', and he was detained only by an attack of food poisoning picked up in a fish restaurant one of whose mussels had the year before paralysed the Russian ambassador for six months, there was, as reporters say, a development.

The delay, as it turned out, proved fortuitous, for he discovered a note in the lobby of the Hotel Nacional advising him to contact a woman called Lola who was to be found in Anzuelo. Having time on his hands before his next assignment – interviewing a hermaphrodite pop singer in a sexual rehabilitation clinic in Aspen, Colorado – he hired one of San Marco's two taxis (the one which was not a hearse) and proceeded, via a two-hour breakdown in suburban San Marco, to a small house overlooking the Bay of Anzuelo where, a hundred metres below the shimmering sea, the rusting hulk of a German submarine encased the white bones of those who had never returned to their homeland to reap the manifold benefits of defeat.

On the porch sat a woman dressed in black holding in her hand a glass frosted with regret for this, so he had been told, was the one-time mistress of Antonio Gabriel Santiago who therefore was the possessor of the knowledge he sought. She watched him approach, lifting her glass and looking at him through the amber glow of Chivas Regal, for though deserted, as he assumed, she was not without money. Hence the villa looking out over the bay, with its startling view.

He lifted his hat and introduced himself. His Spanish was not good but then neither was her hearing, as far as he could make out, since she showed no sign of registering his existence except by that initial raising of the glass. After a moment or two, and feeling overwhelmed by the heat (he was from a newspaper situated in Umeå, in northern Sweden, where it was so cold that children believed all seas were solid and made of ice), he sat down beside her on the gently swinging seat. After a minute or two, however, she said in the clearest of English (and being Swedish he himself spoke that language better than anyone living in Manchester or Birmingham), 'Drinks are inside.' As it happened this was a phrase in which all reporters, whatever their nationality, are fluent and he needed no second invitation.

He opened the door into the cool of a house that was elegantly furnished. On a low table were more bottles than you would see in an average Anzuelo bar. He picked a handful of ice (itself a rarity) from a silver bucket and poured himself half a tumbler of Chivas. So began an evening of which he would later recall little, relying on his tape recorder which he at last remembered he must set between them as this once silent woman began to speak as though her Swedish interrogator was no longer present.

What little he did recall the next day, when he woke as from the dead, his head feeling some distance removed from his body and his throat so dry that he swallowed the tepid water from the ice bucket, was the story of an affair conducted in the shadows, of meetings in hotels, in houses in the middle of the jungle or by the side of the sea where the pounding of the waves echoed the frantic rhythm of their lovemaking. She spoke, he was almost sure, of a manuscript novel Antonio Gabriel Santiago had given her and which she kept out of love, a novel that reflected their affair and told truths otherwise only breathed to her in the midst of passion. All this he desperately endeavoured to recall later that day when he had returned to San Marco and discovered that the cassette had disappeared from his recorder if, that is, he had ever thought to put one in, being befuddled with whisky and the perfume of a woman with whom he was almost certain he had made love, though so little remained of that evening and the night that followed that he could no longer distinguish fact from fantasy.

And had he not slipped the manuscript into his briefcase? Well, if he had it was no longer there, though there were several copies of the Anzuelo newspaper, called, simply, *Anzuelo*, which advertised everything from second-hand corsetry to stillborn lambs. In short, he had nothing to show for his visit beyond fragments of memories and fantasies. And when later that same day he joined local journalists in a bar opposite the cathedral (where a certain young woman, dressed all in white, was stooping to press coins into the hands of a man in the entrance way to the cathedral), and when he mentioned the name of the woman with whom he may or may not have spent a passionate night and who may or may not have offered him a glimpse of a forbidden and unknown manuscript, if not the document itself, there was a sudden burst of laughter.

'Lola,' said a tall man who looked somewhat like Don Quixote, if Don Quixote had decided to wear his hair in dreadlocks, 'so you have been vacuumed up by Lola.'

'You know her?'

Again an explosion of laughter. 'She is a phantom, my man, conjured up by Antonio Gabriel Santiago to bewitch the unwary, to lead you down paths to nowhere. She is his greatest invention. For this alone he is worthy of the Nobel Prize, and you have added the latest chapter to his novel, the novel of his life. My felicitations. Now you in turn will be pursued: for have you not slept with one of his characters and in doing so become one of them? Have a drink, my friend, you join a noble and a varied cast. One day you will inherit the earth.'

The baker worried about his daughter. After her mother's death, when the girl was no more than five (indeed her birthday cake was still moist, a light concoction on which he had worked with great care, folding in the eggs by hand, scattering the frosting like a farmer sowing his field), he had understood that she must be his life's true vocation. He rose each day at five to light the fire for the ovens. He prepared the mixture, lifting the strands of dough like the pale entrails of an animal, preparing first bread and then madeleines, though, out of respect for his daughter, no Geronimo biscuits. He liked the steady sound as he pushed the flat tray far into the oven, feeling the hot draft of air like a wind from the desert. He turned his wrist and slid six shaped wedges onto the blackened surface, chancing a glance into the trembling

167

interior, tears starting to his eyes, before withdrawing the long-handled implement, known in the trade as the devil's hand, using it to swing the black iron door closed.

When he had repeated the action a score or more times in the four ovens, he wiped his hands on a red and white checked cloth, lifted a scarlet coffee pot from the stove and poured two mugs of coffee. Then he went to the foot of the stairs and listened. What did he listen for? Perhaps for nothing at all, simply pausing to let memories, regrets, hopes and dreams wash into his soul. Perhaps there was a second of despair or apprehension, a hesitation at starting his daughter's day for what might lie ahead for her, a motherless child. Whatever may have filled that space in time, whatever thoughts and feelings seeped through from another world, a second or so later he called her name: 'Sabrina.' He called gently the first time, and then waited. If there was no response, he called a little louder, for he was anxious not to start her too suddenly from her dreams. Finally he called again, louder this time, so that she was bound to hear and open her eyes.

He never liked to enter her room when she was in bed. He treated her with great courtesy, as if she were a special guest, as, indeed, he half felt her to be. Instead he returned to the kitchen, sat down at the table and lifted a steaming cup to his lips. Above his head he heard a soft sound as his daughter dressed and then a moment later came skipping down the stairs, eager for the new day.

'Papa,' she cried as she entered, circled her arms around his neck and kissed him gently on the head. As she picked up her coffee he brushed his hand across his eyes. Already the warm and satisfying smell of cooking bread filled the room and seeped under the door to the street beyond so people still in bed stirred in their sleep, their bad dreams transmuted into good so that they would wake, at last, with a smile on their lips and a hunger for fresh bread in their stomachs.

The store opened early and Sabrina worked alongside her father as the door swung to and fro, as fresh bread was drawn from the oven to be carried into the shop at the front of the house and placed on shelves or dropped into wicker baskets. Her father took the money; she reached up for the bread, placing it in front of the customers with a smile. Each in turn said, 'Sabrina', or 'Thank you', before hurrying back to slice the bread and spread it with fresh butter and the strawberry jam they had prepared the previous autumn, filling wide-necked bottles with boiling fruit, a silver teaspoon protecting the glass.

At eight o'clock she would go to school, had, indeed, been going to school for many years. At first he had insisted on accompanying her. He had closed the shop, placed a notice on the door, and held her hand as they walked through city streets and across the junctions until they reached the school, its nuns like a checkerboard as they waited on the steps for the arrival of their pupils. Meanwhile people had stood in line, complaining a little, especially if they were new to the area. But after a time his customers simply rearranged their lives to allow for the thirty minutes when the baker took his daughter to school. Now, though, he no longer closed the shop or took his daughter's hand. She walked on her own or, rather, skipped, for she never did anything so uninspired as merely to walk. She kissed him, as he kissed her, both smelling of warm bread, and then she skipped down the road. He stepped out to watch until she had disappeared from view, and those in the queue watched with him, uncomplaining, understanding how difficult it must be for a man to raise his daughter without a wife.

There was a moment, though, when a widow, herself young and not yet recovered from her husband's death, took him aside, when the last of his customers had gone, and explained that there were certain things that his daughter must know and of which he could himself know nothing or, if knowing, would not be able to communicate to her, for there are tasks for men and tasks for women and this was a woman's task. To tell the truth this was a great relief to him. He had watched her grow and never without a twinge of regret and a feeling of apprehension.

The widow who taught his daughter, however, was prepared also to educate the father, and soon there was another person who worked in the shop, reached into the heat, watched the bread swell and slid the tray in and out. The daughter was released to become a girl again and the father was no longer required to play mother as well. But not all was as it should be, for the daughter remembered her own mother and felt her father begin to share his affections with one who was first employee, working by his side, and then something else, sleeping in his bed. And though they appeared to show no concern, those who queued each day began to worry that the girl should be raised in such circumstances, and when a new baker opened only a street away many transferred their business to him, feeling awkward as they lined up and watched the baker and his woman touch hands and then reach up for a loaf of bread, for who knew where their hands might have been before. The priest at last, urged by those who liked the man's bread but not, as they explained, his tart, paid a visit and explained that it was time for them to part or to marry.

He could no more think of parting from her than he could of separating from his daughter, for had she not brought him back to life, taught him that duty alone is a cold companion, or so she said? Accordingly, he proposed to her one morning when he reached his hand deep inside the oven and felt his flesh tingle

170

with the heat. She agreed before his hand had been withdrawn and they kissed as the dough began to pucker and swell. He told his daughter when she returned from school. Sabrina was sixteen and had all her mother's beauty fresh-minted. She looked at him with a cool eye and for the first time he felt a barrier rise between the two of them. She nodded, allowing each word to slide into her heart, and then stepped forward and kissed him. So Sabrina relinquished her power, knowing that she had no choice but to agree to the terms and cut the strings that bound him so tight to her heart. Yet they were not so cold as not to have tears in their eyes, for both knew that something was ended, though he had not, perhaps, understood the implications of what he had decided to do.

The young girl was the bridesmaid at her father's wedding. Her new mother wore a smart red suit with red shoes and a pink bow in her hair, and looked to her stepdaughter like a decorated cake. Sabrina herself wore white, as if she, and not the woman by her father's side, were the bride. The baker was far from wealthy but his bride had been poor indeed, though none knew how poor for what little she had she invested in the finest clothes. Her house was rented and the small inheritance she had received from her first husband (who traded in this and that and offered the world a face which was not his own) had soon been exhausted. But two (or three), as we know, can live as cheaply as one, at least they can if one of the two (or three) has not accustomed herself to spending more than she should on dresses and shawls and a ring or two to sparkle in the light of the virginal moon.

Did the baker love his new wife? Suffice to say that she had become as necessary to him as daily bread which, incidentally, he was now required to produce in greater quantity as his expenses began to climb. He rose earlier, purchased more flour, lowered

171

his prices a little to compete with his rival. As a result he became ever more tired and his wife ever less satisfied with their nightly encounters.

'It is the girl,' she said. 'As she grows older she becomes more expensive. There are clothes to buy, books to acquire, and now she begins to speak of the university.'

'But my wife and I,' he began, and then stopped, realising that that wife was in the ground and with her many of his hopes.

She stiffened, as which second wife would not, hearing her new husband refer not to her but her predecessor?

'I am your wife,' she announced, as a judge pronounces a sentence, slowly and deliberately. 'The past is the past. She should work for her living. At her age I was working.'

'But we had always planned . . .'

'We?' she queried, her voice rising, 'who is this we? Are we to become paupers in order to educate a girl who will find no employment but learn to despise her elders and betters? You must make up your mind. If we continue like this we shall end up on the streets.'

He felt like remarking on her new dress, which flared out, a spinning circle of scarlet as she turned on her heel, she having a liking for red and for loose-fitting clothes. But he held his tongue. And so it continued for many months. He tried his best to keep the arguments from his daughter, who retreated to her room each night with an armful of books, there to travel freely on the ship of imagination and knowledge. At last, one day, his wife took him fiercely by the arm as he closed the door of the shop and turned to the shelves still half full of bread since, though he baked more loaves, people still ate the same amount.

'What kind of man are you,' she asked, 'who is content to see his wife go about in threads?'

He looked at her standing before him in a red blouse and black skirt, new only the week before.

'You are content to pour money out to keep that girl in books and paper. You pay for her uniform and we give her money each week.'

'Little enough,' interrupted her husband.

'More than enough,' she replied, sharply. 'Either she goes or I do.'

'Go?' he queried, 'And where should she go?'

'To work. Or to relatives. You have relatives, do you not?'

'But she is my daughter.'

'And I am your wife. The time has come for you to decide which is the more important to you.'

And at that she went upstairs, slamming the door of the bedroom behind her. A moment later he heard a soft tread on the stairs and his daughter appeared, dressed for school.

'Papa,' she said, and raised herself on tiptoe to kiss him before opening the door and disappearing down the street.

The next day when the woman came down to breakfast two hours after her husband, who rose as usual to prepare the dough and begin the baking, she found on her plate a row of small figures, baked and coloured with confectioner's paint. The figures, though crude, could easily be made out for they were small mannequins, dressed all in red, with silver buttons down the front and a skirt which flared out. But they were incomplete, for where the heart might have been there was a hole cut out, while the head of each had been neatly severed. On another plate, however, set in the daughter's place, was a perfectly formed gingerbread girl, with currants for eyes and a marzipan halo. In the third place was a large bread man, glazed with egg and shining in the light. But most significant of all was his outstretched hand and on the end an outstretched finger pointing towards the door. She stood and looked at the figures and then at the baker's knife, sticking into the breakfast table. In front of it was a pile of banknotes and a message written on a scrap of paper. She picked it up and read. It said: 'PLEASE CLOSE THE DOOR BEHIND YOU.'

When the young girl graduated from the university her father sat in the front row and smiled as she walked across the stage to collect her certificate. And as she walked he smiled to himself and thought that his first wife had at last returned to him.

Captain Fernandez sat dozing in his wooden-backed rocking chair, gently swaying back and forth, tensing and relaxing his feet, as in his dreams the ship he commanded eased itself up and down on the swelling waves. He smelt the salt air and his nose twitched as a gentle wind blew through his window carrying the smells of the fish dock into his third-floor room. The cries of the gulls, that fought over the pink strands of flesh tossed into the sea by women with bandaged hands streaked with blood and flashing silver knives, pierced his mind. They conjured images of those same birds, rising and falling in the spittle-flecked wake of the *Esmeralda* which trembled and shook beneath him like a woman, also called Esmeralda, he had once known in Buenos Aires, a woman with no tongue to speak but whose passion was eloquent and inexhaustible.

There was no one else in his dream. He sailed alone through the blue-green of the sea that rose and fell as he rocked in a sleep that was a voyage without end. He felt the wood of the wheel, soft against his calloused hands. It seemed alive, resisting, tugging as though it would take him on a journey of its own choosing. He tensed in his chair as he set his muscles to resist such a seduction. Somewhere to the port bow were the sleek black shapes of porpoises threading themselves through the heavy sheen of a sea that was no less than a piece of the sky floated down on the earth by the hand of God. 'Bring her around,' he shouted in his dream, and his cracked lips moved in the cool shadow of his third-floor room, as though he were praying. 'Bring her around.' And around she came, sails crashing and throbbing. He leant in his chair as the pillow slipped on the polished wood, polished by the thinning hair of the man who pressed back against it. 'There'll be rain before nightfall.'

Somewhere a belch of bubbles sounded through the pipes of his building, the plumbing being as old as the Captain. But in his dream those same bubbles chased along the barnacled sides of his fretful ship, sounding like the tinkling bells of heaven, distant and beautiful. They kissed the green-smeared planks, drawn along by a sliding sea to disappear into the incurving spume of the wake which traced a white path across the ocean, laying a trail, perhaps, for lost mariners to follow. The sun floated overhead and the mast cut a line across it, a razor through an eyeball, spilling its red light over the swim of blue sky. The *Esmeralda* yawed from side to side, as that other Esmeralda had done so many years before.

Far ahead the edge of the world arced around, a protecting arm cradling his desires, containing his dreams, shaping his hopes, consoling him for his regrets, and where the blue of the sky met the blue-green of the sea there was a blur of grey and indigo and violet that he sometimes thought of as the line which would some day be drawn across his life. It was always there, a distant fact, marking the edge of his mortal reach, sometimes clear, sometimes obscure.

The sky seemed to darken suddenly, a thin mist drifting across the now copper sun, the ship shuddering a little with a shift in the wind. In his threadbare room, with its spartan furniture and peeling walls, he stirred and a frown passed across his face like the mist across a November sun. A darker memory was beginning to ease its way into his dream. He tugged at the wheel, as though he could deny it access, turn it aside. In his sleep his hands tensed, his fingers closed tight around the invisible wheel. He was no longer alone. Ahead he could see the town and its ancient harbour, though not clearly because while he felt warm inside and content with the world, his eyes were blurred and his movements awkward. The sea itself, but a moment before calm and smooth, danced a broken jig while the deck seemed to sway as if it were on the outer edge of a typhoon.

He gripped the side of his chair and made a sound in his throat that was not speech but a kind of drunken cry. He opened his eyes but was still asleep, staring unseeing through the window at a blank grey sky, while in his dream he drew ever nearer to the town and its harbour wall. And then at last he relaxed, as if there were nothing more to be done. And indeed there was not, for he sailed, as he knew he would, into that wall and heard again the splintering of wood. He heard, too, the cries of men he would have sworn were not on board and indeed were not for they were now in the sea, fighting for their lives, tangled in the nets and broken wood and drowning before those on shore could launch their boats or throw ropes from the harbour and bring them safely home from the sea. He himself floated in that selfsame sea, clutching a bottle tight in his hands as if it could rescue him instead of plunging himself and his crew into an ocean so cold that it stopped the heart even as a cry for help forced its way up from lungs full of salt sea like the lungs of the fish they had hauled from the dark depths, fish that saw the sun once, like the face of God, and died, fish that did not have lungs or souls but which fought for life as though life were something worth fighting for.

He woke now, as he always woke, tears, as salt as that sea, edging down his wrinkled cheeks, so wrinkled that they seemed to have been scored there by a carpenter or a saddler working on leather. He looked at the grey rectangle of the window as though searching for the faces of those who had died, but there was nothing but the darkening cloud, no sound but the cry of the gulls as they sliced down through the air for the entrails of fish that had once swum, silver and free, in an azure sea. He reached out a hand to the small low table beside his chair, and lifted the bottle that stood on it. He pulled the cork out with his teeth. The sound was hollow and when he put the bottle to his lips the merest trickle of cold fire burned its way down his throat, offering him memory without consolation.

He was known in the town, reviled by some, pitied by others, ignored by most as a captain without a command, a sailor without a vessel. Now he sailed only on an inward sea. He closed his eyes on the visible world to see another not available to the outward eye. And slowly his attachment to the world of others, a world in which accusation and blame existed alongside the drudgery of daily toil, slackened. His room became his cabin and he would ring out the hours on a ship's bell he had made by the bell makers of San Marco. It was delivered one day by a young man who mounted it for him. It cost most of the money he had set aside for a future in which he had now lost all interest, but its sound was a consolation and a key to unlock the door to his memories. The boy had looked around at the room and at the man who spent his days and nights there and saw no more than an old man in a bleak and decaying space. But when he rang the bell both leaned forward together and heard something in the echoing purity that brought them together, at least for the moment, as the sound slowly blended into that which came through the single window. The boy went away, the Captain stayed, though he was captain no more, except of the phantom ship that set sail whenever he chose to swallow the dark brown liquor and close his eyes on a world that had closed its eyes on him.

His neighbours complained when he sounded the bell, as he did both day and night. He was visited by the municipal authorities who reminded him of his civic responsibilities. Still he rang his bell. Once again the neighbours complained, banging on the wall, shouting out of windows from which spilled the yellow light of lamps switched on by those whose anger also spilled through those selfsame windows. The municipal authorities threatened to confiscate his bell and take him to court, but he rang it just the same. And after a time the neighbours ceased to complain, incorporating the sound into their own restless dreams. Indeed, in time people came to rely on the sound from the Captain's room, always accurate to the second, for he kept a chronometer which was the only object, other than a bottle of rum, that he kept on his table. It became one of the sounds of the city and more than one citizen laid a hand on the arm of a stranger he was showing the town and told him to listen for the sound of the Captain's bell.

He slept in a hammock he had slung from the walls. At first the landlord had thought to take him to court for damaging his property (his brother-in-law was a lawyer, and what is the point of a brother-in-law who is a lawyer if you do not use his services from time to time) but by then the damage was done; and besides, he was not anxious to draw attention to the state of disrepair in which he kept this and other properties. So the Captain lay motionless in his canvas cradle and imagined he was swinging side to side, as those on ship have been known to imagine the opposite. Nor was he quite as solitary as this account has made out, for he did have a single companion. The Captain was not the only soul to survive the accident that had taken the lives of his friends and his reputation; not, at least, if we grant that

178

cats may have souls, and none who have kept them can doubt this, for how can such independent, arrogant, contemptuous and endearing creatures not have their own claim to immortality? The ancient Egyptians certainly knew as much.

This cat was, in a sense, no less damaged than his master for he had lost a leg in the accident, while something had happened to his voice so he could wail but make none of the other sounds we associate with his kind, thus adding one more sound for his neighbours to endure. For the most part he kept to himself, lying perilously on the window ledge in the sun or slipping, like black liquid, through the door whenever it was opened, tracing a figure-of-eight between the old man's legs, scratching insistently hours later when he returned from patrolling his territory. But every now and then, detecting some need in his master, he would leap from the floor onto the lap of the man who sat rocking gently with tears in his eyes, and trample himself a kind of home, his claws pricking through the rough canvas trousers before, at last, he curled himself into a ball of comfort.

So they lived together many years, cat and man, their days divided by the rising and setting of the sun, the silver sound of a bell and the perfunctory meals they took side by side if not together. The Captain continued to sail on his phantom sea and the cat to chase imaginary mice, twitching in his sleep, extending a paw to scoop up a passing rat. Outside the window flew the flag that once fluttered from the stern of his vessel and which had been returned to him by one of the few people prepared to be seen with him in public before he had withdrawn to his private realm.

Then, one day, the bell ceased to ring and that night the flag was not lowered. The municipal authorities were summoned by those who doubtless now believed that he was failing in his civic duty. They found him sitting motionless in his rocking chair,

179

staring blankly through the window at a rectangle of sky. The cat was stretched beside him, stiff and cold. An empty bottle stood on the table. The only sound was the regular ticking of his chronometer. He was buried in the seamen's cemetery, despite a protest from the widow of one of the sailors whose death he had precipitated. He would have been astonished to know that more than a hundred souls stood in the rain to see him off on his final voyage. And among that hundred was a young boy, who had travelled from the capital and whose skills had fashioned the now silent bell.

There were those in the neighbourhood who had difficulty sleeping in the weeks ahead as the bell, which even in their sleep they had come to rely upon, no longer sounded. In time, however, they ceased to notice the loss and slept the night through, as in time the name cut into the cross above his grave would fade and become obscured. But the gulls continue to swoop and dive above the graveyard that looks down on the harbour where the women still gut the fish brought back from the blue-black sea, and the salt spray of the ocean, blown by the wind, runs down that simple cross like the tears of heaven shed for one who was lost but has now come home safely to harbour at last.

Justina stood in front of a mirror in her room, a mirror whose liquid silver had tarnished and flaked so her image was mottled as though it were rendered by an impressionist painter. She inspected her face, blue eyes framed by a tumble of hair that shone in the light of a golden sun whose glitter filled the room, turning its faded paintwork and exhausted furniture into a king's palace. She looked at her skin, glowing in that same wash of brightness. She turned her head from side to side to see what others might see and acknowledged that, yes, she was as beautiful as they said. Then, on an impulse, she slowly slipped her night-gown from her shoulder, having only a short time before slipped it on for her regular siesta. She edged it slowly and artlessly down, watching the gold flow over her skin until, at last, she pressed her hands to her sides and let the cotton shift fall down-wards as gently as a leaf from a tree. She lowered her eyes and looked at her breasts, full and perfectly rounded and ready. For what? Life is full of many mysteries and one among them is the knowledge, suddenly born, that a moment has come, that some-thing is finished and another thing is about to begin.

Something indeed stirred within her – a kind of poetry whose words were unknown but whose rhythm she acknowledged. She thought of the bell-maker's apprentice, arms so strong and with a smile that could light the day. Could this be he? She trailed her hand down the satin of her body, brushed nipples with the palm of her hands, trembling as she did so, and then down again across the smoothness of her stomach. And there she stopped, looking at herself again in a mirror whose decayed state was such that the lower half of her body was broken up and in part concealed where humidity and time had destroyed the foil which reflected the light. The effect was disturbing, for it made her body seem old and wrinkled and when her hand trailed lower the mirror gave back no true reflection but only a series of broken planes, jagged and incomplete images, as if thereby to censor her for her thoughts and still more for her feelings.

She looked back at her face again, so young, so pure, so perfectly shaped, and smiled. It was not entirely a natural smile for she was endeavouring to see what others saw. She turned her head at angles to see if she might have some aspect that pleased more than others. She had that absolute confidence which comes to those who know that they are beautiful and seek only to display such beauty to the best effect. Then, at last, she bent down to pick up the nightgown which lay in a rumpled circle about her feet. It was as well, however, that when she did so she did not look at the mirror, for as she bent her knees and sank downwards that area of the mirror where the tarnishing was at its worst threw back an image that might have disturbed her. A line of wrinkled and puckered flesh flowed swiftly up her body and eclipsed all of that in which she rejoiced. It was as if the mirror predicted the future, offered a glimpse of that reality which must sober us all and mock our immodesty.

A moment later, however, time was put into reverse. She rose and the wrinkles and blotches were smoothed away as the tide retreats and leaves the soft sand with a satin sheen and a freshness that makes the world seem reborn. She looked at herself again, turned a little one way and then the other and finally lifted the nightgown above her head, her breasts taut, her skin supple and soft. Then she let it fall over her head and slide down her body, brushing against her like a lover's hands as she was once more clothed in a white shift, stained now with the blood of the afternoon sun.

She turned at last, pulled the virgin sheet of her bed back so that it formed a triangle, and lay in an angled shadow where the sun was cut off by the straight edge of the window frame. She lay for a moment, her mind blank, watching the bright fireflies of dust rising and falling with infinite slowness, and then slid effortlessly into a dreamless sleep as somewhere far away a bell began to toll and dogs barked at a stranger who passed the houses they guarded.

One day, when Manuel was working in the cool and musty shadows of the library, a pool of yellow light framing the piles of books through which he was obliged to work his way like a farmer picking weeds from the dry soil, he felt the presence of someone in the darkness. He looked up expecting to find the shrivelled librarian who, from time to time, would shuffle forward and place another tome on the pile like an executioner sliding another rock on the chest of the condemned. But in his place there was the vague form of a woman, dressed somewhat archaically in a gown gathered at the waist that seemed to balloon out at the back as though to balance the equal weight of her breasts, which even in his sudden shock he could not but admire. Perhaps she was no more than a projection of his adolescent lust or of his frustrated desire for Justina or perhaps she was inspired by something he had read, for in his youthful need he found that he could be stirred by almost anything. Since in his search for fiction he was obliged to work his way through every form of writing, hoping to discover some sliver of a fable, some hint of a story, squirrelled away in an otherwise unpromising treatise on philosophy in a multi-volumed history, or interleaved in a reference book for *Manufacturers of Candles and Other Sundries* (a copy of which was in front of him), he had become sensitised to every word or phrase which might stir his sexual instincts. So it was that he would find himself responding to the specialised vocabulary of a historian of horology – spring, tension, balance, screw, turn, key, wind. Even the words 'backwards' and 'forwards' could cause him that mixture of agony and ecstasy which would lead him to turn his reading light off for thirty seconds or so until his body had returned to some kind of equilibrium. Whatever the cause, however, he believed he saw a buxom woman of some thirty years beckon to him from the folding shadows.

He looked around, but as ever was quite alone. His was the only light that glowed in the room labelled HUMANITIES, a word he liked as though it graced his labours with the whole authority of mankind rather than simply the whim of a professor who he suspected had mislaid his senses along with his spectacles. Still the woman beckoned, a pale finger first pointing to his heart then bending like a silver fish hook. He pushed his chair back and closed the book in front of him, sending a cloud of dust into the halo of light like a puff of spores from a ripe mushroom. He stood uncertainly and watched as she turned, the hem of her dress fanning gently out, fluted like the underside of just such a forest plant. She walked slowly into the darkness and he followed, feeling he had no choice but to do so. She glided in front of him, her dress sweeping along the unbrushed floor but disturbing not a particle of the accumulated grime, not an atom of the discarded skin cells shed by generations of scholars and librarians.

There were, of course, women who worked in the library. Their duties were to stack and sort and shelve the books. They fetched and carried as needed and conducted their business in the respectful silence required of all those who cohabit with the dead. Some of these, indeed, dressed in outfits they judged suitable for such a profession, black and long and hinting more of the past than of the present. But he had never seen one such as she whom he followed down the length of the reading room and through an open doorway at the end to a smaller room beyond.

Having sat for many hours at his cramped desk, looking at texts which became so many black lines cancelling out his future, he felt a little dizzy and disoriented, focusing with difficulty on a figure always just too far ahead of him to make out with any clarity. Then she disappeared. He stooped to pass through a doorway constructed long ago to accommodate citizens of Sagrado Dios far smaller than himself, and when he straightened she was nowhere to be seen.

He stopped, for the first time a little afraid: for though he was enough a product of his times to believe he must be fantasising as a result of overwork or more likely, he suddenly thought, as a consequence of chewing too many coca leaves (a habit he shared with many of his compatriots), there was something about this figure and, even more, its subsequent disappearance that made his pulse race. There was, however, another possible explanation, for he found himself confronted by a door, closed, to be sure, and low, but with an elaborate key in an equally elaborate keyhole. A dirty window high above let through the barest of light, and that coloured a lurid yellow. What choice did he have? He could return to his seat and resume his search amongst the annals of the *Manufacturers of Candles and Other Sundries*; or he could reach out his hand and turn the key.

I may to this point have presented the young man as unadventurous and conservative, bending to the wind, lacking the courage to beat a path of his own through the tangled undergrowth of his life, but he was young and none who are young can be defined so casually. Those whose bodies are a tumult of change can never be fully known. He was a seeker after knowledge. Sometimes such a search leads to unknown valleys and distant mountains. But there are those who never stir from their book-lined rooms, yet stare into depths more vertiginous than a mountaineer confronts. They hang from a rope over voids that have no bottom and seek in vain for a secure place to prevent their downward plunge. I am not saying that this was one such, but he turned the key, where others might have resumed their seats or placed another coca leaf in their mouths to forget the key, the door and the woman who had beckoned him there.

The door swung open with difficulty and when it did there was a gentle hiss as though he broke a membrane, liberated something sealed within. A sigh of air, cool and dry, brushed his cheek and even disturbed his hair. He breathed in and detected a perfume that was gone in an instant. Perhaps there had indeed been a woman and this the sign of her passing. Inside the doorway he could detect stairs going down into the dark, but there was no sign of a light switch. How, then, was he to see? And yet, after a moment or two, it seemed there was a kind of steady glow, a faint yellow blur like a weak sun seen through parchment. He put his hand out to steady himself on the door frame and then tentatively set his foot on a stone step which he noticed, to his surprise, was not worn down with use, as were the other stairs in the National Library in which everything seemed to give the impression of dissolution and decay.

He had, of course, seen no apparition. How could he? We live in an age of science and rationality and know such visions for the illusions they are. Not a day passes without the discovery that what we once accounted moral flaws are in effect defects in our internal wiring, that the shape of a smile, a sense of humour, a liking for a swift drink, were all imprinted on us at the moment of our conception. We know that a little dusting of powder can transform the world just as can the sight of bare flesh. So, doubtless, it was with him for the leaves he chewed stimulated parts of the brain in such a way as to reinvent the world. And what, then, of the imagination of the poet or the spinner of stories? Are the warp and woof of fiction themselves no more than the brain's desire for shape and order that leads us to see shapes in a cloud?

None of this, of course, occurred to the young student who descended stone steps into the long room below where boxes and trunks of donated books, confiscated texts, the detritus of pen and typewriter, were stored against the day that there would be time and labour and money enough to disinter them. But if there is reason and logic enough to explain how he came to rise from his desk, follow a phantom and descend into these cool depths, how explain his choice of one box rather than another to open?

It was distinguished by nothing. On the outside it was no more than a crate of a kind that could still be purchased in the city square, though he could see in the thin light from the single light bulb, which now flickered fitfully once he had found the switch, that it was of greater antiquity than this. It was made of better wood than was to be found today and fashioned with greater care and skill than any of its modern counterparts. It was, to be sure, locked, but his mere testing of that lock was sufficient to snap it through, so rusted was it, so weakened by time.

He swung the lid back and saw that it was full of manuscripts, with an occasional crudely printed, crudely bound book amongst them. And on top was a list compiled in black ink and stamped with the authority of some functionary. It was difficult to read but the heading was clear enough. It read: FORBIDDEN TEXTS. He stared at the words as if unable to make sense of them, as if in some sense the two words could make no sense when brought together in this way.

He placed the official document on the table and picked up the first bundle of paper, tied together with a piece of green twine turned white at the knot. He pulled gently and it snapped with a puff of dust. He lifted the pages and disentangled the twine, dropping it on the table where it lay, vermicular, a hieroglyph awaiting decipherment. It was almost impossible to read in the feeble light, so he took the first page and stood directly under the fluttering bulb. The sheet was covered with green ink, turning black-red where it bled into the paper. At the top were two words, underlined thrice: MARIA'S DREAM. He started to read.

In the village of San Isidro, where the magical waters of the Blanco River sparkle and dance and the Madonna smiles

187

down on rich and poor alike, there was born a girl who was trebly blessed. She was born at midnight on her mother's saint's day, at the place of the Miracle of Maria, to a father who had completed the pilgrimage to Compostella. From her earliest days she brought joy to all around her and as she grew revealed such powers as have never been seen before. She was a teller of stories but the stories she told came true. It was a gift that alarmed her but which she treasured nonetheless, though she used it sparingly. And being truly blessed, her stories contained no darkness. It has been said that all stories, if continued long enough, end in death; but her stories were brief and never came near to the grave. To be sure, they sometimes touched on illness and disease but only insofar as both would pass, disaster giving birth to new life.

But there came a time when a man arrived from the city. He carried a decree that he hammered to the door of the church before going to the cantina with the priest, the Church and the state toasting one another as they ever have. Because of a storm, when the villagers came to the mass the following day and saw a piece of paper fluttering there the rain had caused the printer's ink to run so that they could read nothing. Nor could any of those who saw it later that day, when the rains had passed, though each imagined that he or she could make out what the notice must have said. Some insisted that it was the announcement of a tax on mules, others that it declared a new national holiday. It was only when the young girl was arrested, therefore, and charged with storytelling that they learned that it was an injunction against precisely this. And from that moment good things ceased to happen in San Isidro. It was as if the stories themselves had created what they prophesied. The end of the stories thus signified the end of good luck.

He put the sheet of rough paper back on the pile and picked up the official list again, its status confirmed by the squashed rose of the sealing wax which carried the imprint of officialdom. He looked again at the date. It was true. Here was a story about the suppression of story which dated from the very time when stories were suppressed. Here at the heart or, more accurately, in the bowels of authority's storehouse he had discovered a cache of fictive subversion. He replaced the paper from which he had read, but as soon as he took up the other sheets the ribbon snapped again and they spilled out of his grasp. He gathered them together, placed the list on top and closed the box. For a full minute he did no more than stare at it. In truth his discovery was such that would concern one citizen in a hundred thousand. What if he had discovered stories one hundred and fifty years old? What were they but a curiosity? Yet he had, almost unbeknown to himself, become so absorbed in the task assigned to him that he had come to feel that there must indeed be some real significance in a job to which he had committed so much of his time.

He lifted the box. It was heavier than he had thought. Nonetheless, he carried it up the stone staircase towards the yellow light of the room above. He walked through that room and the next until he came to the desk where the librarian sat on a high stool and looked at him through glasses so thick that his eyes seemed to bulge out of his head like those in the cartoons which the young man had once seen projected onto the near white wall of the priest's house, a priest who had run his hand up the brown shorts which his mother had ironed with a heavy black iron taken from the stove so that he should look his best for the instruction he was to receive, little knowing the nature of that instruction.

He placed the box on the desk in front of the librarian.

'Yes?'

'More papers to catalogue.'

The Professor had an agreement with the library that his pupil-researcher would have full access to the holdings of the institution but that in return he would aid in the cataloguing of material deposited over many years but never adequately noted or described. And if from time to time this might require that such material be transferred, for a day or so, to the Professor's house, well, where could be the harm in that? The National Museum and Library was, to be honest, seldom visited and when it was few showed any interest in the kind of material that interested the Professor. As to his being mad, what should that signify so long as his assistant was not and, besides, mad professors were more commonly to be encountered in libraries than anywhere else.

'Name and details,' said the librarian, stabbing a blunt finger in the general direction of the desk since his glasses, though thick, were not thick enough.

The student wrote: 'Case of sundry papers' and placed the official form in the hands of the man for whom the world was too vague and unfocused to command much interest. He had a wife, after all, who could guide him where he had need to go, a wife of uncommon plainness who took care to keep just beyond the range of his vision except at night and whom he believed to be as beautiful as the sunrise which he had not seen in many a year but of which he retained a vivid memory.

The box, heavy to lift, was heavier still to carry through the streets, but he was drawn onwards by his desire to uncover its secrets, probe its depths. At times he was obliged to set it down and wipe the sweat from his brow with the back of a dusty hand that left his forehead streaked with dirt. Still he struggled on until he came to the Professor's house.

He had been entrusted with a key, large and awkward to carry. He kept it on a string around his neck so it pressed against his chest. Sometimes he forgot to take it off at night and woke to find its outline impressed upon his skin. It was emblazoned as though it were a brand seared on his flesh to indicate his profession or his sin. He inserted the key and turned it. A bell set above the door rang as he swung it back. He lifted the box and stepped into the cool, pushing the door closed behind him. The bell rang again. It was now the siesta hour and everyone in the house had retired to their beds. The study was thus empty when he entered and placed the box as gently as he might on the table.

He sat for a moment to recover and then stood in front of the box as though it were a reliquary. At last he lifted the lid and began to remove the papers one by one, laying them carefully on the table before a kind of exultant madness overcame him and he lifted three or four of the manuscripts at a time, each one written in a different coloured ink – red, blue, green – and let them spill on the table top, a cascade of stories, a rainbow of fiction, a palette of pictures, a spectrum of lies from a time when only authorised lies were permitted and the imagination had been sentenced to prison for three hundred years.

He felt his heart race and when the door opened and Justina stepped inside for a moment it raced faster still.

'Oh,' she said, 'what's that?'

How to explain? 'Stories,' he replied.

'Oh,' she said, in a disappointed voice. 'Have you seen papa?'

He shook his head and she stepped back into the hallway, closing the door behind her. He looked down at the table,

191

scattered with dead words. The bloom seemed suddenly to have gone off these long-ago flowers. What, after all, were they beside the living beauty of Justina, whose story had yet to be written? Where a moment before he had thought he held a key to a room of miracles, now he saw no more than a pile of old papers. He had allowed his employer's obsession to become his own, had sentenced himself to the obscurity and dust of the past when he should have been looking for tomorrow. What was once upon a time beside young breasts pressing against white cotton? What was long ago in a distant land beside an urgent present when he would kiss if not her lips then the shadow she cast? And yet there were secrets in this slithering heap of suppressed visions as there were secrets concealed by that white cotton and he longed to search out both.

When the Professor returned from his walk to the bakery, a bag of madeleines in his hands and his lips still stained with the story he had told, he found first his daughter and then his pupil. She met him as he crossed the threshold and chided him for leaving without giving her the money he had promised, money with which she absolutely must buy some pearls she had seen in a shop. Such subjects meant little to him; but he could deny her nothing and accordingly went to his room where he upended a leather purse and counted out the coins she requested.

'Why pearls?' he asked.

She stamped her foot and then, thinking better of it, smiled and said, 'Because they are beautiful.'

'Ah,' he replied, 'and does beauty have a price?'

'This beauty does,' she answered, and spun about and ran to the outer door. The bell rang as she opened it and rang again as she stepped onto the street.

When he came upon his pupil he found him sorting through a pile of manuscripts and making notes in a careful hand. The boy rose to his feet as though about to make a speech, but the only word he uttered was 'stories'.

'Stories?'

The boy nodded then, taking a breath, added, 'Forbidden stories.'

'Forbidden stories?'

The pupil then told the Professor how he had come to discover the stories, though without mentioning the mysterious lady who had led him to them. He knew that his employer disapproved of his chewing the coca leaf and knew, too, that this would be the explanation he preferred. At last he finished and withdrew from the table, thereby inviting the Professor to take possession of the prize. But instead of stepping forward he looked troubled. The truth was that the existence of such stories threatened his thesis about the seepage of fiction into the general life of the state. For if fiction did not die but continued to spring into being then it was never truly lost, and if not lost then why should the instinct for fable be thus diverted?

'Who read them?' he asked, seizing on a vital fact.

The young man shrugged. How should he know? 'They were seized, sir. So perhaps no one read them.'

The Professor leaned forward, reaching for the official cover sheet which his pupil had placed to one side. He read the words 'FORBIDDEN TEXTS' and ran his finger down the list, written in a careful hand by one who could never have imagined the future in which his words would be read. He let the page fall back onto the table, a leaf floating down from the tree.

'Leave them,' he said, 'leave them until tomorrow.'

The student looked at him uncertainly, used as he was to the Professor's elliptical manner of speaking. At last, when it was apparent that he would speak no more, he turned and left the room, half hoping he would see Justina. She, though, was walking swiftly along the street, clutching a purse and dreaming of the pearls that would soon rest coolly against her neck. She was entirely taken by surprise, therefore, when she was seized by that neck, swung around and pulled into the deep shadow of an alley. A hand reached down, snatched the purse from her hand, and pushed her forward onto her knees. There was a flash of silver above her. She fell into the sunlight and as she did so saw the legs of someone run past her. She turned in time to see a struggle as two figures wrestled in the gloom. There was a sudden crack and the one she took for the thief staggered back into the light, scarlet blood flowing down his cheek, a knife in his hand. He looked down at her. She saw the blood, his dark hair, the flash of hatred in his eyes, and he was gone, running down the road.

Only then was she aware of the pain in her wrist. She pulled herself to her feet and rose, cradling one hand with the other. And as she did so a figure stepped into the light and held out her purse. He was the young bell maker whom she had first seen in the cathedral square and then again when she was Queen of the parade and then in the café, each time pulling closer to her, the boy who had entered her life and her heart, a thief himself though of something more precious than a purse. Who else would have been here to rescue her? If hers was a story did it not require a hero and was he not there to play his role? He bowed and stood, his arms outstretched. She walked towards him, her hands shaking, her soul aflame.

The banker Doreme was large in his sympathies, large in his appetites, and indisputably large in his girth. He was the size of an opera singer raised on pasta, as large as the Santos twins, who had been joined together at the stomach and hence ate twice as much as they should, taking it in turns to evacuate the conse-quences of their logical gluttony. Each day at ten he would rise, wash, shave, breakfast on eggs and a little fruit, cream cheese, some cooked meats and the fine bread baked by a baker who sold madeleines to a crazed professor and raised his daughter alone until a widow set herself to share his bed. It was that daughter, indeed, who delivered his bread in a wicker basket and had, he noted, suddenly blossomed, making each morning a delight when he welcomed her with a smile and a wave of a podgy hand.

At a quarter to twelve he would set out for the bank, rolling a little and perspiring, with, sometimes, a piece of country bread in his hand spread with a little paté, pimpled with pepper. He lived within sight of his workplace, but it took him a good ten minutes to reach the brilliant white columns of a bank which resembled the state theatre, or would have had that not followed its predecessors in burning to the ground. So frequently did this occur, indeed, that members of the fire brigade were always issued with free tickets so as to be on hand when the flame of a candle licked indecorously at a gossamer curtain or a cigarette was dropped by a member of the stage crew into a basket of costumes or a scene painter's bottle of spirits.

He was greeted each morning (or, rather, afternoon, for the clock above the bank would frequently strike the noon hour before he had begun to climb the marble steps) by his head clerk. He handed him a copy of *Rayo de Esperanza*, one of the city's four official newspapers (opposition papers, nothing but a cause of discontent, having been closed down), which had been carefully ironed by the wife of the Chief Clerk to remove any wrinkle, just as the editor had smoothed out his news to remove any inconvenient wrinkles of a political kind. Whereupon he would step into the cathedral cool, the echoing sanctity, of the bank where the sound of a single coin dropped on the polished floor (with its mosaics, its tessellated portraits of former managers staring up, as it were, from the grave) would reverberate as though to remind all of how easily an O'Grady might slip between the fingers (O'Grady being the currency of Sagrado Dios, unconvertible, of course, into any other currency but convertible into temporary pleasure, fleeting satisfaction).

The Manager sat in a glass cubicle at the far end of the hall from where he could observe and be observed. For an hour he read his paper. Then he took a coffee and some ice water and a biscuit or two, Geronimos by preference. There followed an hour of what he called 'Bank Business', which in these days of ruinous inflation frequently meant writing his signature in purple onto documents authorising the seizing of assets and occasionally the institution of legal proceedings. A bank manager is never liked. That is not his function. He exists to embody probity, the implacable nature of finance. He is an expression of causality and hence morality. You do this then you shall suffer that. You were good enough to deposit your money with us; very well, we will return to you interest and if the value of this shall some day decline as inflation nibbles away at the capital well, then, there is a logic at work which is not without its beauty.

Mathematics, numbers, figures: these are the foundation stones of society. Politicians come and go, dogmas are propounded, embraced, abandoned, ideologies rise and fall but ten per cent is ten per cent and interest is well named, for the bank has an interest in everything, from the widow's mite (well, no, to be honest, not the widow's mite) to the rich man's millions. It has an interest in land and the houses built on that land. It has an interest in business, since its business is interest. It has an interest in the newborn and the recently deceased. It uses such words as 'security' and 'trust' to comfort those in distress and relieve them of responsibility for their financial affairs by relieving them of their finances.

These were difficult times, however. Let no one believe that banking is without responsibilities and anxieties. As the Manager takes a second break for coffee and a cake or two, or occasionally more, he is doubtless concerned at the extra work which a ruinous inflation brings to an economy. For beyond the foreclosures that are daily adding to the bank's portfolio of property, and which must eventually, of course, lead to still further work and hence further rewards for assuming the burden of that work, each day sees a recalculation of the currency. He doubtless recalls the day when the price of everything was known to all and such stability had led to a stable country, beyond the necessary revolutions which were cyclical and had their own regularities. But this is no longer so. There were even those who presented themselves at the counter of his bank and offered to pay their debts in the form of food or family heirlooms or personal services. At first he had refused, for what should a banker do in entering such transactions? But after a while he began to see that there might be advantages to be had in a handsome painting for, after all, it might be of greater worth than mere money by the day's end (if the words mere and money could ever come in such close proximity in the mind of a banker), while some of the services he was offered were of a kind he began to think he might avail himself of, provided only that they should never appear in any ledger. And besides, this was San Marco and not Geneva or London. There were local customs to be respected so that, as he progressed to lunch, at around four in the afternoon, it was often to consider several offers best contemplated over a nest of young eels, a haunch of lamb cooked with rosemary, and a bottle of the country's best wine, though in Sagrado Dios the best was not necessarily a guarantee of quality. Even the word 'wine' was thought by some to be something of an exaggeration, though words, in this country of inventions, had been known to have a life of their own.

On his mind at the moment was a certain Señora Rico, whom we know as burning a candle of love for the Mayor, blessedly ignorant as she is of his disregard for the proprieties as she writes her passionate letter each day only to destroy it. The Señora owed a little to the bank and he had begun to wonder whether a certain arrangement might not be made that would involve his visiting her in her white-painted house with its discreet shutters, at a time when citizens would retire to their beds in the heat of the day. He might thereby, he considered, be rendering her a double service. And so he whiled away his day, this symbol, in every respect, of solidity, inheritor of the double-entry book-keeping that has been one of history's gifts to the world, wondering, as bankers have always done, how they might effect a transfer of what others might be persuaded to offer in return for the simple pleasure of receiving it. Nor should we despise the bankers of this world for they are storytellers, too. Borrow from us and a world of possibility will be opened to you. What you desire can be yours as what we desire assuredly will be. In our vaults are stored away against tomorrow the money with which you plan to wed, to visit faraway places (should the laws against such ever be revoked), to raise your children; and if our invest-ments should disappoint and hence what we pay to you be less than you had hoped, less than you need to survive, have no fear, we will be only too happy to accept more from you to restore the balance. At the same time, we are sure you understand that the cost of borrowing will have to rise for who can turn back the sea of costs that confronts even the best regulated concern.

So the banker Doreme spent his days, planning to do to one what he did to all, secure in his own good estimation and com-manding the respect of all those for whom wealth is a sign of probity and a good suit a sign of good intentions.

The Professor sat at the table, the steady ticking of a clock measuring out his silence. At first he simply looked at the profusion of forbidden stories, each written in a different hand and in an array of coloured ink, dulled somewhat by the passage of time. So a current had continued to flow in those years when the sea of stories had seemed like stagnant water. What was banned in public was practised in secret. When had it ever been otherwise? He was not so unworldly as to suppose that political, sexual and literary pursuits deemed dangerous and subversive had not continued in the past as doubtless they did in the present. But he had never suspected that any of those might survive, that he might hold them in his hands. Now he was about to do so he was unsure how he felt about such a prospect. In part he was thrilled to read what no others had done for so many years, and few enough even when they had first been penned, but he was apprehensive that the mere existence of such work might bear adversely on the theories of which he was so proud.

He noticed that not all the papers had been removed from the box and before touching any of those spread across the polished walnut desk, which shone like amber in the lamplight, lifted these out. They were, he quickly saw, not stories at all but official papers. Like all the stories they bore the stamp of officialdom, but these also bore the name and title of a legal officer who, he quickly gathered, had been required to read each story, digest and analyse its content, and render a judgement on the danger it might represent. No doubt these reports were to be the basis of whatever legal actions were brought against those who had been caught with such contraband in their possession.

He started reading, almost without meaning to. The first paragraph was no more than a formality. The reader had the honour and etc. . . . submitted his report in the hope . . . assured the addressee that he was his honoured servant . . . and continued in that vein. The second paragraph, however, began the process of analysis, first setting out to describe the narrative line, to unfold the story, elaborate its fable. It did so in such detail and with such perception, however, that the Professor came to feel that should the original author of the story read the account he might have taken great pleasure in finding such a sensitive audience, such an intelligent reader. Next he took each character in turn, describing him or her in loving detail, exploring the subtleties concealed beneath appearance, discovering subtexts, super-texts, urtexts. Finally came an assessment of the meaning of the story to the state. It was with surprise that he found not an arbitrary dismissal, not a harsh invitation to censor and ban, but an infinitely subtle explanation of why such a story should be published and the degree to which it would blunt, divert and obviate any subversive impulse the reader might have carried into the text. So persuasive was this analysis that it seemed impossible that anyone should have resisted its logic, refused to accept the innocence of its provenance or intent.

It was a story, to be sure, and stories were indeed banned, argued the analyst, in a hand neat and ordered yet with an occasional flourish of the pen, a curlicue, a swoop and rise which suggested the lyric, the rhythmic, the free, but it was a story so close to life that it was almost tantamount to a simple account. For if people live thus, he argued, what purpose could be served by denying a mere account of that truth. The story, in short, merely confirmed what was while appearing to contemplate what might never be and hence could be no more than confirmation of the status quo, and what could his master require beyond that? Indeed was that not the whole purpose and intent of the state, to accommodate all to the present mode of being and the present apprehension of the real?

He had signed his name with a flourish, though it was not a name the Professor recognised, and had then pressed what appeared to be the embossed design of a ring into what must, for a moment, have been warm and pliable wax, though it was now a brittle seal, flakes of which lay at the bottom of the otherwise empty box, small pellets of red as if he had bequeathed calcified drops of his own blood to the future that was now the present.

The Professor picked up another. It was written in the same hand. Not having read the story to which it referred he could not be sure of its accuracy, but the characters stood out from the page in their pain and exultance. The journey on which they were launched was full of wonder so that anyone would wish to accompany them as they set their feet upon the path. It was a fable of love and death, of hope and despair, that left them at one moment in fear for their serenity and the next encased in a security which seemed born of the story itself. The Professor laughed; the Professor cried. The sound of the clock was stilled as other sounds filled his ears. The man was a storyteller himself, as compelling as any he had read before. Set to patrol the imagination of others, he released his own; and in displaying it defended the other. The Professor picked up one of the man's accounts and read:

Don Pablo Escabar, returning to his house from a journey to the interior where he kept a second wife, reined in his horse and watched as a bright light descended the sky, like the tip of a heated dagger slicing through black velvet. The writer evidently intends us to see this as a moment of truth as he leaves the tangled darkness of the forest for the ordered existence of the town. A sudden enlightenment floods his mind as he realises that he has divided his life in two, creating two contrasting worlds. As the light of the falling star fades so he urges his horse forward, determined that he will seal the gap between the two. He decides he will tell the woman towards whom he rides of the existence of the woman away from whom he is inexorably moving. This, he believes, will heal the breach in his own life and perhaps the breach in the country itself, which is divided, we learn, by its own secrecies, held apart by its differing needs.

The story then tells of his return to his wife who greets him and lays before him a feast to welcome him back from his journey. He thinks to tell her at once, to confess and speak of the vision that came to him on the forest's edge as the heavens offered him a sign. But it seemed churlish to say this when such a sumptuous meal awaited him. So he deferred saying anything but sat down to dine with her, for, as we are told, he is certainly hungry from his ride, having long since consumed the sweetmeats provided for him by that other wife who had wished him well on this, one of his regular visits to the far city on business she knew nothing of.

The food was better, it seemed to him, than any she had provided before, as was the wine, which she had secured, she told him, from a passing trader who told her that it was a special wine with special properties. And when the meal was over and he thought to recall what he had seen and the conclusions he had reached it felt even less appropriate to say anything for it would seem that he had been happy to eat and to drink everything she had supplied before telling her truths she would surely not appreciate. So he accepted a little more wine and then carried it and her up the winding staircase, placing her gently on the bed and the wine and glasses on a table beside it. It is clear that husband and wife then made love, though the writer is discreet in his description, using conventional images which would, I believe, disturb no one and inflame none. Excellency, since this is a husband and wife, albeit a husband who has acquired one more than the usual tally of wives, no moral law is breached.

Then, as they lie together, he thinks once more to make her privy to his thinking, blurred though that is by now from an evening's carousing. But if it was difficult before, it is surely impossible now: for there are plainly more proprieties to be respected than those adduced by the Good Book. So instead he lies back and looks up at the ceiling on which are painted a series of stars. And as he looks so he imagines that he sees one of these stars fall, silver, from the painted sky, like that other on the edge of the forest. Then, for a reason of which he is unaware, or none which the author sees fit to tell, he asks suddenly about the origin of the wine he has been drinking the whole evening long. It was, she repeats, purchased from a strange man with a still stranger story. He had travelled through the snow and presented himself at the door with a bottle in each hand, glowing blood red against the white snow. 'Good evening, Señora,' he had said, and asked if she would wish to purchase his wine. Knowing that her husband was due to return she was greatly tempted but nonetheless thought to ask of its origin. The man replied by saying that it was made from grapes harvested from the vineyard of a master magician and hence had properties beyond that of even the finest vintages.

The man who lies in a soft bed listening to this story thinks little of it. To be honest he is no longer too clear in his mind, being on the verge of sleep. His wife continues with her story nonetheless, answering the question he might have asked were his eyelids not already closing under the influence of his journey, the wine, the food, and his other pleasures. She had asked him, she explains, what special properties the wine might have. 'Why, many,' he had replied, 'but the first, perhaps, is that whoever shall drink it shall be obliged to tell the truth so long as the wine shall be within him.' His wife then pauses, as though she wishes the implications of what she has said to penetrate the mind of the man who lies beside her. And, Excellency, here is one of the strengths of the story; for this is in essence a comic tale. The slow dawning of the knowledge of his situation is exquisitely handled, for though before he had been determined to explain his situation he now realises that at some stage in the evening he had come to reconsider this. And besides, even if he were still to do as he had planned he wished to tell the story in such a way that some details must necessarily be suppressed.

'Tell me, my dear,' begins his wife, and immediately he holds his hand up, fully awake suddenly and aware of his plight. 'A moment, my dear. Nature calls.' He then takes himself to a water closet where he hopes to relieve himself of as much of the wine as he can manage. But all drinkers will recognise the fallacy of this approach. The body has its own clock, which will not be speeded no matter how hard we try. He has other resources, however, and when he returns he climbs into bed, closes his eyes and announces that he must sleep immediately.

'Oh, my dear, I wish you had told me you were anxious to sleep. I felt so sure that you would wish to stay awake tonight that I thought nothing of another property of the wine. Apparently, my dear, it prevents sleep for several hours, but there is no need to worry for we can talk the night away.'

Excellency, at this point the story becomes a delight, for the husband may only protect himself from his wife's enquiries by talking of inconsequential details, though, knowing that he may only speak the truth, he struggles to restrict himself to subjects on which he can expound without risk that it will lead back to the central truth. He thus cannot speak of horses or journeys or clothes or the forest or his work or, indeed, he realises with increasing alarm, anything; for what, in some degree, does not bear on his plight? But at last such desperate irrelevancies as he can summon to a mind still clouded by the wine which is his chief enemy are exhausted and he falls into silence.

His wife has herself remained silent throughout; but now she turns and faces him and in a voice low but not tender begins to speak.

'Tell me, my love, and tell me the truth I charge you, is there . . .' She gets no further, for he has just remembered what he should never have forgotten. His wife had drunk from the self same bottles as himself. Thus, before she can say anything further he blurts out, as fast as he can, 'Do you have a lover? Where have you placed the money your father left you? Why do all the women of Madre de Dios smile when they speak of the schoolteacher Tomas Diez? Where does our daughter go each Saturday night?' and so on and so on and so on. The next day he left for the forest, his conscience as clean as that of a young girl at her first mass, for by the time his wife had finished reciting her own sins he was entirely sober and now followed his fancy with the added spice of moral justification.

Excellency, this is a story that might be said to offend against morality and good taste, but I ask whether humour may not relieve the sting and the pleasure of the conceit mitigate its subversiveness, for if it suggests that truth may have its price it also warns that truth will out, unless it were wholly better that it should not, a principle surely well known to all those of us who bear the burden of public office. I am, as ever, your humble servant.

The Professor looked from the report to the story and back again. It seemed to him, suddenly, that there was a certain similarity between the writing of the one and the writing of the other, a certain flourish here and there, but, as he well knew, each century has its style, favoured by tutors, enforced by institutions. He placed the form back in the box, his hand shaking gently. Where there had been silence there was suddenly sound, where there was no more than a blank sheet there was a splash of colour, a shape, a form. And if there was one box were there not perhaps more? He snatched the form up again, looking for a date. And there it was, 1821. He quickly searched for other forms, interleaved at intervals and placed at the beginning of each story on which it reported. He looked again for the date before riffling on through the papers with his gnarled fingers. He stopped at last, the final sheet floating down onto the papers now fanned across the sheen of the table. They covered no more than six months. And if so much treasure could be gathered from so short a time, how much more might there be and where was his theory, except that if they were indeed suppressed then their mere existence meant nothing more than that the need survived and if the need survived, but was not publicly satisfied, why, then, there he was again, surely, back with his theory after all?

Later that day, with his student helper by his side, summoned back to the Professor's room by an urgent message, he went to the National Library. It was some time since he had walked up its marble steps (marble once brought from Italy by an Italian entrepreneur who had been misled into believing that San Marco awaited the construction of an opera house – hence the diva who travelled there only to be disappointed when she found not an opera house but a library in which silence was preferred to sound). The librarian got to his feet and half bowed. It was seldom enough that anyone entered and even more seldom that the winner of the country's premier award for scholarship, the Steiner Award (signified by a single thread of blue silk worn on the lapel and frequently picked off by well-meaning ladies who fancied it no more than an errant piece of thread), would be seen in a place when they might more reasonably have been expected to gather at the Writers and Readers Club where they slept and drank and spoke of the research they would undertake one day.

The Professor swept past him and followed his assistant as he led through the various rooms devoted to history and philosophy and natural science (but not literature) until he came to the door which led to the stairs which in turn led to the subterranean room where he had discovered the box of stories. Together they descended, like prospectors entering a diamond mine, but instead of glittering jewels all that faced them were row upon row of boxes, each one covered with dust and with locks encrusted with rust.

The student had thought to bring a lamp with him and this he placed on a table. He pumped it to create the necessary pressure then, illegally it must be said, struck a match and applied it to the delicate mantle. Their shadows leapt into life. The Professor drew up a chair, dusted it with his handkerchief, and sat. He then instructed his assistant to bring one box from each shelf and place them on the floor. There were many shelves and soon he was surrounded by boxes as though some severe judge had condemned him to be walled in with fiction, immured with lies for some unspeakable crime. And so he began to read as above him, invisible in the gloom, the portrait of a woman, whose dress was gathered at the waist and ballooned out behind, smiled down at him as if pleased that the treasure she had guarded should at last have been brought into the light, even if it be only that of a lamp which hissed away as though in disapprobation.

The virgins were weeping again. It was a regular visitation. First one village would announce sanguinary tears, attracting the middle classes from distant San Marco (always more superstitious if not religious than the peasants), then another would declare an outbreak of lachrymose statues. The tide of dyspeptic buses would reverse itself and the sellers of religious icons, pilgrimage shoes, embroidered prayer sheets, would set out as best they could across country to get to the next place of miracles before yet another settlement announced its own visitation.

Such things, noted *Perder la Esperanza*, the country's most popular daily, happened not during carnival or the football season or at harvest time, when there were distractions enough, but when there was little to be done but greet another day of unwavering sun and relentless poverty. By the same token the newspapers, having nothing else to report, would send ever more jaded reporters to be shown ever less convincing statues in mud huts or cool churches. They once persuaded a scientist at the University of Sagrado Dios to reproduce the effect and reported it on their front page, anxious to kill off such stupidity. The result was that pilgrims marched to the laboratory and priests spoke of scientists denying the Virgin's power. The editor shrugged and acknowledged his mistake. He, after all, should have known that faith cannot be disproved and that to challenge it is merely to give it added strength. The scientist, meanwhile, was dismissed from his post and sent to the jungle to investigate contagious diseases, succumbing swiftly to the first of those he encountered.

They were not fraudsters who saw beads of blood swell from the eyes of effigies, often themselves poorly-fashioned and crude.

They were believers. And blood did weep from these eyes, or something that looked like blood. And where it was not blood it was water, liquid silver, reflecting the wavering light from candles placed around them, each light a prayer, a dream, a wish, a hope, a cry, a lament, a desire, a need, a fear, an anxiety, a distress, a belief, a faith, a conviction, a certainty, a doubt. Are these occurrences made out of their own intensities or are they simply sensitive, ready, like warm soil awaiting the seed? For the journalists, sweating their way to hamlets far from main roads (such as they are) and absent from the map, such people are credulous fools, though their readership requires they accord respect to what they despise.

But, for whatever reason, the virgins were weeping blood again and whenever the tears fell politicians had to pack their suits, eat a hearty meal, summon their cars (or rather compete for the one functioning taxi), and prepare to visit the distant miracles observed by their electorate. The problem was that the roads were no longer secure. The Thousand Points of Light had recently taken to sudden appearances on roads, and not only the remote ones, either. They would set up roadblocks and exact a tax on whoever had the ill luck to pass that way. On one occasion, at least, a petty official had met his death, though precisely why or in what circumstance it was impossible to say since his sole companion, and hence the sole witness, had been his wife and she was rumoured to be living with the guerrillas who killed him, fighting by their side. The military, of course, had been dispatched; but since they could do no more than react, and that somewhat tardily, they offered little protection to the anxious officials. But there are votes in sobbing virgins and though elections were a branch of fiction rather than politics (their results being enthusiastically invented by those set to ensure their integrity) it was still thought worthwhile to keep in with an electorate which might produce the next President when the time came for another revolution.

At first there had been more of a boy than a girl in Justina, who favoured climbing a tree over brushing her hair. There came a moment, though, when tomboy gave way to young woman, when her body swelled and tingled with new energy, when blood was spilled and in spilling seemed to precipitate the transformation it marked. Men seemed to grow hungry in her presence, boys nudging each other as she walked along the street. For the first time she felt embarrassed about her father, whose eccentricities had formerly seemed as natural as the wind. She looked in the mirror, seduced by her own sudden beauty.

She began to write poetry and to read it in bed at night as moths bruised themselves against the window and singed themselves on the light. She read in particular the mournful verses of a young man, dead at twenty-three, who had set the country alight with his poetry a hundred and fifty years before. Eduardo Fernandez had been born in Anzuelo, this being the principal reason why visitors continue their pilgrimage to a town otherwise only known for its squid, the reason, too, why a certain Nobel Prize winner chose this as a home for his mistress, if mistress she was.

His father was a carpenter and Eduardo was to follow him in that trade, central to any town or village. But his talent was for working with words and not wood. His father could neither read nor write; but who had need of such when he could inscribe himself in the boats he fashioned and the houses he built? Eduardo was taught by his first love, Théresa, daughter to the town's only lawyer. It was an affair which many have written of since, as much for the sweet pain it represents as for its significance in the life of the country's principal poet. For the fact is that the girl suffered from consumption and as the light of his talent strengthened, so the candle of her life guttered and failed. Two thirds of his poems place her at their centre and the last word he uttered was her name.

His verses use a simple language so that the words may more easily slide directly into the hearts of his readers. He was a man of the people who thrilled with the language of revolution yet always returned to death in verses that every schoolchild to this day is taught to recite by heart. He spoke of the permanence of art and the transitory nature of life ('Ephemeral', indeed, was the title of the first poem Justina wrote in homage to her master). The words themselves were thus victorious over their subject and Théresa kept alive by his poetry, who in fact lay in a simple grave in the cemetery of Anzuelo, where lay also a certain sea captain who made a single mistake and lived and died with regret.

The poet, too, suffered from consumption, no doubt having caught that along with love from his Théresa, joining his mouth to hers and drinking in death. Yet he did not die of the disease which left him coughing into the scarlet handkerchief, scarlet to hide the death he knew was approaching. He met his death one day in a café called Verona, that today is a shrine where, for a few coins, you can see the room he rented, with the single bed and the desk on which is laid the very piece of paper (now under yellowing plastic) on which he had been writing his last poem before going down for a glass of wine.

> In the heart of the heart is a place called sorrow
> Where nothing may stir but the thought of the dead
> It is here that the dream of a different tomorrow
> Is born from the hope that the soul may be fed
> By a vision of beauty, a memory of

The next word plainly gave him difficulty, for he laid aside his pen and was hence downstairs, sitting at a table with a glass of wine in front of him, when the assassin approached. A single bullet was all it took to end his life, though a woman – a stranger dressed all in black – who rushed to his side said that before he died he had spoken a single word: Thérésa. But since she disappeared immediately thereafter there was no one to confirm the truth of this or even of her existence, for the landlord, to whom she repeated this, had drunk a deal of his own stock that day.

The doctor who was called judged that he would have died within the year without benefit of an assassin's bullet, but such a death guaranteed that he would live for ever not only in the hearts of young girls pierced by his sad beauty but also in the minds of those who believed that freedom will always need its martyrs.

Justina read his poems because he wrote of love and death and made them beautiful and because there was a pleasurable ache which came from the knowledge of his death. He was buried beside Thérésa, and young couples in Anzuelo would, on their wedding day, pause at the graveside to lay a posy on the flat grey stone as though this gesture were as important as the vows they had just exchanged in church. She cried when she read his poems and she cried when she read her own. And when she began to receive letters from admirers – ill-spelt and scarcely felicitously expressed – she gathered them together and tied them with a scarlet ribbon whether she liked those who sent them or not. She was ripe, in other words, as an orange on a tree is ripe. Time alone would precipitate a fall. Meanwhile energy was stored, as the fruit stores sugar, and soon one would come who would taste that sweetness.

It was clear that it would not be the boy who arrived each day, his fingers stained with ink and with papers in his hands that fluttered in the wind as though he held a dove struggling to escape. He had his uses, for he would occupy her father and thus leave her free to buy dresses and see how her hair might look if coloured this way or that or cut in a certain way. Nor was she frivolous, for the poetry that she read made her think profound thoughts about life and death and the meaning of things, though that meaning seldom seemed to amount to much more than a transforming love which must soon reveal itself to her.

She performed well at school and was admired by her teachers, though rather more by the men than the women who shook their heads and recognised that her beauty must be her ruin. Her literature teacher especially believed her capable of great things and at her persuading organised a visit to Anzuelo, to the home of Eduardo Fernandez. They travelled in a bus that bounced and rolled and spluttered along a highway strewn with rocks from the hillside and pitted with holes. Though there were only six of them he contrived to sit beside Justina and watched, with a mixture of misery and exultance, as the countryside bounced up and down through the grime-smeared windows, reflecting, as it did, his own sadly fluctuating feelings. He had survived ten years' teaching without succumbing to the young girls who flaunted their swelling breasts, as it seemed to him, at their mentor. Nor was he entirely wrong about them, for some were indeed discovering what power was locked up in their bodies. But now he could feel reality begin to slide away from him.

She had handed him her poetry and was it so perverse to read in the passion he found in their lines an admission of her need if not for him then for what he could so easily represent? He moved closer to her on the plastic seat, feeling the pressure of her presence, smelling the cheap scent transformed into a seductive perfume by the warmth of her body. He wanted to cry out, was half convinced, indeed, that he had. Her eyes were bright with

213

anticipation, his dull with despair. To be next to her was agony; to be apart was intolerable.

At the museum he took over from the resentful curator and conducted his brood from room to room. He saw that she had tears in her eyes and wanted nothing more than to crush her to him. He did put his hand on her shoulder to steer her through the door and into the café where the poet had died. They sat at the very table where his blood had been spilt and there, for all to see, was the red stain sunk into the grain of the wood (and renewed, had they but known it, each season with the benefit of a little coloured candle oil). The other girls chatted inconsequentially and drank sugared water, coloured with vegetable dyes and cooled with crushed ice. He and Justina fell silent. He took a glass of red wine, hoping that she might confuse him with the one he knew she admired beyond others and, indeed, she watched as he lifted the glass to his lips and stained them scarlet.

Justina, however, thought no more than how great a gulf of time and talent intervened between the poet who transformed the world he entered and a man whose cuffs were dusted with chalk and whose elbows were heavily patched with leather. Nonetheless the circumstances did have such a power that when his hand first closed on her knee, a knee bordered between a blue sock and a pleated skirt, almost as though it were a work of art, she did not at first respond. For a second he felt on the verge of entering paradise. But when that same hand began to stray upwards over the warm flesh, seeking he knew not what, she suddenly jerked back in alarm, forcing him to do likewise so that the table lifted up and the bottle tipped over, spilling the wine in a puddle which looped its way to the edge of the table and started to pour onto his thighs. It added its stain to that of the martyr's blood. The dying poet had uttered the name of his beloved. Justina, involuntarily, shouted 'sir', while he, equally involuntarily, whispered 'shit'.

On the return journey Justina sat on her own, staring out at the rain already turning the highway into a stream, while he sat next to a fat girl in glasses who insisted on reciting the state capitals of America for a geography test. In his hand he still carried the two-page guide to the home of the national poet, though since the rain had started while they walked the streets of Anzuelo waiting for the bus to return it was a sodden mass on which it was impossible to make out anything more than the name of the man who had written of the pain of love and then died so that he no longer had to suffer it.

He came from the south, where the land cooled as it neared Antarctica. Like his fellow southerners he was not a passionate man. He prided himself on his rationality. The religion he embraced was severe and Protestant while that of the north was permissive and Catholic. In the north, confession led to absolution. You sinned, you confessed, and were free to sin again, a rhythm he despised. Where he came from the temperatures were sometimes so low that metal snapped. People were the same. Men were not permitted to bend. They must stand tall against the wind. But it is the nature of things that when the winnowing wind blows strong it is those who bend who survive. His religion allowed him no suppleness.

So he turned to an analyst who would allow him to explain and explore the strange feelings he had, feelings which on occasion frightened even him: for the fact was that he felt promptings that he found the greatest difficulty in resisting. He felt the flesh to be an abomination and indeed had heard such a conviction voiced by others as though it were a doctrine. And if the flesh was an abomination then what of those who tempted him in the flesh? Were they not the cause of his falling away? The psychiatrist felt increasing alarm. He, too, had the power of

215

absolution. He, too, knew that without confidentiality he could do nothing for those who sought him out. Yet there was something in this man that disturbed him, something that made him feel the downward tug of the whirlpool.

The man felt the withdrawal of trust, saw the eyes slide across his own, watched as one soft white hand washed the other. So he left and retreated to his room and in his room he had a revelation. He would leave the south, with its harsh codes and rigorous customs, its unforgiving religion and radical ways and go to the north, where the sun burned off excess and the body sanctioned its own needs. He would run away from the self of which he felt a victim in order to embrace a new self he was sure must be awaiting him there. Accordingly he submitted his resignation, gave notice that he was leaving his lodging, visited the local graveyard to discover the name of a man whose birth certificate he might acquire, becoming, thereby, if not this person then at least the shell of a person he could later fill with events and thoughts and feelings of his own.

He arrived in San Marco without making any arrangements in advance. This would have been impossible for the self he had left behind, which patrolled itself with the discipline and rigour of an army guarding the frontiers of a state. He stood in the sun outside the railway station, stunned and immobile. The heat was more than he could believe. He felt like an actor surprised on the stage. The light seemed to bleach all colour from the world. Behind him the train sounded its whistle, a strangled screech of pain. The crowds jostled him and a man tried to take hold of his case, urging him towards a dilapidated taxi, streaked with rust. He swung round and stared at the man, who stepped back as though stunned. The air seemed so thin that he could hardly breathe. Then he saw a sign reading TEL, the first two letters having dis-appeared along, it appeared, with any sign of paint or decoration.

He picked up his case and strode out into the road, oblivious to a passing hearse.

The man behind the desk was asleep, the sound of a fan blade catching its metal guard blending with that of a drill on the street outside. Flies flew heavily about him and grit from the street crunched beneath his feet. He hit the bell with the palm of his hand and the clerk reanimated. Neither spoke. The clerk pointed at a sign which announced the room rate. The man nodded. The clerk held his hand out. The man counted notes into his hand. The clerk took a key, hanging from a hook in a cupboard of hooks, and held it out towards him. He took the key and looked around in disgust before mounting the stairs.

The key turned easily in the lock. He kicked the door with his foot. The sound was not reassuring. It was plainly made of the thinnest wood. Inside, it was dark. The shutters were closed against the light and the windows against the sound of the traffic which nonetheless created a vibration that pressed on his ear-drums. He switched the light on and the low-wattage bulb of a desk lamp glowed feebly. He put the suitcase down, kicked the door closed, walked to the centre of the room and pulled a short chain which hung down from the ceiling. The brass and wood fan began to turn infinitely slowly. The air barely moved. Some-where the pipes juddered, a man shouted, someone punched the wall, someone else began to cough and did not stop until another shout and another punch on the wall. The fan stopped and then restarted. He looked up and watched as the shadow of the blades strobed across the flaking ceiling. He was in the north. He had signed his false name in the register. He was reborn. The pipes began to judder again. A man shouted. Someone punched the wall. The man began to cough once more.

He found a job easily enough. There was a wood mill in the commercial district where he laboured contentedly for a while.

In the south he had worked in a bank, sitting behind a desk totalling amounts in a ledger, balancing one column with another, dressing respectably, listening to the echo of quiet voices in an echoing hall. Now he discovered his body. For the first weeks he ached so that even walking back to the hotel through the dry streets was painful to him. Each day he lifted and carried. He watched as great trees were turned and fed into giant saws which rendered them into so many planks of wood. He fed these same planks into other saws, blurred circles of light from which a fountain of sawdust sprayed upwards. He slid the wood into piles, breathing in the smell of resin and running his fingers along the soft inner heart of the tree. He wore large leather gloves for much of the time but would slip them off occasionally for the sheer pleasure of touching the satin sheen of the wood.

After a time the aches began to fade and he could feel his body begin to firm with muscles. His pale face tanned from working in the sun. He found himself lifting planks on his own which had required the help of another only a short time before. He began to feel that he was in control where in the south he had felt no more than a victim. He moved his lodgings, locating a room closer to his work. He rented an upstairs room from a family of five. One of the family caught his eye. She was a young woman of eighteen, ten years younger than himself. It was a simple room but clean and neat, a woman's room. No pipes juddered and shook here and no one coughed the night away.

He took to walking the streets in the evening, feeling that he was taking possession of the town. He grew to know it but he himself remained an enigma, unknowable and unknown. The city no longer bewildered him nor did the sun stun him as it had that first day when it seemed to rivet him to the ground. He could feel his tension ease and for a while he might even have regarded himself as happy had he thought to interrogate himself and had anyone thought to ask him. But no one did. At work the noise of the whirring saw made conversation difficult and, besides, those who worked there were not as he. Their talk was crude and their interests narrow. Nor was there companionship when he returned to his lodging, for they all had lives of their own and paid no attention to the man who let himself in every evening and went directly to his room.

Nonetheless, happiness or contentment, or some such feeling, came for a season. But it was not long before he sensed an insufficiency in what he did. He began to feel a lack of rigour in the lives of those around him. He arrived at work at the appointed hour, as he had at the bank, but none of his work-mates felt so constrained. Shops seemed to open and close at will. The streets were dirty, the air felt rancid and there was a flaccid spirit to the people. None had ambition, none sought change or complained about their lives beyond a desire for more money, and though he took pleasure in his own company he began to feel the lack of contact with others. He would sit in a bar and drink, but none joined him; nor did he feel it possible to open a conversation with others. One night he paid a woman money and followed her to her squalid room, but when she turned around and began to undress he was overwhelmed by a sense of disgust and struck her in the face, flinging money at the tangled sheets of a bed she can have left but a short while before. But hurrying away through the streets he felt alive as he had not since his arrival in San Marco.

Perhaps it was that one incident that marked the beginning of his decline. Perhaps it was merely a symptom of a problem that had begun long before and in another place. Whatever the truth of that, the girl was followed by another and another. The blow was followed by another and another. There are women, of course, who trade in such assaults, but he was not interested in them. He would always bargain for a simpler exchange and then attack them when they least expected it. And the assaults became more violent as, in his mind, he became more real.

He bought himself a knife. He went to a shop whose window was stocked with them as though the world were full of those who wished to slash and cut and stab. Some were large, with grooves down which blood could flow; others had serrated edges for sawing. He chose a plainer blade that would fold into an ebony handle and spring out with the pressing of a button. He would sit in his room for minutes at a time flicking the blade out and pressing it back into its handle. He sat in front of a mirror and watched as the blade reflected the lamplight. He carried it in a front pocket of his trousers, pressed against the slope of his stomach. He felt better as soon as he had bought it. Almost serene. He never showed it to anyone, but knowing it was there gave him great confidence and even pleasure, for there is a pleasure in such things to such people. In particular, he walked the streets each night and felt a new sense of power over those he passed. He smiled at those he encountered in bars, knowing, as they did not, that he had their lives in his hands.

It was not, however, at night that he made his first attack. He reported sick and walked the streets in the flat heat of the day, a heat that crushed and exhausted, drew all the energy from the air. He avoided the city centre with its people, its cars, buses, animals drawing carts. He walked down roads where the houses shrank back into the shade, the ground-floor windows criss-crossed with elegant black bars twisted like liquorice sticks. These houses rested in the shadow of trees whose olive leaves glistened, sweated in the feverish heat.

There were people there, he knew, who were protected from the noise and frenzy, the lazy buzzing of persistent flies, who poured cold water from earthen jars and placed food on white plates as though they were artists creating geometrical designs. There were dogs and cats who ate better than he and had their food prepared by starched-aproned maids and placed on cool tiles criss-crossed with grouting, white and unstained. He knew that behind the dark windows were books and records and radio sets, crisp sheets and simple beds whose simplicity was the essence of their elegance. He did not need to enter them to know that silver and gold taps poured clean water into enamelled baths and showers fanned cool water over unmarked flesh, flesh not soiled by toil, brute need or despair.

And if there was alcohol, and there was, it was contained not in warm cans or discoloured bottles hidden inside brown paper bags but crystal-clear flasks. The liquid itself, he was sure, was a rainbow of flavours and sensations that dulled the sting and softened the harshness of a fire which purged despair with despair of its own.

Knowing little of such people, he presumed they owned telephones on which they spoke to others so that they had no need to venture forth (though in fact the Sagrado Dios telephone system seemed primarily designed to frustrate rather than facilitate communication). And if they did so, he presumed, then they must rely on cars that glided to their door so that they could step from one coldness into another with no knowledge of the stench and heat of his reality (having failed to register that cars of any kind were a deal rarer than the truffles which featured on the city's menus but seldom if ever made an appearance on the plate). He hated them as much as he wished himself one of them but knew they must have a charm which protected them from such as he.

Except that as he passed one door it opened and there was the sound of a bell, pure and clear, and a young girl dressed in white stood for a second in the doorway framed against an interior which seemed composed of nothing but light. Then she turned, pulled the door closed behind her and walked to the wrought-iron gate that opened, as he knew it would, soundlessly. As she stepped into the glare of the sun she was blinded for a second, and hence did not see the man who stood across the street.

He had nothing in his mind beyond the need to see her again, that girl in white, that and the necessity to run through the viscous heat towards his fate. There was no one on the street except a white dog with black ears, a dog which pressed itself to the ground as he passed. Then, when he judged he was well ahead of her, he cut back down an alley, moved into the sullen shade, sweat pouring from his shirt and dripping into his eyes. He ran until he reached the end of the alley and then pressed himself back against the warm bricks. Only then did he begin to pant, like the dog he had passed, its tongue hanging out, close to the ground as he was to the wall. There was a pain in his chest as he fought to draw air in. He had never been an athlete. Even though his time in the sawmill had given him muscles he had not suspected, it had not prepared him for this running in the sun.

He felt the rough abrasion of the bricks as he edged towards the corner and risked a glance. She was there, moving forward now, a white mirage in the wavering heat haze that seemed to flow endlessly upwards like a reverse waterfall. He ducked back and pressed his head against the wall, a head now throbbing with the sun and the running and the fighting for breath. He tried to think, but everything seemed so confused and confusing. He did not will himself to reach for the knife, did not think about opening it, the slender blade clicking into place, reassuringly precise, satisfyingly slender and light.

What did he want? He wanted nothing. He did what seemed necessary, what seemed required. He raised the blade above his head like a priest with the sacrament and waited and listened for

222

the sound of her footsteps as she came to meet him, as somehow he felt she surely would. And then she appeared before he was ready. Her soft shoes had made no sound. She simply appeared in the bright light and had almost passed when he stepped forward, looped his arm around her neck and pulled her back into the alley. If the clock had been stopped at that moment, time been frozen, he would not have been able to tell you what he was about to do, though to anyone watching it would surely have been clear enough. He quite literally had nothing in mind. He obeyed a necessity that required no thought and his whole body sang as if it had discovered a purpose.

Except that that purpose was aborted, the rhythm disrupted, for he himself was now seized from behind and spun round. He clasped his knife the tighter. It flashed like a sudden star but a blow grazed his mouth as a knee came up into his groin. He felt a sharp pain that swelled out and up and now he had only a single objective – flight. He swung his own fist and felt a jolt as it came up against bone. The arm released him and he staggered back, glimpsing his assailant and the white figure, now grey in the shadow. And then he was running, the pain passing through him as, heavy-footed and tasting blood, he emerged into the bright-ness and urged himself onwards, listening for the sound of pursuit.

When at last he was back in his room he turned the key in the lock and stood with his back against the wood fighting for breath. The fear had seeped away. But where fear had been there was a strange exultance. He had acted. Just as his journey from south to north had given birth to a new identity, so the moment when he flourished the knife had brought him a purpose that such an identity could serve.

Not a victim of fate or an agent of history he was, rather, a maker and unmaker of worlds. He was chosen and had accepted his task. He was come to purify the world, cut out its disease.

And that is why, in the backroom of the Green Parrot, he joined the Thousand Points of Light and why, one day, and in their name but without their approval, he took out his knife and stabbed the Chief of Police as he walked down the Boulevard O'Grady, thinking of his weekend wife and watching the sun glinting on the open window of his house, where his weekday wife awaited his return.

The Chief might well have lived, for the blade reached no vital organ. But he had the ill luck to be hurried to the Sisters of Small Mercies who performed their usual miracle, turning the living into the dead without intent.

The Thousand Points of Light was not the first terrorist group in Sagrado Dios. It was, however, the first that did not consist partly or wholly of members of the security forces working under-cover. Always anxious that there might be those who resented the constant corruption and occasional violence of the state, the four separate security organisations frequently sought to set up small units or factions in the hope of flushing out dissenters. Either the dissenters were rarer than supposed or the agents pro-vocateurs were so recognisable (regulations requiring uniform haircuts and suits) as to discourage others from joining them. In one raid all twenty-three members of the Red Liberation Faction turned out to be members of the organisations con-ducting the raids.

This was different and the difference was itself the cause of alarm. When the Chief of Police died the people were inclined to shrug, cross themselves and think of the Sisters of Small Mercies, especially since the press were kept in ignorance of the claim made by the Thousand Points of Light. The security forces took a different view. For once none of them had been represented in the group if that is what it was, and hence set themselves to discover what it might be. The Chief of Police, before he died as a result of the ministrations of the Sisters of Small Mercies, had identified his attacker, recalling a man with cold eyes he had watched enter the Green Parrot.

The fact was that the Professor and his followers had removed themselves to the mountains from which they hoped to conduct their revolution. And in a few short weeks they had drawn others to them. The very simplicity of their message was the essence of the attraction. It was necessary, they declared, to begin again, to reach back before corruption and division, beyond colonial exploitation and the residue it left – 'scum around the bath' was a favourite expression – to a world of simple virtues. Their leader distrusted the mind as only an intellectual can, for was it not its seductions that had led him astray for so many years, that had cut him off from the lives of others? The need now was to put one's faith in the common people, though the common people were, of course, the victims of false consciousness and must hence be re-educated. The Professor had not, you see, strayed quite so far away from his origins. What to do with the intellectuals, the politicians, lawyers, doctors and even the teachers who taught pernicious values? They would be swept aside.

What form such a sweeping away might take was left a little vague. Policy and practice were held conveniently apart for the moment, but there were those who thought they saw the logic of such teachings and awaited only the signal for action to set the purging in motion. There were few of them, to be sure, but when did that ever do anything but strengthen those who felt the need for solidarity? Their faith must shine the brighter, their example be more sufficient.

The death of the Chief of Police changed everything. Until that moment words were words and nothing more. A divide had been crossed. Authority had been challenged and its vulnerability displayed. It was inconvenient that he had died in the hands of the Sisters but the symbolism remained clear. It certainly seemed clear to the President for whom paranoia was a wise and rational policy. When news was brought of the Chief's stabbing he saw himself joining a long line of dead presidents, a company he had no desire to enter, though if history taught anything (and in Sagrado Dios it seldom did) it was that he was unlikely to lay aside his office for the pleasure of retirement. He summoned a meeting of the heads of the four intelligence agencies.

When he asked them for information about the Thousand Points of Light they endeavoured to look both knowing and confident while, in fact, knowing nothing beyond the name found on a piece of paper dropped in the street beside the wounded Chief of Police and thereafter on walls throughout the city sprayed through a stencil and accompanied by what was evidently the movement's symbol, twelve stars. Later this would be simplified to a single star; but for a while the city's walls had seemed like the night sky.

After a few moments it became evident that none of those in the room could enlighten the President and evident to the President that he was doomed, for never before had a group emerged whose membership list had not been placed on his desk before the ink on the manifesto was dry. He considered firing these men who owed their position and salaries to a knowledge they plainly did not possess. Instead he dismissed them with such finality that two, at least, of them took action that day to transfer their assets to Switzerland. But the President had other cards to play, for if there were four official agencies there were two others known only to himself. These had helped to place him in his present position and hence he knew both their methods and their ruthlessness. He therefore turned to those to whom brutality was a kind of science. They asked no questions,

226

accepted the proffered evidence, such as it was, and disappeared as silently as they had arrived, though through the rear entrance into a car which exhaled a black and oily smoke, not least because in Sagrado Dios there were none that did not.

The People of Light, as they now thought of themselves, issued their first declaration. It was sent to the press and was immediately suppressed on the orders of the Executive Council, which is to say the President. It announced a first blow for the People, a first Flash of Light, which would illuminate the dark workings of power. It argued against the elite, against business, against those who believed the mind superior to the natural skills of the artisan. One was a builder, the other a destroyer, it announced, though since no one but the four editors, the President, the heads of the four official intelligence agencies and the heads of the two unofficial agencies saw it, it could hardly be said to have had a major impact. It was a sign of the naivety of the movement that anyone had thought such a document would have been allowed to see the light of day and a sign of the naivety of those in power that they believed it could be so easily suppressed since within days it was found pasted to walls, nailed to fences and scattered in streets and squares throughout the capital.

The ease with which this was accomplished, along with the scale of the distribution, further alarmed those who privately hoped that a deranged individual rather than an organised group had chosen to assassinate the Chief of Police.

The funeral was a state affair, only slightly marred by the arrival at the graveside of two women claiming to be the wives of a man so recently described as a national hero. It was shown live on television, a service that was admittedly received by few (mostly members of the President's family) and ran for only two hours a day on alternate days. It was paid for and run by an American evangelical church whose leaders believed the popular

227

arts to be a bulwark against godless communism as well, they fervently hoped, as the source of welcome revenue. The ceremony had had a certain dignity until the moment when the two women stepped forward together when the President invited the Chief's wife to speak some words. It was some moments before the producer noticed the precise nature of the pictures he was transmitting to the nation and switched to another camera, itself moving vertically down the body of a young woman in the crowd.

The President, virtually invisible behind a dozen security guards, themselves jostling each other, made a speech that was moving if inaudible, a production assistant having kicked the microphone lead from its socket in crossing her legs. Desperate at the consequences of silencing a man whose nominee was the head of the state television company and, indeed, whose niece was the production assistant whose legs he had been watching only a moment before, the producer called for a caption to be displayed, apologising for the lack of sound, and a record of suitable music to be played to cover the silence. But when fate has once turned its hand against you there is nothing to be done. By ill luck the record on the turntable was not the *Funeral March* or Verdi's *Requiem* but 'Come Along, Binga Banga Señorita Dorita' which had been placed last in the pan-American song contest and was particularly hated by the President who, against his better judgement, had agreed to appear on the promotional film dancing with a scantily clad Miss San Marco. The failure of what he and, it has to be said, the rest of the country readily agreed to be an execrable song had led to an immediate decline in his popularity.

Panic ensued in the studio and panic is seldom conducive to the solving of problems. A caption appeared on the screen announcing that the transmitter was being repaired. This gave way to another apologising for interference in vision. 'Come Along Binga Banga Señorita Dorita' came to a sudden halt and was replaced with 'Do Me Like I Want You To', sung by Montezuma and the Carlos Boys, banned the previous week by the Archbishop of San Marco. The producer now did what producers do in such circumstances: he went to the commercials. The country was thus treated to the sight of its first permitted commercial for sanitary towels, 'Free As a Bird and Fully Absorbent' sung by Evita Martinez, the country's leading singer of sentimental ballads, who had the ability to make even the mundane seem appealing. Her 'Pancho's Lubricant and Valve Cleaner' had made it into the charts until this, too, was banned by the ever vigilant Archbishop whose radio was permanently tuned to the popular music channel.

Suddenly the President's speech returned, the studio manager having found the microphone lead and plugged it back into the socket. But although the sound was restored the advertisement continued to run, so that as the President asked, rhetorically, 'What do we think of when the word "politician" is mentioned?' the viewers were treated to a picture of a talking ass, eating banknotes, while his question, 'What do we all want?' appeared to be answered by a line of young women in bikinis bouncing up and down on a bed while a reprise of the earlier advertisement, now complete with sound, seemed to reply: 'Free As a Bird and Fully Absorbent.'

The producer was, of course, peremptorily fired and joined a small documentary production company which the following year won an Emmy for their film 'The Voiceless One', voted the best foreign language television programme for a small audience. It told the story of a deaf mute alcoholic who finds a purpose in life by befriending a stranded whale. Later filmed by Hollywood as *The Princess and the Sea* it won an Oscar, this time for Best

229

Supporting Actor, the first time the award had gone to a non-human mammal.

The country was, to be sure, not unduly alarmed by the death of the Chief of Police or moved by the President's address, even when it was published in full in the following day's papers, primarily because there were few who bothered to read it. His reference to the Sisters of Small Mercies was sufficient to ensure that his comments about 'certain forces' and 'foreign-inspired anarchists' were not taken entirely seriously. Had they known that it marked the beginning of something more ominous they would undoubtedly have responded differently.

In fact those most shocked by the event, beyond the President and those who served him, were the would-be revolutionaries themselves. In their mountain headquarters they had spoken much about the need to smash the state and its representatives and even trained with half a dozen weapons they had 'liberated' from state armouries, but the notion of actually killing someone was alien. There had been a certain comfort and security in speaking of deeds which if performed must in some sense evidence the purity of their aims. Theirs, though, was a Platonic Revolution in which reality was what they declared it to be. To act was to enter a world in which the refinements of their philosophy were elbowed aside by the brute force in which they had assured themselves they believed. Yet how to build unless decaying buildings were first pulled down? Demolition is thus a constructive trade. Could retreat not be a progressive movement? To miss the correct turn necessitates the traveller to go back in order to go forward correctly. So, too, with a society that has taken the wrong direction. First it is necessary to destroy because destruction is an essential element of construction.

Thus their leader announced the death of the Chief of Police as a first and necessary step towards enlightenment, though in private he cursed the fool who had perpetrated it when the organisation was as yet ill-prepared for what must follow. But, like the mad Captain Brown's lunatic raid on Harper's Ferry, it must serve as a trigger for a wider explosion. Indeed John Brown of Potowotamy was a special hero of the Professor who, when he had not been delivering lectures on Aristotle, Hume and Kant, was exploring the life of a man he secretly admired. Had he, after all, not acted for himself when freedom was threatened? Was he afraid to stain his hands with blood when the abolitionists had been slaughtered at Lawrence, Kansas? Did he not sacrifice his sons' lives as readily as his own in order to pull down the rotten superstructure of the state?

After a few days the Chief's death had indeed begun to seem a necessary step, a line drawn across time. Yet the death of one would not suffice and so it was that they began to plan the death of many until the *how* of that began to replace the *why* and people were condemned for crimes they could not know they had committed, the crime of learning, of ambition, of separation from the land and those who worked it. And they began to spread the word throughout the country.

Curiously, they found little echo amongst those who did in fact work the land. Indeed such people had a respect for doctors and teachers that could only be seen as further evidence of their enslavement and false consciousness. Those who did respond lived in the cities. But even here it was not those without work or those who laboured in the heat of the day who listened but those who might seem blessed with all the advantages a corrupt state can offer. They were the sons and daughters of the rich, who despised the wealth which they believed had separated them from those whose company they would keep, the true people, the simple people, who understood the ways of the earth and who evidenced this in working for them as gardeners and maids. In coffee shops and bars they listened to the People of Light, as they called themselves, and felt a new sense of purpose and direction rendered void by wealth and what they now saw as a sterile education. They listened and they made contributions, withdrawing money from accounts established by the parents against whom they now found themselves in rebellion. Meanwhile the very secrecy gave a charge to their lives as the mysteries of the Church did not.

There were those, too, who worked for the state which they despised and who longed to serve a nobler cause than corruption and self-interest. They signed forms, removed documents from manila folders, identified where arms were stored and, later, where officials might be located at certain times of day. So, like a cancer growing, the People of Light grew in numbers, power and influence until even those who shared nothing of their faith, and even abhorred their methods, kept silent unless they in turn should attract undue attention and be seen as legitimate targets by those who thought to sculpt a new Sagrado Dios.

If the death of the Chief of Police had seemed more like an act of God then the bomb which exploded at the annual conference of San Marco's medical society was clearly an act of the devil. There were those in the Movement, indeed, who were shocked into reality as doctors were taken to the Municipal Hospital, having refused, even in extremis, to be carried to the closer Sisters of Small Mercies. An assault on false knowledge was one thing, but where were people to turn when they suffered from illness and disease? There were, they were told, folk remedies ignored by pharmaceutical companies concerned only for their millions, companies, indeed, which had sponsored the very conference at which the bomb had exploded. And besides, who received the best medical care? Was it the people? What was needed was not doctors but peasant nurses who would take their remedies on bicycles throughout the country so that nobody would again be without help.

Everything ended with the second bomb. It was market day and the cobbled square was covered with brightly coloured blankets and lengths of cloth laid on the grey stones. There were vegetables in piles, pots and pans, simple dresses and baskets. Lemonade sellers walked up and down with trays on their chests and metal flasks at their side. At the centre were tables and chairs where you could eat tortillas and bat on a stick. It was a place where people bought and sold, a place where they shared gossip, the stories which pull life together even as they seem to pull it apart.

The bomb went off in the café. It was where two teachers and a doctor friend met each Thursday for a cup of coffee and a sandwich. At lunchtime they would make their way to the square from school and surgery and come together, as they had at university, and as they had many years ago at their old school which still taught those who believed that tomorrow would be better than today. They were the target. They were what stood between the people and their glorious future. They had been declared an historical irrelevance by those for whom relevance was a favourite word. They were arrogant in their knowledge and presumed to know what was true and what was false, they who defined it in such a way as to support their own self-image. Well, there were those who had lessons of their own to teach, those who were the true surgeons dedicated to cutting the dead flesh from the living tissue. And so two young men, their hearts beating, their eyes bright with certainty, pushed their cart through the crowds, past the stalls where children's windmills whirled and cotton blouses jerked and fluttered in the breeze as if they longed for someone to dance a dance of passion in them, past the woman who offered a single melon and the man, eyes

233

clouded and cheeks hollowed with pain, who held a chipped cup and rattled the few coins it held, until they came to the café.

They set their cart beside the table where the three friends sat, one facing the sun and shading his eyes with a hat whose brim had been turned down. The two boys stood for a second looking about them and then, for the briefest second, caught one another's eyes, seeing, what, a puzzled look, a tremor of doubt, a confiding smile? Who can say? For no one who might have seen such an expression survived, any more than did the two young men who offered their lives for a cause they could hardly be said to understand. For what did they or those who sent them know of the explosive they had mixed and primed? They had worked, after all, from a scrap of paper written in a language that was not their own. They had mixed the fertiliser, readied the detonator, attached the clock, believing that those who ordered them to do so knew what they ordered and understood the processes they sanctioned. But in fact they knew nothing but had faith in the paper as they had faith in what they were told, believing the more because of those who said it and because those who heard offered their belief in return.

The bomb exploded and killed the three friends who were together in death as they had been together in life. It killed the two boys, who became martyrs, two boys who shared nothing, indeed, but their ignorance. It killed the man with the tin cup who was thus cured of his blindness in being cured of his life. It killed the woman whose head exploded along with the melon she had held and it killed the children who saw the windmills spinning blood red in the sky and the women who longed to dance in the cotton blouses which flamed red for a moment and then shrivelled to black, gone in the instant in a swirl of wind. It killed one hundred and twenty-one human souls, whose blood flowed on the grey cobbles turned crimson as the floor of the cathedral is transformed into liquid red when the light streams down from the heavens. There were those who survived who never heard again or never saw another shred of light. There were those who survived who never slept again, though they might dream in wakefulness of a swirl of light and of darkness and a rain of paper and cloth and fingers and legs out of a sky as blue as Christ's eyes.

There are lines in history which once crossed change everything. There are some lines, we have noted, which mark the paths trodden by those who would go where they will rather than where others bid. These are the true lines and they speak of freedom. But there are others drawn by fate or perverted will and which mark a boundary that may never be recrossed. There was a line in Eden, the line of knowledge. Step across it and there was no going back. The Terror of St Lucia Market defined such a moment, for the bomb in the square killed the soul of a country. From that moment on the people would never follow those who set themselves to determine where they should walk. From that moment onwards they would walk only down paths of desire.

For a day the People of the Light themselves were in shock, unable to understand the meaning of what they had done, for most of those who had died were those in whose name they had placed their own souls in peril. But the Professor rallied them. These people, too, were martyrs, he explained, for were they not also laying down their lives for the future that others would inherit? Would the sheer scale of the slaughter not convince those who clung to power that it was time to release their grasp? Would it not also convince them that they were confronted with the truly implacable, for those who are prepared to sacrifice their friends will surely stop at nothing to secure their aims? Indeed, he added, was it not their task to cap each horror with a still greater horror until it was clear that their demands would have to be met? And besides, were they not all forged together by this deed? For if they were to stop now and abandon their objectives then those deaths would be drained of all meaning and become a purposeless slaughter. The only way to give them meaning was to see them as part of a greater story and thus no guilt would attach itself to those who had sent the martyrs on their way. No change was ever effected without suffering, no revolution ever concluded without the spilling of blood.

By degrees, however, those who stood in the dirt of the mountain retreat and looked up at their leader, his grey hair catching the dying sun, began to turn aside until, when he was finished, he stood alone on that mountainside as the dark of night began to close about him and he faltered in his speech and stood silent, at last, in the face of their judgement.

If Justina had ambitions to become a poet then so, too, did her teacher. Indeed, he had published a poem in the city's evening paper, in the days when the capital could boast such. It was his last year of high school and it brought him sudden fame, for how many could claim to have seen their work in print before seeing their final results? It was a poem that had come to him so naturally he imagined that others must flow out of him as easily as the waters of the Angelica (named by Jacques the Navigator for his childhood love, who later married a horse butcher) flowed through the centre of the city.

He plotted a career for himself as a journalist who each evening would retire to a loft to compose the national epic. The editor of the newspaper, however, was a deal less enthusiastic since he included a poem each day only at the insistence of a wife he could not abide and hence detested any and all of those who filled space which could more profitably have been filled with crime, scandal or even, in the last resort, news. The young poet thus found himself on the street no less than five minutes after leaving it having applied for a job. He then decided, as had so many before him, that if all other avenues were closed he would condescend to teach and thus earn himself the time to write, for did not school vacations stretch for ever?

Accordingly, he progressed to university where he quickly established a poetry magazine – *Life* – and since he was both founder and editor published a deal of his own work, though it no longer came as readily as it had that first time. It is the great advantage of such publications, however, that they attract few critics and, it must be confessed, few readers, so it was possible for him to maintain an idea of his accomplishments shaped primarily by the response of his mother and the literature master of his old school who had earned himself an extra increment on the appearance of a poem by one of his pupils in the evening paper.

For four years he acted out the role of poet, having all the accoutrements required short of actual talent, which is to say he wore a beret, drank a deal of wine or, when possible, anisette (in truth, since import duties precluded this, a drink made of fermented ass's milk with a dash of dogwort, poisonous in all months except April), and slept around a deal, though not as much as he would have liked for few of the young women who went to the university saw marriage to a poet as forming part of their plans, and this was a time when marriage came high on the curriculum for the relatively few women who found themselves favoured by the admissions tutor, a man for whom women and education seemed unnatural bedfellows. Many decades later, he would have been dismissed for failing to include the requisite quota of women's texts in his course on the Peloponnesian War, but at the time of which I speak enlightenment lay a deal further off.

It was the good fortune of the young poet, however, that one girl at least was impressed by his velvet jacket and velvet voice. A girl from the country, who had no ambition but to find a good man, she had been so misinformed as to believe that such were to be found at the university. The two formed a partnership that might have proved unbreakable were it not for the Paulo Panama Poetry Prize, awarded each year in memory of a young man who, thirty years before, had met his death in the cause of literature by standing in the middle of the campus and reciting verses which had ridiculed the political and sexual shortcomings of the then President, a short man with a shorter temper who had arrested writers for no better reason than that it was a traditional thing to do. Married to a woman half as tall again he did what small men often do: he climbed on his dignity, mounted atop his office and, as a result, fell victim to ridicule. But before he was swept from power by Fernando the Incorruptible (a title given to him by the parliament after he had bribed a sufficient number to be sure of a majority), he arranged for the arrest of Paulo on a charge of sedition.

When Paulo Panama died three months later, and on the eve of the uprising that would sweep Fernando the Incorruptible from power (toppled by the minority he had failed to bribe), his death was announced as a martyrdom, though since he had been transferred, under guard, to the hospital of the Sisters of Small Mercies, there were those who thought his death might have been occasioned by something other than the assaults of the military, the Sisters being, as we know, women of faith rather than knowledge, to the benefit of the city's morticians who were thus enthusiastic supporters of the hospital.

The Paulo Panama Prize was presented each year by the Mayor of the city, who used the occasion, as he used all occasions, to further his career and ingratiate himself with that admittedly small section of society which regarded literature as of some significance. Our scholar poet had submitted a poem that dealt a little with myth and somewhat with dreams and, to a degree, with subtle references to other poems, which is to say it was a trifle derivative. But what poetry is not? Can it be said that there is any true originality when even the language we use has passed through so many mouths before our own, like the water supplied by the Municipal Water Company?

The event was presided over by the President of the University, a man who owed his position to having made a substantial contribution to the ruling party which had campaigned against the giving of donations to political parties but naturally needed funds if it was to be in a position to carry out its promises. What he had not realised, however, was that while his job required very little besides eating expensive meals and dismissing politically oriented students (incorrectly politically oriented students), he would occasionally have to give a speech. For others this would be no great burden; but he had a disability. He was a stutterer and had only learned a little earlier in the day that he would not only have to speak but present the Paul Panama Poetry Prize, a near impossibility as he well knew. He came from a village of stutterers, a village originally called after Thomas Torquemada but which had been renamed Ayoo in an attempt to save time.

The President was not, however, a man without initiative. Even to be in a position to bribe the government it is necessary to have the skills which might have won him a place in that government in the first place. He had learned to give speeches in which all words began with vowels and had prepared one for this occasion but had left it in the urinals, placing it in the care of an old woman who sat there collecting money. Unfortunately he had come out without any change and she affected to have lost

239

the speech when he tried to reclaim it. He thus now rose to his feet, sure that he could recall the first two sentences but painfully aware that he was unlikely to recall much more.

So it was that, staring out at several hundred students, and in the presence of the Mayor and his wife, he announced: 'I am always amazed at, and appreciative of, eagerness and enthusiasm and am an admirer of art and all evidences of accomplishment and erudition, indeed of all aspects of artistic integrity and I am aware of extensive endeavours and examination achievements. Everybody is anxious and eager, and I am also, about an event of outstanding importance and anything I utter is useless alongside anything else.' The Mayor nodded his agreement. At this point, however, the President's memory bank was exhausted and he set out on a sea for which he had no charts and which he was sure contained nothing but rocks, even though he could never have pronounced the word. Adrenalin, besides starting with a vowel, has rescued many a terrified creature and perhaps he thought it might him. Humankind, however, is born to disappointment and so, it seemed, was he. Though he spoke more carefully, conscious that at any moment he could founder, the rocks were even now breaking surface. 'Actually, I am also c-c-con-con, aware of importance of all artistic expression and especially of p-p-p-p-p, v-v-v-v-v, elegies and other iambic er irrelevancies and Auden and Isherwood' (he was not, note, badly read, merely linguistically suicidal) 'and, er, others equally elegant, elongated and abbreviated at equal intervals as I expect. All entwined, Eliot, effervescent (the word popped into his head because he had read it on a bottle only an hour earlier), exquisite.' The time had come, he realised, to cut his losses. He tried another tack. 'Enough.' He pronounced the word, he hoped, with finality, though aware that even precipitate retreat requires some final gesture; after all the Mayor was rumoured to be preparing a presidential bid and hence might be in a position to favour if not the university then himself. So he took a deep breath, seeing, as he thought, a glimpse of a protective harbour. 'I should like t-t-t-to thank the M-M-M-Mayor who is a pri-, a pri-, a pri-, a privileged member of university (definite articles were, in his book, definitely optional) and his wife, who is a –' he paused, aware, suddenly, of a pit about to open up beneath his feet '– who is a –' he dug his fingernails into his hand, looking out at the upturned faces, and at last, concentrating with the fierceness of a chess grand master about to play his most risky move, managed triumphantly to pronounce the entire word whose syllabic constituent had come close to rendering him entirely speechless. Taking a desperate linguistic run at it, he announced, 'who is a . . . countrywoman of ours.' He sank into his chair sweating profusely and only vaguely aware that he had somehow stirred the students from their practised apathy. Later he consoled himself with the thought that it might have been worse, as he was justified in feeling since it did, indeed, now become precisely that.

The Mayor, who had the capacity both to sympathise with and rejoice in the problems of others, rose to his feet and nodded his appreciation. He then introduced the occasion by referring to improvements in the municipal drainage system and by assuring his audience that he had a special concern for the young, the old, and those who found themselves in between. He spoke eloquently of his commitment to the university, while assuring the audience that his commitment could never be at the cost of . . . there followed a list which itself had something of the rhythm of a poem about it. He smiled benignly down from the platform at the sight of so many potential voters looking up at him. Then he, in turn, committed an error, making an unfortunate reference to the need for student discipline. This provoked a well-known activist to rise unsteadily to his feet and raise his third finger. For the erudite, this was plainly a reference to the country's indigenous peoples; but the Mayor's wife thought otherwise, and though prepared to betray her husband in private was not about to condone an attack by others and in public. She thus rose indignantly to her feet and seized the microphone, forgetful, as her alarmed husband was not, that the dental technician she had consulted (who also serviced the hearse that had brought her husband and herself to the university) had as yet failed to adjust her teeth. 'Shit down,' she shouted. 'My husband is Mayor of this shitty. You are a student. Your job is to shit your examinations. I am going to shit here and I hope you are going to shit there and listen to the beauties of our national language. What are we going to do?' she asked, indicating with an upward motion of her hands that she expected a response. 'Shit,' replied three hundred students dutifully. Satisfied, she resumed her seat, smiling and nodding to her husband, whose face now matched the puce robes with which the university had endowed him. It would be a moment that many students would remember in later years as they recalled what they had been told, rather to the depression of some, would be the best years of their lives.

There followed the ceremony itself. In the audience was the teacher/poet's family and the family of the girl who so admired his velvet voice. The occasion was widely regarded as the most significant, if often also the most boring, in the university calendar, though it now appeared that opinion might be shifting in the latter regard. It was also extremely popular with students, not least because it was preceded by a party on the previous evening to which all were invited and at which the wine was free (Eduardo having been the son of the country's best-known wine maker, famous for developing a grape which was not so much disease-resistant as disease-embracing, the flavour of its various moulds adding to the taste).

Unfortunately the young scholar, partly through fear that his inadequacy as a poet might be about to be publicly exposed (for, yes, even he had begun to have doubts as he sat at his table and tried to think of a rhyme for Navigator in the epic poem he was planning to celebrate one of the country's most famous sons), and partly because anything free has to be enjoyed to the full, had drunk rather more than he had intended. The elderly poet, on the other hand, drank exactly as much as he intended, which is to say a great deal.

The problem lay less with the President or, indeed, the Mayor's wife, than with the judge. He was known as a poet, but he was also known as a drunken and certifiable lunatic, not properties infrequently observed in those who breathe beauty into the world. He had been appointed by those who believed that the one implied the other and were thus reassured by the combination. Having made a few desultory passes at those women students, dignitaries, faculty wives, waitresses, unwise enough to come within his reach, he had been carried to his bed by members of the Guild of Sporting Clubs who painted his testicles green, removed his money belt (empty), and fixed a notice to his head reading: 'PANSY POET', before themselves leaving the party which, according to tradition, they terminated by singing bawdy songs and vomiting in the quadrangle. They were joined in this by alumni who had travelled there on purpose not to miss the vomiting which itself brought back so many happy memories, as it assuredly brought back what they had so eagerly eaten and imbibed.

No one, therefore, was in the best of condition when, on the following day, at last the famous poet rose awkwardly to his feet and moved, like a knight on a chessboard, one step forward, two to the side, towards the podium. He wore a sweater that had evidently suffered the depredations of the Spitting Wolf Moth (which first spat on the wool and then sucked up the dissolved fluid, a habit irritating to those who liked to dress in wool but devastating to the sheep on whom they sometimes descended like children at a birthday party sighting ice cream and jelly) and which also bore an inscription in runic letters, he being fascinated by Old Norse myths, even calling his children (and he had many) after figures from the sagas.

He clutched in his hands a piece of paper that might have been his speech or even the winning poem, but that might just as well have been the Declaration of Sagrado Dios Independence for all the good it did him since the Guild of Sporting Club members had thought to remove his reading glasses the night before. He stood, therefore, and glared out at the multicoloured blur of the audience as though trying to recall who he might be and why he was there. Then, with a jolt, he seemed to recall himself and shot out a hand which struck the microphone. 'Shit.' The Mayor smiled weakly. His wife ran her fingers reassuringly over her pearls. Had she not, after all, just advised the audience in similar terms?

The shock of striking the microphone and hearing his voice come back to him from the loudspeakers seemed, however, to have a salutary effect. He straightened, reached out a tentative hand, took hold of the microphone as though he were holding the neck of a young woman, and began to recite his favourite saga. After a moment or two he stopped, evidently recalling that this was, perhaps, not why he was standing in a large hall addressing a vague but plainly numerous audience (his own readings rarely attracted audiences much above four or five). There followed another jerk, as though a message from his brain had finally arrived.

'Poetry competition,' he announced. There was an audible sigh of relief from behind him. The Mayor's wife relaxed her hold on her pearls. 'Many entries. Several ridiculous.' There was a hesitant laugh from the audience. 'But one,' he said, warming to his text, 'outstanding. Life. Sex. Blood. Perversion.' The audience leaned forward, their interest finally caught. The poet detected their sudden concentration and warmed to his theme. 'Sex. More sex. Roots of life. Pounding. Relentless. Rhythm. Rhythm of sex.' Behind him, members of the platform party moved in their seats, the better to see the winner the moment he or she rose from their seat.

'The poem,' he said, with a sweep of his hand, 'is about a ménage à trois of which the poet is plainly a member. Come forward, poet.' There was a pause while he looked about and then seemed to recall that he would have need to identify the pervert he had announced. He searched his fallible memory and then to his amazement the name materialised and he announced it.

The young would-be poet, his mind still muddled with alcohol, had followed the rambling remarks with growing despair, for it was evident that his own poem, which dealt with the souls of the dead meeting in paradise, had been passed over. He could make no sense, therefore, of the sudden announcement of his name. Plainly a mistake had been made. What was he to do? He remained seated, but all around him his fellow students were looking at him with renewed interest or simple envy. Some made what seemed obscene gestures; others tugged at his sleeve, encouraging him to walk forward through the crowd to receive his prize. At last he realised that he would have to rise. As he did so there was sporadic applause, mixed with what sounded like jeers. He knew that somewhere his mother would be asking what a ménage à trois might be and his future in-laws

245

considering what perversion he might have practised on their virginal daughter.

He walked unsteadily, by no means recovered from his previous night's drinking. There was more applause. A photographer stepped forward and a light flashed in his eyes. Whether it was the light that blinded him or the wine that destroyed his co-ordination, he stumbled on the first of a flight of steps which would have led him up onto the stage to receive his prize. He then slipped on the second and tripped on the third, falling forward and smashing his nose. The Mayor rose in alarm, stepped back and fell off the platform, breaking his leg when he hit the floor. The distinguished poet stumbled back and the string securing his trousers snapped, swiftly revealing a flash of green, a sight greeted with cheers by the Green Faction (the Guilds flourishing at the university) and jeers by the Red, Blue and Yellow.

The Mayor was taken to the Sisters of Small Mercies where his leg was set in plaster and he contracted an infection which killed him within three days. The elderly poet found himself fêted by the Green Student Association, who lobbied for an honorary doctorate, blocked, of course, by the other colours. The young poet, who never received the prize, was estranged from his parents, lost the girl he loved, and six months later ended up teaching literature in the heat of the north to young girls whose swelling bosoms, white shirts and opalescent buttons recalled lost pleasures and unrequited desires.

There can be no end to an account of Sagrado Dios, for its story is composed of many. Its citizens are born and they die. For a space of time they are remembered and then the ripples begin to still. Tears dry in the southern wind and spring returns, its ironies ignored by those who stoop to pick a flower and offer it to another, as if they were the first to do such. Some suffer pain, others discover pleasure and contentment. All go on a journey whether they leave the country of their birth or not, and the government continues to prefer not. All are unique; yet in their essence all are the same. Stories exist to tell us simultaneously how different and how similar we are and there is the wonder of a life that leaves us dismayed and exulted in equal proportions. Who has not looked up at the night sky and asked the meaning of the story in which we play our part? That sky will be there when we leave as it was when we entered and the question will remain, except that we do all answer that question, each in his own way. Like Pedro Romerez, who entered the chapel of the undertaker Hernando Juarez, then functioning as a cinema, and never minded if the film was already under way, we are born into a story that will continue when we leave. And is there not a reassurance in that and would we rather not have entered the chapel to be enchanted by the spell that story casts? But some stories, perhaps, need completing, though I rather think that you might guess the fate of two people whose lives you have brushed against for these brief hours.

Justina and her young bell maker walked through what passed for a park in San Marco, which is to say that there were several trees and what might once have been grass along with a plant which consumed whatever fell into its, well, bell-like flowers, whether that be a Lazy Bee or a cigarette packet. They, though, were oblivious to this. Somewhere behind them, in a city which combined squalor with occasional beauty, a bell struck and it was as though a spark leapt between them. After a moment the bell ceased to toll, but it continued to reverberate in the souls of two of God's creatures. Time, which had hurried them on their way, now relented and they stepped into another world. What need of a storyteller to tell you what you know so well, for who is there who reads this who has not slipped into that world themselves? And having visited it you will know the pleasures and the pains in store for them, the soft bruise of absence and the sudden plenitude of presence. You will know, too, however, that young love may burn for days, for weeks and even months, but seldom for years. Anniversaries come more frequently than in later life. Our first month together! Three months! Half a year! And then the candle gutters, the shadows on the wall loom and shrink, and suddenly there are two strangers once again, walking away from one another as if they had never walked the other way.

So if I say that none of this occurred, that there was no blunting of passion, no slackening of need, no relinquishment of pleasure, you will know that I speak of something that was rare indeed. To be sure, Justina continued with her studies and in the autumn moved to the university where she met others like herself, revelled in the parties, the clubs and societies and occasionally bought the books the professors set for her to study. Federico, too, learned his craft, pressing hand and ear against smooth metal and watching as a waterfall of sparks lit up the darkness of the foundry. Yet this was not the centre of their lives. It was what they did while they awaited their next meeting. It was how they filled the less important spaces in their lives.

Her father noticed nothing. His world was defined by the walls of his study and the boundaries of his enquiring mind, and since to him all knowledge led to further knowledge there were in truth no boundaries to his universe.

There was one who did observe, however, one who kept watch over a relationship that could spell nothing but pain to him. He was a man who went to the National Library each day, who read what other men had written and wrote it down on

248

small white cards. These he gathered into boxes and arranged according to the alphabet, each card cross-referenced to other cards until all experience seemed stitched together. And since new names and concepts were added each day it was necessary to rearrange these cards and their content, constantly forming new patterns, precipitating new juxtapositions. It was a task that required great rigour and not a little time. And since the light in the library was poor, as was that in the Professor's study, he was forced to wear spectacles which, he was sure, must make him look less attractive to the young girl whom he saw each day and whose love he still believed he might win one day.

He knew that she cared for another but he had followed the young man in question and discovered that he was of no account. He worked for a bell maker and had no education. It could only be a matter of time, he was sure, before she came to understand that he had nothing to offer her. And working in the library as he did he saw that time was a friend and not a foe. For what is a library but a distillation of time, such that in a single moment he could look around and see, in an instant, different times brought together as a cliff face, in crumbling, will reveal the centuries.

And yet, as he walked through the parched streets with his box of index cards, he felt a need that could never be satisfied by such thoughts of time's relativity, for it is one of life's unnecessary ironies that we are led to love those who may not offer love in return, and feel pain that can never be assuaged.

In time he too became a professor and continued the work bequeathed to him by his former employer, now retired to a home for the totally bewildered. He took pleasure and pride in his rank and the respect it earned him. He was a conscientious teacher, as the Professor, in truth, had not been, and looked out for a pupil to whom he could in turn bequeath his life's work.

But never a day passed without his thinking of a young girl, dressed in white, who was the love of his life. And though she, of course, grew old in time, she never aged a day in the memory of a certain professor who walked each day from the cool of the university to his house on Cathedral Square. Each evening he stood on his balcony, as the sun faded over the distant mountains, and watched as the pigeons exploded into the night sky and the great door of the cathedral slammed closed to the accompaniment of the great bell, and thought of what might have been.

Meanwhile, in a small white house, a man, a woman, Federico and Justina, and their children besides, stopped for a moment at the sound of the bell and smiled at each other before sitting together while the mother pulled a large book from the shelves. It was called *One Hundred Days: One Hundred Nights*. It contained so many stories and provoked so many more, when once again it was closed for the night, that they often wondered if there would come a day when it would be finished so that they could start once more.

Some live in great cities, amidst a swirl of colour and noise, the night sky and its frosting of distant worlds smeared away by the glow of what we take too readily to be the light of civilisation. Others live in places that barely trouble the cartographer, never part, it is assumed, of the fable we call history or the fantasy we designate the present. Yet in truth such distinctions are without meaning. Boundaries, borders, frontiers are no more than marks inscribed on paper. Ideologies, traditions, conventions are so many letters carved on ice on a summer's day. We live and die by other principles than these. And if nothing more than chance brings two people together then chance has fulfilled its primary purpose, for there is a meaning born at such a moment as there is when a poet forges a metaphor from apparently divergent facts. These two people, then, inhabiting a place with more of fiction about it than fact, serve as something more than one another's destiny. They stand as evidence of what lifts this life above mere existence. They stand as a paradigm of all those encounters that have flooded the world with meaning and made it a place worth inhabiting – even here where beggars sit at the door of a great cathedral where once a young girl stepped into the brilliant light of day, stumbling into the path of a young man who heard what others could not – both suddenly finding what neither knew they sought and what, I can tell you, who have a right to know, they would never hereafter lose even as age edged them towards their story's end. And note where that apostrophe is placed. Those whom story has joined together let no man set asunder.

Today it is possible to take a package tour to Sagrado Dios. None of the major airlines flies there, but by taking a plane from Miami to Florianopolis and then another to San Marco you may reach it in no more than a few more hours, though, since the planes are serviced by San Marco's own engineers, many prefer to reach it by another route. To be honest the tourist trade is not as yet firmly established. The large cruise liners rarely come within a hundred miles or so and there are few facilities to attract them to come closer, though the SS *White Russian*, a Baltic bulk carrier converted into a cruise ship, has announced that its round-the-world inaugural voyage from Riga, via Hull, Reykjavik, New Jersey and Brisbane, will include San Marco provided that the port facility, presently designed only for fishing boats, is uprated with the addition of a modern landing facility and casino, a development which the Catholic Church regularly denounces from the pulpits of churches across the country even as it seeks to diversify its investments to include its shares.

As a result, Sagrado Dios today is much as it ever was. A virgin has started crying in Anzuelo. The Mayor's wife has a new set of teeth. The bank manager still sits and stares down the marble hall of his bank at the door through which he no doubt hopes that, one day, his true love will come. The two wives of the deceased Chief of Police live happily side by side, as do the still beautiful Justina and her husband who together, each Christmas, wrap a silver bell for each of their children to ring out when they all play a tune that others might recognise as a bawdy ballad but which to them recalls the moment when love first entered their lives and they understood the world's true bounty.